Hannah March was .... Peterborough on the e................ on the University of Ea...................... Writing under Malcolm Bradbury and Angela Carter. She is now married and lives in Peterborough.

THE COMPLAINT OF THE DOVE, THE DEVIL'S HIGHWAY (shortlisted for the CWA Ellis Peters Historical Dagger), DISTINCTION OF BLOOD and DEATH BE MY THEME, Hannah March's previous mysteries featuring Robert Fairfax, are also published by Headline:

'*The Complaint of the Dove* has more than a charismatic protagonist. March has created a felicitously realised Georgian mystery, and setting a detective novel in the age of Moll Flanders is a masterstroke ... *The Devil's Highway* is equally as exuberant'   *The Times*

'Written well with a great deal of self-assurance. I liked the period detail and the characterisation of the large cast of suspects'   Deryn Lake, *Shots*

'March writes in an engaging, easy-to-read style and draws the reader in from the very beginning to her well-spun web of a story ... A well-paced, exciting book and I eagerly await the third instalment of Fairfax's adventures'   *Historical Novel Review*

'A clever and accomplished first novel ... witty and convincing; for fans of period dramas such as Moll Flanders and Tom Jones, this will slip down like a cup of sherbet'   *Scotland on Sunday*

'A gloriously rich tale of London at its grandest and seamiest, well told, at a cracking pace'
                     Newcastle upon Tyne Evening Chronicle

A Necessary Evil

Hannah March

headline

First published in 2001
by HEADLINE BOOK PUBLISHING

First published in paperback in 2002
by HEADLINE BOOK PUBLISHING

10 9 8 7 6 5 4 3 2 1

ISBN 0 7472 6628 X

Printed and bound in Great Britain by
Clays Ltd, St Ives plc

HEADLINE BOOK PUBLISHING
A division of Hodder Headline
338 Euston Road
LONDON NW1 3BH

www.headline.co.uk
www.hodderheadline.com

A NECESSARY EVIL

One

'Sir, I shall not be sorry to quit your premises. The fact that you rented the rooms to me as furnished, when they contain a collection of broken-down sticks and rotted draperies fit only for a bonfire, I shall leave aside: likewise, the fact that you charged me what would be accounted a fortune in the most fashionable squares of the Upper Town, let alone in a drab corner of what is inaptly named Cheap Street. Nor shall I allude to the tricks of your lack-witted children, or the smell of the backstairs privy, both equally unpleasant. I shall only say that, intolerable as these things are, my chief delight in leaving the dubious shelter of your roof is going away from *you* – from your dullness, vulgarity, meanness, and pig-headedness. I shall only add that you had the ugliest face I had ever seen, until I saw your wife.'

So said Robert Fairfax under his breath, as he packed his trunk.

Where he went wrong was in repeating it, out loud, to his landlord's face. He had dragged his trunk to the bottom of the stairs, and there the man stood – and out it came.

Not that Fairfax was afraid of his landlord – or former landlord – as he was being evicted. But the man was a butcher, and had a dog. Fairfax should have remembered

1

that dog, which seemed determined to uphold the reputation for ferocity of butchers' dogs everywhere. As soon as the man's clotted brain registered that he had been insulted, he gave a sharp whistle. The dog came up from the kitchen as if it had been fired from a cannon. It was already biting the air.

Without the trunk, Fairfax could have just run. But the trunk contained all his worldly goods and he couldn't leave it in the butcher's hall. So his exit contained the maximum of indignity and pain, as he staggered down the steps into the street dragging the trunk by one hand and the dog by one leg. At least he only screamed a little, and the street was not at its busiest. Only about fifty people saw his humiliation.

He tried to shake the dog off, but it was like being caught in a live man-trap. Letting go of the trunk, he tried to grab the beast by the scruff and found it had him by the arm instead. He supposed he might have gone on for ever, transferring the agony to different portions of his body, if a man had not come to his aid. The man had a stick, and used it – but he also had that simple authority in his 'Down! Down, sirrah!' that Fairfax had always lacked with dogs. The softest spaniel would detect this, and terrorize him from its cushion.

'You're hurt, sir, I think,' the man said, as the dog slunk back to its master, who stood in his doorway looking fatly triumphant.

'Thank you – a thousand thanks – it's nothing.' Fairfax's stocking was torn and there was blood, but no longer being chewed was bliss enough.

'You had better put on some salve, and bind it.'

'I shall – as soon as I may. You are very good.'

' 'Tis a matter of wonder to me,' the man said, 'how folk *look on* in this world.' He spoke meditatively. He was a stout,

2

blunt-featured, weathered-looking man, plainly dressed, wearing his own grizzled hair: his voice was a deep slow growl with some odd inflection that Fairfax could not place. The way he stood planted in the middle of the street, indifferent to the bustle around him, bespoke a certain serenity. It was only after a moment that Fairfax noticed the man had no left hand: there was a short iron hook instead.

'Look on, and laugh,' Fairfax said, aware of two little boys nearby who were doing a spirited impression of a man running in terror from a dog. He bent and put his hands to the trunk. He had some idea of lifting it and carrying it on his shoulder. It was not a large trunk and he had seen sailors do it.

After a few moments' grunting, cursing, and nearly falling over, he concluded that sailors must be made differently from him. Meanwhile, the two boys were vastly entertained. He couldn't remember ever seeing anyone truly doubled up with laughter before, rolling on the ground and kicking.

'That is too heavy for you, sir,' the man said in his rumbling way. 'Come, let me take a hand. Have you far to go? The coach-office, mebbe?'

'No, no. I'm not travelling anywhere. Only shifting to new lodgings. Avon Street – no great distance. This is very kind of you . . .'

The man only shrugged and lifted one end of the trunk with his big roughened right hand. No great matter, he seemed to say. But, in this civilized nation in the year 1765 of the Christian age, an act of disinterested kindness was so rare that you felt yourself embarrassed by it, Fairfax thought. Or perhaps that was just a reflection of the way he was feeling after being turned out of his lodgings. Such a thing had never happened to him before.

Well, that wasn't true: he had been turned out of his lodgings frequently in his younger days, when he was struggling as a Grub Street hack, and was often unable to pay the rent. But the point was he was *young* then, whereas now he was in his thirty-fifth year, and it just wasn't the sort of thing that should happen.

It happens because of the way you are living lately . . . He pushed that unwelcome thought away.

'You were lucky to find another lodging in this town, I think,' the man said as they went along, carrying the trunk between them. 'Half the country must be here. What folly!'

Folly? Well, Fairfax supposed it was, if you stepped back from it: the way society flocked to this town a hundred miles from London, cramming themselves into it for several months of the year at great expense and some inconvenience. But that was Bath: that was fashion. It was fifty years ago that a man called Beau Nash had begun the transformation of a plain spa town into an elegant resort of society, and it was still growing, in size and prominence. It was the place to see and be seen: for many, the idea of *not* appearing at Bath at least once a year was as unthinkable as leaving off wearing wig and powder.

And if it was folly, then Fairfax was one of the fools. For, of course, the place was a honey-pot. The great might gather here to nod at each other across the Pump Room just as they did at St James, but they were only a small proportion of the whole. New wealth came here to parade itself, and old names without money. Prosperous tradesmen on the spree rubbed shoulders with half-pay officers on their uppers: place-seekers and fortune-hunters, climbers and sinkers, the marriage-hungry and the unmarriageable, gamblers and rakes and fops and heiresses and speculators and swindlers, all were scrambling for advantage beneath the veil of Bath's strict ceremonial. They even outnumbered the invalids and the ailing, who came for the traditional curative properties of the waters – but the principle was the same. All wanted Bath to do them some good.

Fairfax too. Through an unfortunate confluence of gentlemanly birth, a brain, and no money, he earned his bread as a tutor. At the end of this summer his latest pupil had gone off to Oxford to complete his studies with the usual course in drinking and whoring, and Fairfax had found himself quite unable to get a new position in London. It was a bad time of year: many of the gentry were still at their country places, or else . . . or else on their way to Bath.

So to Bath he had come. There was no better place in which to advertize yourself 'for sale', as it were. Something else had prompted him, too: some vague notion that by going to Bath he would be taking the cure, and that this would be a good thing. He didn't examine the notion any more closely than that. It might have revealed a suspicion that he was drinking too much, and that, of course, was nonsense.

'Move aside, there! Damn your eyes, move aside!'

For a moment Fairfax did not realize the rasping voice was addressing them. They had come to a tangle of horse and foot traffic by the entrance to the Bear Inn Yard, which was, inconveniently, the way through to the Hot Bath. A dray was trying to get out and a cart was trying to get in and, sensibly enough, Fairfax's companion had put down his side of the trunk and was taking a breath while the congestion cleared.

'What are you doing there? Make way, damn you!'

The voice came from behind them. Fairfax turned. It was

a gentleman being carried in a sedan-chair, who was thrusting his florid face out of the window – his hand, too, which brandished a long silver-headed cane.

About to say something, Fairfax was forestalled by his companion who was closer to the chair. 'You must wait, friend, like us,' he said, composedly taking out his handkerchief and wiping his face. ' 'Tis all a moiling of wheels here, and best let it clear.'

The gentleman plainly did not like that 'friend'.

'Are you deaf, or a fool? I told you to move!'

'If you'd *asked*, I would have said the same,' the man with the hook said stolidly. 'But as for being told . . .'

'Get out of the way, d'you hear?'

'Aye, I hear,' the man said, putting away his handkerchief. ' 'Tis all one to me, friend. You must wait.'

'Damn your insolence, do you know who I am?' The gentleman had pushed open the door of the chair, as if better to display himself – or to hurl himself at this impudent obstacle. Fairfax saw a gaunt frame beneath the velvet and silk: the hand that grasped the ornate cane was clawlike, more wilful than strong. The gentleman suggested a seedy eagle, with his sharp-drawn face, gimlet eyes, and fleshless jaw. He was ugly, but the ugliness was of handsomeness wrecked, and like all destruction it was rather fascinating. 'Do you know who I am?' he repeated.

'You are a man, as I am.' The shrug was unconcerned. Fairfax didn't think his companion was deliberately choosing the words that would most enrage the gentleman – but he could hardly have made a better job of it if he were.

'Pah! I've had enough of you. Stand away, I tell you!'

As he spoke, the gentleman made a slash in the air with his cane. A gesture, no doubt: but that veined and bony hand was unsteady and the cane swished within an inch of the stout man's nose.

For a moment something flashed through his rugged composure, but when he spoke his voice was level.

'Friend, I'll take that stick from you and break it over my knee, if you like.'

The gentleman in the sedan-chair gave a whoop of hard laughter. 'And now you threaten me! I don't think, my man, you quite understand—'

'I understand well: you are grander than me and so I must give place. But where I come from, these fal-lals don't matter, friend, that's all.' He bent and picked up his side of the trunk. 'Well, I think now there's room to shift—'

'What, you are a Scot, are you?' the gentleman said, studying his antagonist with new penetration. 'Always a pert set of people . . .'

'I speak of America,' the man said, casually. 'D'you have a good grip there, sir? We can soon—'

'America!' The gentleman spat the word out. 'I should have known. That parcel of rogues! I have read their treasonable bleatings, all because they will not pay a penny towards their own defence. This is their loyalty to the crown that shielded them in the late war.' He flourished the stick again. 'I'd see you all horsewhipped – every last man of you—'

'That would take quite a time, I think,' the man said, moving on so briskly that Fairfax had to hurry to keep up.

'Don't you walk away from me, sirrah!' The gentleman seemed determined to have the last word. 'I'll know you again, damn you – I know your face, d'you hear?'

'A fiery disposition,' Fairfax observed after a while, not knowing what else to say. He was rather relieved to have been left out of it: he had had enough confrontation for one day.

His companion seemed to jerk out of deep thought. 'Eh? Oh – yes. Too much choler in the blood, I fancy. Which way now?'

'Just the next turning – I shan't inconvenience you much longer. I was about to ask, before our interruption, whether you are a stranger here, but my question is answered. I have always had a great curiosity about the American colonies. The Red Indian tribes and their customs – they have seashells for currency, I hear – and—'

'A stranger,' the man said heavily. 'Yes, that is what I am. It is all very strange to me.'

He was silent then, and Fairfax forgot about the Red Indians and their seashells as a young woman crossed his path with a startling display of half-bare, uplifted and powdered bosom. Yawning and scratching, she walked up the steps of the nearest house with a similarly startling display of leg and let herself in.

Well, he had heard there were brothels in Avon Street. At least this wasn't actually next door to the house where, after an urgent search early this morning, he had found a lodging to rent. (It was two doors away.) Why this should bother him he didn't know. The nastiest things, he had found, often went on in private households, not in well-ordered businesses like brothels. But then the mantle of respectability was hard to let go of. Hence, no doubt, his outrage at being evicted.

Shabby-genteel, he thought, that's what I'm becoming. Dread phrase.

'Well, here we are. Sir, you've been most kind – and if you'd like to step in then I can offer you refreshment as soon as I unpack this—'

'Thank'ee, no. I'll bid you good day.'

An odd fish, Fairfax thought, watching the man stump away. For a moment he had wondered whether he should offer money, but decided it was inappropriate. When someone who was plainly needy did you a service, you gave money and they accepted it with no awkwardness on either side. But that man, despite his broadcloth coat and rough-hewn way, had an independence about him . . . Dear God, thought Fairfax, another dread phrase: you couldn't quite *place* him. Perhaps that was what had infuriated the gentleman in the sedan-chair.

He knocked at the door and was let in by his new landlady's maid. He had put down his fifteen shillings this morning with another five shillings 'for candles', the landlady had said – really a sweetener to stop her renting the rooms to someone else in the time it took him to fetch his things. But at least she had given him only an averagely suspicious glare, which she gave him again now, poking her mob-capped head out of her ground-floor parlour as he manoeuvred his trunk up the narrow stairs.

Was she going to complain of the noise? He would explode if she did. Noise was what had got him into trouble with the butcher of Cheap Street. To grumble about noise, in Bath! The place was a cacophony. Not just with the endless hubbub of traffic in a town grotesquely swollen with company – even in the autumn season, which was slightly less fashionable than spring – but with the discordant music of the town-waits, bands of strolling wind-players who made a living by honking and tootling until you paid them to stop, and with the repeated pealing of the Abbey bells, which were rung whenever a prominent visitor arrived. ('Prominent' meaning with their own carriage: Fairfax, rattling in on top of the public coach a fortnight ago, had been spared.) And all the noise he had made was to play his flute in his rooms of an evening.

Very well, of a night. The small hours, sometimes. But that was when the muse visited him. And yes, perhaps the muse visited him because he had been drinking wine till late, and then he just had to play his flute and be damned to the consequences . . . Still, it was no excuse for the way he had been treated. And as for being called a young sot . . .

'Flattering to be thought of as young,' he grunted to himself as he thrust open the door to his rooms and, with a final heave, dragged in the infernal trunk.

He sat down to get his breath, and took another look at his new home. Well, two rooms were better than none: narrow and cramped, but the whole house was like that – this was still unfashionable Lower Town Bath, not the lofty new squares and parades. Cane-bottomed chairs, brass candlesticks and tin snuffers, a worn rug, a couple of framed prints; and in the bedroom, an old sagging half-testered bed with shiny-worn flowered hangings and a faint odour of mildew.

Shabby-genteel. But at least in Bath he was not alone in that. From somewhere above he could just hear the squeaking of a kit-fiddle and the decorous tramp of feet. A dancing-master, no doubt. Yes, this was his place, amongst the dancing- and drawing-masters, governesses and companions, scribblers and barber-surgeons and half-pay officers . . . Like the one looking at him now. He hadn't closed the door, and a young soldier in regimentals stood there smiling.

'Couldn't help but notice new arrival, and forgive intrusion and all that, and before I extend hand of welcome, may I ask – do you sleepwalk, sir?'

'Never, to my knowledge.'

'Not a sufferer of night terrors, a moaner and screamer-out, or generally a party liable to hammer on another party's door at two in the morning and ask him to shoo the porcupines away?'

'I should hope not,' Fairfax said, laughing.

'Then here's the hand of welcome from your neighbour,' the soldier said coming in. 'Only you've guessed, no doubt, that those were the sort of tricks the last occupant of these rooms got up to. I won't say it didn't amuse at first, but even ghostly porcupines pall, you know, they do pall. Poor fellow. Francis Locke. Me, not him.' The soldier gave him his hand.

'Robert Fairfax.'

'Fairfax, eh? Like Cromwell's old general. Lot of fighting around these parts back in those days. Prince Rupert and all that. Odd to think of it now, ain't it? Englishmen killing Englishmen. All that burning faith. Different world. What would we kill each other for now? Money, perhaps? Root of all evil, they say. Scripture. Don't know my Bible as well as I should, mind.'

' "The love of money is the root of all evil",' Fairfax said. 'That's the text, I think. All very well, but I fancy the lack of money has much to answer for as well.'

'You're a philosopher. I am too. Here's something that sets me thinking. D'you remember a few years ago, when we thrashed the Frenchies in the wars, all over the globe?'

'I do. The church bells never stopped ringing.'

'Ah! And a man in a red coat was liable to get cheers wherever he went. I'm glad you remember it, sir, because damn me if it don't seem everyone else has forgot. And fellows like me, who were so much wanted then, don't seem to be wanted now. That's what makes me philosophize. But I'm only a lowly ensign. What do I know?'

'You fought in the late wars?'

'I think so. That is, I went with my regiment to Pennsylvania, and fired my gun in a lot of noise and smoke and infernal confusion, and fell down a slope and broke my arm, and afterwards I found we had retaken Fort Duquesne from the French, though I wasn't wholly aware we had ever lost it. Of course, you are a man. When I tell it to ladies, I stormed Quebec single-handed.' Ensign Locke yawned vastly and blinked about him. 'Your quarters look very much like mine. As if an old miser recently died in them. And what do you do in Bath, Mr Fairfax? Pardon infernal curiosity. I just like knowing other people's business.'

'I am a tutor. I came to look for pupils.'

'Found 'em?'

'Yes, I am engaged to teach French to . . . some people.' He wasn't supposed to say who: it was a curious business.

'Wish I had such a string to my bow. My father wasn't a great one for schooling. "A man knows enough who knows the value of a guinea" he used to say. Alderman Locke, of King's Lynn. You won't have heard of him. Brewer, fat belly, fat purse – I won't say fat head because that would be unkind, wouldn't it? "Money will do more than my lord's letter" was another saying of his. Still saying it just before he went bankrupt, alas. And alack, too, if you like – I always think alack is a little neglected, don't you? Anyhow, fortunately he was able to buy me a commission in the army before he went under. But alack again, that's all I have in the world. So naturally I have come to Bath to see what offers. A man can gamble decently here if nothing else. Now hark'ee, Mr Fairfax, I've got half a bottle of canary, unless you're a Methody, in which case I ain't.'

'I'm not, and I've got half a bottle of malmsey. We might put them together.'

They did, Locke fetching his bottle and two chipped glasses, and remarking as he poured that it was past ten, which made it practically noon, and so all right for liquor. Fairfax realized that he hadn't even thought about the hour . . . then pushed that thought away again. In truth, it was rather flattering to have his company sought by someone so young: thirty-five was hardly dotage, but many young blades saw it as such. And besides, he had been through an unpleasant experience this morning. As Locke caught sight of his torn and bloody stocking, he explained.

'Poke your thumbs into the brute's eyes, that's what you should do. Better dress that wound, though, in case it turns nasty.'

'You've seen worse, I dare say,' Fairfax said, feeling the wine go down. It was like the waving of an enchanter's wand.

'Well, I saw a man with his arm blown off to the elbow. Curious; all he did was swear like a tinker – or a trooper, which he was. It didn't look real, in truth.'

He was very tall, this young ensign – half of him legs; and handsome, with a fresh complexion and friendly brown eyes that seemed always to carry a twinkle of fellowship. When he got restlessly up and went to the looking-glass above the mantel, what he said was: ' 'Ods bobs, I look like the very devil,' but it was plain that he really admired what he saw. There was just a touch, too, of affectation about the way he carried himself, a reined-in swagger; and his long fingers were not very clean. But there was something irresistible about his laugh, which was a shout so explosive that it startled you into laughter before you knew it.

'I must be careful,' he went on with a last glance in the mirror. 'I'm a military man, and a toper. Therefore I'm doomed to end up with mulberry cheeks and blue lips and mad staring eyes – and living here, probably. Being carried to the baths every day and snarling about the iniquities of the young. God, what a vision!'

'I saw such a vision in the flesh today. A man was helping me with my trunk and we dared to obstruct this gentleman's chair. He was all ready to deal out a horse-whipping. His face was more plum than mulberry, though. A sort of awesome ruin of a man—'

'Heyo, that sounds like my colonel. When I say my colonel, I don't mean colonel of my regiment. *He* married a Creole heiress and then dropped dead of West-India fever before he could enjoy a doubloon of it. No, I'm talking about Delabole – Colonel Sir James Delabole. Mouthful of a name. Devil of a character, in all senses. Let's see, pigeon-wing wig? Hawkish sort of nose? Carries a silver-top cane . . .?'

'You have him.'

'That's Sir James, for a thousand pounds. And the horse-whipping of innocent strangers is quite in his line. Oh, he's delicious. I must introduce you – you'll be monstrously entertained. Oh, I thought he was fearsome at first. It was a fortnight ago when I came to Bath, travelling in the public coach of course, and we stopped to change horses at Marlborough. I was stretching my legs and having a cup of ale when in comes this spanking carriage, and out of *that* steps our singular friend and begins browbeating the inn-servants as soon as he's on his shaky legs. Like a fox in a hen-house. I dare say you stopped at Marlborough coming here, Mr Fairfax – excellent inn, ain't it? Fires lit, booths swept, every variety of comestible. But our friend wants pigeon-pie.

And it so happens that they haven't any – only a last piece that *I'd* bespoke. Up goes our friend like twenty fireworks. There's beef and mutton and pork and broiled fowls – but he won't have anything but pigeon-pie. Well, of course I steps up and invites him to have mine. I wasn't particular and, in truth, I feared he would have an apoplexy on the spot otherwise. Remarkable transformation of fierce old cuss into tender lamb – I'm not talking about meat now, by the way. "Sir, you are a true gentleman, give me your hand," and all that. Of course, this helped.' Locke tapped the breast of his red coat. 'There was no doubt he was a military man from the way he barked at those poor serving-wenches as if they were so many troopers. And it turns out he knew my commanding officer – said my behaviour was everything he'd expect from that gallant regiment and where had I served and what-naught – and the upshot was he invited me to dine in his booth. And when we were done, actually pressed me to finish the journey to Bath in his own carriage. Well, of course I wasn't about to decline. You'll agree, Mr Fairfax, that a man without prospects goes to Bath precisely in the hope of cultivating influential acquaintance. But besides that, the man was plainly a character and I love a character above all things. And so most unexpectedly I made my entrance into Bath with the Abbey bells ringing. Not a thing I ever expected. They're more likely to ring the bells when I *leave* a place. Ha! And since then, I've been encouraged to consider myself one of Sir James's party here. Take a turn with him about the Pump Room, call whenever I please at his house in the Circus – oh, yes, he's taken a whole house for the season, he's monstrous rich – and generally consider myself a lucky dog.'

'My congratulations. He has a large party?'

'Oh, just wife and daughter. Agreeable creatures, mild as

he's spicy. Well, that's the party for *now*. There's a curious story here and it's still unfolding. Don't worry, it ain't a dull one – plenty of scandal in it. Fact is, the colonel's current wife ain't his first. Twenty-odd years ago, when he was a dashing young captain – forgive the circulating-library language – he fell in love with a pretty wine-merchant's daughter. I mean the daughter was pretty, not the wine-merchant. And do I mean *love*? I think it must have been on her part because she threw up everything and eloped with him in spite of her father, who didn't approve of the attachment at all. Then, Sir James was just plain Captain James Delabole, an officer with a racy reputation and few prospects, as it seemed. He was of good family, but he was a younger brother: it was his elder brother who inherited the baronetcy and the estate in Hampshire, and all James D. had was his commission and a clutch of debts. But the wine-merchant had done well for himself: and so one does wonder whether, when the captain whisked the girl away and married her, he was hoping her father would do something financially handsome, once he was reconciled to the marriage. But it appears the merchant never was reconciled to it. He did not unlock the coffers, or give the couple his reluctant blessing. The captain and his young bride went abroad, in the fashion of elopers with nothing a year to live on; there in France, it seems, it all went tragically sour and they parted. This is the point where you must take your pick on what you believe. Did the captain feel she had misled him about her prospects of an inheritance? Or was he just a rogue? At any rate, they quarrelled and he decamped, leaving her alone and pregnant.'

'Hm. A rogue, whatever the circumstances.'

'It don't look pretty, I admit. I speak no secrets, by the way: all this is a musty tale of yesteryear, though no doubt it made delicious tattle in its day. Well! The unhappy bride had her child and made her way back to these shores, and her stern father, the wine-merchant, at last gathered his erring daughter back to his relenting bosom. I'm quite catching the style of this thing, aren't I? Well, the poor girl's spirit seems to have been quite broke, and she went into a consumptive decline and soon died – leaving the merchant in sole charge of the little girl-child she'd borne. So he brought her up himself. She had her father's surname, but nothing else, and that seemed the end of their connection. The old wine-merchant wanted naught to do with the villain who'd taken his daughter – and the captain showed no great interest in claiming his child. Viewed the whole thing as a youthful indiscretion, I dare say.'

'You are not making me like this Delabole very much.'

'Oh, my dear sir, I don't *like* him particular, myself, but there's no denying he's a character. And there's no denying either that when a gentleman's handsome and well-born, society's apt to forgive him a good deal. Especially when he starts gathering honours to himself, as that penniless young captain did. First he was promoted major under Cumberland, putting down the Pretender in 'forty-six. Then he married again – the heiress of a rich lawyer this time, getting past her bloom and counting herself lucky to have hooked him, and with no disapproving parent to spoil things. Then, wonder of wonders, his brother the baronet died young and childless and suddenly he had an estate. In the late wars he was made colonel, and he swelled his fortune with various pieces of jobbery in the Ordnance, and a grateful sovereign gave him a knighthood.'

'The reward of virtue,' said Fairfax, putting aside the empty canary bottle.

'Dry, sir. I like it. Well now, here he is, Colonel Sir James Delabole, fifty going on seventy – all that good living, you know – full of gout and full of honours. He's lived abroad a good deal – Gibraltar – then Jersey where he was governor – and there's a hint of laying down the old bones about him now. Sink to his rest in his dear homeland and all that. Now what goes through a man's mind when he gets old and decayed I don't know – hope I never find out – but it seems Sir James has got to thinking of the past and the daughter he's never known, that neglected flower of his first love – am I nauseating you?'

'Well, *he* is. So, he fancies himself as a repentant rake now, is that it?'

'I don't know about repentant. That would mean admitting he was wrong, which is . . . well, not his way. But it is reconciliation he's after. The wine-merchant retired here to Bath some years since, with his precious granddaughter; and that's what brings Sir James here, besides the waters. He wrote to the old man to make his first approaches, I believe, and got a stony answer. But he's persisted, and they *have* met without tearing each other's throats, though it's all still quite ticklish.'

'It was forgiving of the wine-merchant, I think.'

'Well, there's the girl herself, don't forget. Suddenly here's the father she never met, a man mighty grand and distinguished in his way: natural if she's curious to see him. And it ain't just a matter of embraces and fine words. The nub is, Sir James is a rich man – God, he's rich! And hearing time's chariot at his back, doing whatever time's chariot does, he turns his mind to where he's going to leave his property. Ah yes – that's the interesting question! D'you know, I've had more entertainment out of these people than a dozen plays!'

'And what will he do, do you think?'

'There you have the suspense of the piece. I don't know – he certainly don't confide in me – and I fancy no one does know. But I'll say this: I reckon he's as sentimental as only a hardened old rakehell can be, and he's mightily struck with this brand new daughter of his. I've seen that for myself.' Ensign Locke drained his glass and smacked his lips. 'See for yourself! Aye, that's my cordial invitation to you, Mr Fairfax. The wine is gone and the morning is fine. Let's go and parade ourselves in the Pump Room, like every other Bath booby, and there you're sure to meet Sir James at the least, if you're equal to it.'

'He can't be worse than a butcher's dog. All right: let me just change my stockings.'

Even primed with wine as he was, some part of Fairfax inwardly protested that he hadn't even unpacked. He ought to be settling himself in properly . . . Oh, but that was old and fussy. He contented himself with pulling a clean pair of stockings from his trunk and hastily retying his cravat. The face in the mirror reproached him, in spite of himself. Thirty-five, Robert; and see how the wine is drawing these lines under the eyes. For a moment he imagined his former mentor, Samuel Johnson, frowning over his shoulder. *So what is this, Robbie? You are setting yourself up as a man of sorrows, is that the shape of it? You lost a lady-love who was never yours to begin with, and so you cease to care for yourself. And you pledge bumpers with some young coxcomb of an ensign, because it gives you a sickly fancy of being young yourself.*

Yes, that was about right. But acknowledging it changed nothing.

'By the by, Mr Fairfax, you don't know of a good bone-setter hereabouts, I suppose?'

'I can't say I do. Do you still carry a wound?' He thought Locke looked as lithe as a tumbler.

'Oh . . . fetched a crack in the ankle-bone at Fort Duquesne. The surgeon fixed it but he was always half-seas over, in truth, and it still gives me trouble now and then. I fancy it wasn't set right, and you hear of these fellows who know how to give a twist and a wrench in the right way and all's well. I thought Bath was a likely place – every sort of leech and quack here – but never mind. Ready?'

On their way out, Locke pushed open a door standing ajar on the ground floor.

'We'll see if Macleod wants to join us. He won't, though . . . Holla, Davey! Here's a new inmate for the madhouse. Mr Fairfax. He teaches pupils, like you, except you scare yours off.'

'I'd say come in, Locke, but you are in. Sir, how d'ye do? Forgive me not shaking hands, but I'd only daub you.' A young man dressed in a threadbare banyan, a loose cap on his unwigged head, was painting at an easel by the window. He greeted Fairfax with a lift of his pugnacious chin, his eyes hardly straying from his work. It was a very large canvas, for the most part roughly blocked, but marble limbs and a fluted column suggested a classical subject.

'Macleod's a drawing-master,' Locke said. 'Or at least that's the idea, isn't it, Davey?' His tone was affectionately malicious.

'Go boil your head, you puling redbreast,' Macleod said robustly. 'I have a new pupil to visit this afternoon, as it happens.'

'But will you keep this one?'

'The slubberdegullion is referring, Mr Fairfax, to the matter of my last pupil. No great secret. She was a young

20

woman of uncommon stupidity, whose fond parents wished her to learn fashionable accomplishments. She had already defeated a music-teacher who could not get her to understand that the keys of the harpsichord were different from the key that unlocked it. With me, it was a simple sketch of Prior Park that did it. "Sketch the foliage lightly," says I, "like this." "Foliage?" "Leaves, madam, leaves." "But must I draw every leaf, then?" says she. "Damn your eyes," says I, "can you *see* every damnation leaf?" That was the end of that. No great loss. I am a drawing-master by necessity: but *this* –' he made a sweeping gesture at his canvas – 'by avocation.'

'That don't pay, though, does it? There's the rub,' Locke said.

'Ach, you think of naught but money, Locke.'

'Consequence of not having any.'

'The subject, sir,' Macleod said to Fairfax, 'is the grief of Niobe for her dead children. A most beautiful and sublime fable, calling for the most elevated treatment—'

'And a deal of naked flesh. No one would give a hang for those old Greeks and Romans if they'd worn a lot of clothes,' Locke said. 'Come on, Davey, we're going to take a turn in the Pump Room. Join us. Feast your eyes on real beauties instead of pretend ones in togas.'

'Women didn't wear the toga, ass. Go, go, before I find a place for this maul-stick. I'll come another time.'

'He never does,' Locke said as they left. 'Dedicated, you see. Or mad.'

Fairfax found he rather envied the young Scot. Walking with Locke to the Pump Room, through the singularly aimless bustle of the Bath streets, he found himself entertaining an ascetic fantasy: himself in a room like Macleod's, solitary and rapt, hard at work. (At what? He couldn't paint

21

but he had scribbled in his time, and he had entertained thoughts of an epic poem on the subject of King Arthur – though he doubted that would ever appeal.) Yes, that was the life, surely... He felt the gravely mocking presence of Johnson again. *So, instead of a disillusioned wastrel, you are now a dedicated artist. Which is it to be, Robbie? Who are you?*

Indeed, Fairfax thought, as they plunged into the stifling throng of the Pump Room, who am I?

'You,' said a harsh voice in his ear, 'are that villain I saw earlier.'

Two

'Or you were with him, at any rate,' the gentleman went on, as Fairfax turned. 'I was a touch intemperate, I think. But I have an invalid's crotchets, and I must make my visit to the Hot Bath every morning at exactly the same time, else I am put out of humour. But give me a round cursing, by all means, and we shall be even.'

It was the same gentleman he had seen in the sedan-chair earlier – the same face, at once hawkish and fleshy, the same ruined complexion, the same gaunt frame supported by the same long silver-headed cane – but now gently smiling and exerting such a degree of charm that Fairfax was quite taken aback.

'The trouble with Bath,' the gentleman went on confidentially, 'is that it is still neither fish nor fowl. Mr Wood the architect has wrought wonders, but at the heart there is still the cramped medieval city. I suppose medieval people did not find it cramped. I always imagine them smaller than us. At six feet Henry the Eighth was accounted a giant.'

This man was certainly six feet tall, or rather had been. Infirmity had rounded his shoulders and thrust his head down: indeed to look at him was almost to see the hands of mortality, a dexterous torturer, at their work – twisting his spine, attenuating his limbs, caving in his chest. A touch of grotesquerie was added by his feet, which were so swollen that he wore specially-made shoes, wide as dinner-plates. Finest leather, though: embroidery and pearl buttons on his coat and waistcoat, and a jewelled pin nestling in the lace at his neck. I am still a figure, they said. I am still very much alive, said the hard eyes scanning Fairfax from head to foot.

'Well, Locke,' the gentleman went on, tugging at the ensign's sleeve, 'be a good fellow and introduce us.'

'Of course, Sir James – though, as usual, it seems you are ahead of me. This is Mr Fairfax who has taken lodgings next to mine. Colonel Sir James Delabole. I believe, Mr Fairfax, I may have mentioned his name to you,' Locke said, with a straight-faced look.

'I'm honoured, sir,' Fairfax said. 'Do you find the bathing of benefit?'

'My physician says it is. And he is infallible, of course. He lost a patient last week. "What," I asked him, "went wrong?" "Nothing," he said, "nature took its course." Fine profession! If they cure you, they take the credit: if you die, then there was nothing to be done. Like gaming with loaded dice. But as to the baths, they must be miraculous indeed if they can make a whole man out of *me* – don't you think?'

He said it with a sort of grim boastfulness. There was no reply to be made, unless a flattering one: it was Locke who came up with it.

'You look uncommonly fine, sir, as anyone in this room would say; and such infirmities as you bear come from a life dedicated to your country's service, and only do you credit.'

'You needn't lay it on so thick,' Sir James said – though he looked pleased. 'You make me sound like some sort of saint. It's good living that's broken me – but not what the parsons call good living. Play, women and wine undo a man, they say. Well, here's the proof. Damn me if it's not the women who take the most out of you – eh?' He gave a yelping laugh, with which Locke joined in, and poked Fairfax in the ribs with a skeletal finger. 'Come, man, never tell me you're a prude. You know I'm in the right of it. Are you married?'

'No.'

'Then count your blessings. I've been caught twice. Where *is* my lady? Oh, I see her. And that doltish daughter of mine gawking at the bathers again. They look rum enough, I'll warrant, but the novelty should have palled by now. She came in for her mother's brains as well as her looks, I fear. Come, we'll take a turn that way. Give me your arm, Locke. Abominable crush in here today. Half of 'em people of no account.'

Well, Fairfax had no doubts about which half he belonged to. On entering the Pump Room he had seen the Master of Ceremonies give him a look, as if wondering whether he was worth his time, and then turn away. It was fair enough: Fairfax had not written his name in the subscription-books for the coffee-houses, the reading-rooms and the Walks, nor had he paid calls, nor frequented the Assembly Rooms, as people did who sought to be noticed. As for the more spectacular means of advertizing oneself socially here – being attended by a quartet of horn-players, and treating the company at the hotels to turtle-soup dinners – they were wholly beyond his means.

But no matter: though the Master of Ceremonies might ignore him, he could not have him thrown out unless he wore a sword or molested ladies. And that was one of the things Fairfax did like about Bath. The public rooms, like the Pump Room, genuinely were public. The company gathered here today was as varied a mixture as you would find anywhere. The wasp-waisted dandy strolled past the stout bumpkin in a tie-wig who might well supply his candles or blacking: the skirts of the tradesman's wife brushed those of the duchess. Fairfax thought that, at least, was healthy. In other ways the place was an instant headache. The press of bodies made it hot and airless, and conversation was a trial against the babble of voices and the sawing of music from the gallery. Sir James Delabole's ladies, Fairfax thought, had the right idea: the best entertainment to be had was watching the bathers in the King's Bath, which was below the windows of the Pump Room. Reconciling total immersion in the healing hot water with public decency had led to this strange spectacle, with the men in drawers and canvas waistcoats and the women in great loose gowns of linen that swelled out in the water; a straw hat with a handkerchief tucked in it to wipe the sweating brow completed the unusual ensemble. The bath-guides, strapping creatures of both sexes who helped the bathers in and out, wore nothing stranger than a tasselled cap, but the ultimate absurdity for Fairfax was the broad-brimmed hat with the crown cut out that you donned to have your head pumped – a good sluicing on the skull being supposedly good for palsy.

There were sobering sights too: a blind man openly smiling at the feel of the water, a dreadfully crippled little girl of six or seven being lowered in with infinite gentleness by her own father.

'Well, my dears, it feels a lot better than it looks, let me assure you,' Sir James Delabole said to his women. 'Here's a friend of Locke's to meet you – Mr Fairfax. Are you a Yorkshire Fairfax, sir?'

'I come from Suffolk, like thin beer and hard cheese.' And

my father was the Justice Fairfax who ended in disgrace and suicide. Fairfax preferred not to speak of his origins, though he didn't much care if Delabole caught on to them. The colonel would no doubt disapprove, with all the moral loftiness of the unprincipled seducer. 'Lady Delabole: ma'am, an honour. Miss Delabole: charmed.'

The two ladies, who had turned from the window at Sir James's approach with the nervous promptness of over-trained dogs, were alike in being finely dressed, and as pale as Sir James was purple. As for the rest, the daughter was a quivering miss of seventeen or so with great moist eyes and a pursed mouth of surpassing sulkiness. She looked at Fairfax as if he had done her an intolerable, irreparable wrong. Lady Delabole – tall, very fair, more lean than slender – was glacial in her polite composure, as if she had been introduced to a hundred Fairfaxes that morning, all in a line. Poised, Fairfax thought – but then one could be poised over an abyss. He had an intuition, the source of which he did not care to examine, that Lady Delabole drank.

'What the devil does that creature mean,' Sir James said, turning to regard a much-dressed lady sailing by in a cloud of pomade, 'wearing patches at a morning gathering? I declare this place has no more *ton* than Billingsgate of late.'

'Oh, sir, you are harsh. That poor woman has need of artifice. The trouble is, you're spoiled by the continual presence of beauties, already amply supplied by nature.' Locke directed his gallantry, with a bow, at both ladies. Lady Delabole just momentarily modified her expression of genteel boredom, but her daughter lit up.

'Oh, I love nature above everything,' she said. 'I wish everyone felt so but they don't. They are most horribly artificial and have no sensibility—'

'Pooh, this is some new nonsense you have got in your head, Selina,' her father snapped, 'from reading foolish novels, no doubt. These damned circulating-libraries have much to answer for, filling girls' heads with stuff. Nature's all very well, but it ain't nature that makes those frizzles in your hair, or puts that fine gown on your back. Unless you'd prefer to go barefoot, and wrap yourself in skins like a savage, hey? Well, would you?'

'No, indeed, sir,' she said in a spiritless manner. Fairfax had seldom seen anyone so swiftly extinguished; and though he thought she talked nonsense, he was sorry for her. Perhaps she divined this, because she gave him another glare of bitter hostility.

'Do you go to the Assembly ball tomorrow, Mr Fairfax?' Lady Delabole said, staunchly summoning up the energy to speak to him.

'I have taken up no subscription, and do not think to, ma'am.'

'Why, that was before you met me, you dull dog,' Locke said. 'I have tickets, and I insist upon your going. I promise you'll find it diverting, if only to see me cut a caper. None of your minuets, though. Country-dances for me, cotillions, plenty of leg-work – when I dance I dance, not mince like a clockwork toy . . .' Laughing, he did a jig on the spot. Selina Delabole, Fairfax noticed, gazed at him worshipfully.

'Your ankle will not prevent you, then?' Fairfax said. Locke certainly did not look like a man with an ill-set break in his leg. But perhaps he had a touch of the hypochondriac in him.

'Eh? Oh – it takes you unawares, you know. Unpredictable. Like the fair sex. All sweetness and peace and then suddenly

– bang!' Locke cocked a smile at Miss Delabole. 'You're flattened.'

'Ah, time was when I'd have danced you all off the floor,' Sir James said, loudly: he seemed to be a little pushed out of the picture, and not liking it. 'Dance till two in the morning, then go on to cards till dawn, and never a moment's weariness even then. There's many a Covent Garden nymph who'll testify to that.' He grinned harshly at Fairfax, who did not grin back. Accustomed, obviously, to ready sycophancy, the colonel took him up. 'What? Do I shock you, sir? Are you a curate, or a Methody or some such?'

'No, sir. Nor am I shocked. I supposed you simply stating the facts of your past. But pardon me, perhaps I mistook you, and you were only jesting.'

Sir James studied him sourly. 'Pah, any man who claims to have been a saint in his youth is a liar or a milksop.'

'Well, there is no late dancing here, at any rate,' Locke put in, 'not a step after eleven – all propriety and decorum. They say in Beau Nash's day he even refused Princess Amelia one more dance, and made her put up her fan and go off to bed.'

'I knew Nash. Father was a damned glassmaker – had no more breeding than that footman, for all his airs,' grunted Sir James. 'Locke, help me to that bench, will you. My legs are all red-hot pins.'

Solicitously, Locke gave the colonel his arm and helped him to a bench near the bar where the spring-water was served.

'Very bad, my dear?' Lady Delabole said, her hand on his shoulder.

'Of course not, I'm groaning for the fun of it.' He jabbed his cane in the direction of an old man who was being pushed in a wheeled chair. 'Hm. Barring a miracle, that will be my next conveyance. That or a hearse.'

'Papa, you mustn't speak so,' Miss Delabole said.

'Oho, I mustn't, eh?' The colonel was all acid. 'So I am to be dictated to by my own little chit of a girl, am I? I wasn't aware you'd become head of the household, my dear, but there, my wits must be more enfeebled than I thought.'

'I only meant that it is upsetting.' Miss Delabole was so very whiney: Fairfax found irritation getting in the way of sympathy.

'Well, well, I am touched, my dear. Touched to think of the tears you will shed for me. Perhaps they will be as copious as the tears you shed over that damned canary-bird. So giddy-headed she forgets to feed it,' Sir James said with a grimace at Fairfax, 'then weeps like a waterspout when it drops dead . . . Ah!'

The colonel had just seen someone come in and his face changed completely. Suddenly it was wistful, uplifted, vision-ary. He creaked to his feet.

'My dear . . .! Over here . . .! Ah, but that's a sight to cheer a sick man's heart. How do you do, my dear? And Tiverton, good morning to you – give me your hand. Well, this is a merry meeting!'

The newcomers were a young woman and an old man. This, Fairfax thought, must be the long-lost daughter and her grandfather. A glance told him that she was a beauty, one who made heads turn, and he a big hale hard-grained fellow, twenty years older than the colonel but looking as if he would outlive him by another twenty. But his attention was chiefly on the faces of Lady Delabole and her daughter. For he had been thinking, whilst making Sir James Delabole's acquaint-ance and disliking him as much as he had expected to, of the story Locke had told him; what intrigued him was how the colonel's current family felt. Here he was, seeking out the child of an early first marriage, about whom he had never bothered his head before, and lavishing attention on her . . . and from the gallant way he bent to kiss the young woman's hand, treating her with a good deal more consideration than he showed to Lady Delabole and Selina. Were they not put out? Jealous? Or were they simply too cowed by him for any independence of thought?

It was hard to tell. Lady Delabole was all colourless correctness. If pressed to assign an emotion to her ivory face, you might say she was vaguely concerned about whether she had sent all her handkerchiefs to the wash yesterday. Even that was overstating it. As for Selina, she looked prettily sulky – but then she continually did, except when Ensign Locke spoke to her.

'Please, sir, don't stand on my account. Take your ease, I beg,' the young woman said.

'I will, my dear, as you're good enough to suggest it – but will you sit by me? That's well. And how do you find yourself, sweeting? The last time I saw you was at the Spring Gardens, and I was concerned, for just as you went home there was a rain-shower and I feared you would catch cold.'

'I am quite well, I thank you, sir.'

'Aye, that I can see from your bloom. Who would suppose we are kin, eh, Locke? Roses in those cheeks. I don't know what in mine – plums, probably. You've met Ensign Locke, of course, my dear. Mr Fairfax here is a neighbour of his. Sir, this is my daughter from my first marriage: Caroline Delabole.'

Pleased as Punch, Fairfax thought – appropriate given the colonel's looks and temper. He bowed over Caroline

Delabole's hand, and for once thanked heaven he was not ten years younger, for he would have fallen in love with her in short order. It was not just the beauty, but the cool, low, fluty voice, the air of simplicity set off by the chip hat and the plain blue gown, the strong white hands, the direct gaze. Nothing finicky about her. The old man, her grandfather, who was introduced as Mr Gilbert Tiverton, had a watchful look on his leathery face as he shook Fairfax's hand. Well, Fairfax thought, it isn't me you should fear taking her away.

'But Tiverton, I didn't think to see you in the Pump Room. Not your usual habit, hey? I don't complain of it, mind,' Sir James said, patting Caroline's hand.

'We come here but seldom,' Gilbert Tiverton said, pulling a snuff-box from the folds of his black stuff suit and taking a hearty pinch. 'Visitors do, though you incline to it less when you are settled at Bath. But I have had some trifling indisposition of the stomach, and the waters are a sovereign cure for that.'

'What, you are going to drink the stuff?' Sir James said. 'Rather you than me. I find a dip in it eases my legs, or I fancy it does, but as for swallowing it, I'd sooner drink a horse-puddle. But there, 'tis your stomach.'

'As you say,' Mr Tiverton said stiffly. 'It is my stomach.' He stumped over to the bar, indicated to the pumper the largest of the polished glasses ranged there and, when it was filled with the hot spring-water, drank it down in slow deliberate gulps. Loath as he was to agree with Sir James on anything, Fairfax found himself growing queasy. He had tried it once, and had been put in mind of drinking his own shaving-water.

'Your grandfather don't much love me, I'm afraid, my dear,' said Sir James smiling to Caroline. 'I can't say I blame him, in truth. It's been a great jolt to him, I dare say, my popping up again after all this time, and has stirred some melancholy memories, perhaps. But we shall rub along splendidly soon enough. I have tried to be discreet, you know: since coming to Bath I have not pressed myself upon you or him, I hope, but have taken things most gently, one step at a time. I know well 'tis a ticklish situation, and if I had met with a complete rebuff, from him or you, I would have taken it like a gentleman. But come, I have managed the matter pretty well, have I not, Caroline? We are getting to know each other, day by day, by these gentle degrees – and I'm sure you are beginning to find I'm not such an ogre as I'm painted, eh? Or does your grandfather still call me so, when you're alone? Whisper it in my ear, my dear – no harm in that!'

'Sir, you know indeed I can't go tattling tales like that – it would be unfair on everyone,' Caroline said, smiling, and very composed. 'And besides, you know there is no need to speak so. When you first communicated with us, and declared your intention of coming here to see me, I own I was surprised and a little fluttered. But the choice was generously left to me, whether I wished a reconciliation or not: my grandfather said he would abide by it and you know he is most staunchly true to his word. I chose, and do not regret it. Whatever the unhappiness of the past, it is still a great joy to me to find a father. And what is more, a sister,' she added, leaning forward to throw a friendly look at Selina, 'and never mind that silly word "half". I hope we can be wholly sisters to one another, in affection if not in law.'

She spat that out well, Fairfax thought. A pity that she couldn't have included Lady Delabole, but it would have been simply off-key to say she had found a mother – and stepmother didn't have the same ring. He studied Caroline Delabole's broad-browed, firm-lipped face.

Statuesque described her handsome figure, so what was the corresponding word for her face? Bustesque? Something suggesting luminous repose, at any rate. As for underneath, she was either a genuinely sweet-natured young woman or a mistress of pretence and self-serving manipulation.

'And you never thought, I hope, that your absent father – well, that he had no love or care for you?' Sir James said haltingly. 'It was not so, believe me. But the unhappy history of your late mother and I . . . the jealous tenderness of the grandfather who raised you . . . the unsettled life thrust upon me by the army . . . all these made it seem that my absence was both best for you and unavoidable. I thought of you much – and now in the days of my retirement I can turn thought to deed.'

In other words, he feels he's not long for this world, and he's not greatly impressed with the way his other child's turned out. And in a spirit of holy sentimentality he's fixed on you to give a fillip to his self-regard now that he's an old corrupt wreck . . . Fairfax reproached himself for his cynicism, but he thought he was right.

Mr Tiverton came back. It was plain that he did not like having his granddaughter out of his sight. As for her sitting next to Sir James, he surely did not like that either. But there was little choice except to stand sturdily by, not quite knowing what to do with himself – especially his hands. He tried grasping the lapels of his coat, but that made him look as if he were about to give a speech. Not funny, though, this man: no lightness about him. Oak-solid, solemn, he looked as if he could be every bit as difficult a customer as Sir James if he chose.

'Well, Tiverton, d'you feel the benefit of that? It don't appear to have improved you, but you know best,' Sir James said. He unscrewed the heavy silver top of his cane and drew from it a miniature flask of pewter. With a sigh he put it to his lips. 'This is the stuff for me. Do you know what it is, Caroline? A spirit, but not brandy, no, nor rum. Usquebaugh, our Celtic friends call it. It means water of life. And upon my soul, it's well named. You should try a little of this, Tiverton – for thy stomach's sake, as scripture has it.'

Mr Tiverton shook his great full-wigged head. 'I abstain from liquors, sir, as you well know.'

'And yet you deal in 'em! That's a curious thing, ain't it?'

'As well you know also, sir, I retired from active business some years since. I retain some small interest in a firm at Bristol –' Mr Tiverton, as if it irritated him too much to look at Sir James, addressed himself to Fairfax – 'a share, an advisory word, no more. I was formerly an importer of wines, with a place in the City. As for not drinking them, there is naught uncommon in that. A man may deal in horse-fodder, but he doesn't serve it at table.'

'Or petticoats – but let us hope he don't wear 'em,' said Locke, to a muffled squeal from Selina.

'God's life, that's enough talk of *trade*, I think,' Sir James said with a look of distaste, replacing the top of his cane. 'Tell me, Caroline, what you have been a-doing since last I saw you.'

'Me? Oh – well, I have been netting a purse. And I have practised hard upon the harpsichord, for I have some new pieces by Mr Bach come from London. And we took a walk in the Grove and then went to call on an old servant who is poorly with an ague, and I read to her for a while from the newspaper, which she dearly loves, doesn't she, Grandfather? Her favourite is the King of Prussia. If she hears nothing of him for a time, she is quite concerned. The American colonies, though, she has no patience with.'

'She has taste, my dear,' Sir James said smiling. 'My blood boils when I hear the bleating of those rogues. Our arms have performed valiant deeds in their defence – here's a young fellow who has been there and braved the Frenchie cannon on their behalf,' he gestured at Locke, who struck a mournfully heroic pose that made the girl smile. 'Yet they grumble, and call us tyrants . . . but there, my physician has warned me against boiling blood, so I'll say no more. Well, 'tis a delightful picture, Caroline. Mild – very mild and domestic. Naught wrong with that, of course: but there is so much more in the world, my dear, for a young lady like you. Twenty-one, well educated and accomplished – I congratulate you on that, Tiverton, she's a credit to you – with beauty and address, and of course with *expectations* . . .'

Was there a little cruel mischief in the way Sir James let that word hang in the air, with Lady Delabole and Selina looking on? Fairfax wondered. But Caroline only shook her head and said gently: 'Sir, you are very kind – but really you know you are talking nonsense.'

'Ha! Am I? Why, you don't know the stir you would make in London, my dear. Bath is all very well – and I believe even here you have lived in a sheltered way, and kept out of society – but London is the place for you. Damn it all, if I had my way I'd whisk you off there in a twinkling, and you would see for yourself—'

'You know, sir, this is a matter to be talked of only with due consideration,' Mr Tiverton said, glowering. 'Not lightly – no, no. And Caroline's life in my care has not been as you represent it. Her childhood was spent in London, before we retired here, and so—'

'Pooh, a City man's London – stock-jobbers and prentice-boys and a trip to the tea-gardens twice a year. Come, Tiverton, you know what I mean: society, man, the season. That's the place for her. She's equipped for it in all respects. Not least, in who she is: the eldest daughter of Colonel Sir James Delabole.'

Something of a gauntlet thrown down there, Fairfax thought. It was Caroline who took it up, very gracefully, saying: 'So I am, and happy to be so: just as I'm happy to be the granddaughter of Mr Tiverton of Bath; and I don't see why I can't be both. We are all a family now, are we not?'

She looked in appeal to Lady Delabole, who said: 'Of course, my dear. Whatever you say,' so remotely that she might have been up in the gallery with the fiddlers.

'Indeed.' Mr Tiverton – whose eyes never seemed to blink, perhaps because that would mean losing sight of Caroline for an instant – cleared his throat noisily. 'Well, it is in that spirit that I wish to extend an invitation to you and yours, sir. That's partly why I came, knowing I would find you here. If you will dine with us this evening, I shall be . . .' Plainly he couldn't say *delighted*. 'I shall be obliged. Nothing on the grand scale, but we have a little occasion, and if you would care to be of the party—'

'My dear fellow, I should like nothing better. An olive branch indeed, eh? – letting me across your threshold again? Nay, I jest,' Sir James said. 'But what's the occasion? Are you another year older, and deeper in credit?'

Mr Tiverton's habitual frown deepened. 'The occasion is by way of welcome to a friend of ours: Mr Pinner, an excellent young man who has been abroad some while on business. He is the son of my late overseer, who set up on his own account as a Bristol merchant. I took an early interest in promoting his career: he has talents and industry, and a sound character.'

'Ah, a protégé of yours, eh?'

'I suppose so,' Mr Tiverton agreed cautiously. 'I have been his patron, and over time he has come to stand somewhat in the light of a member of the family. Caroline has known him many years, and can testify to his qualities.'

'Heyo, is this fellow a beau of yours, my dear? Is that the shape of it?' Sir James said. 'Well, 'tis no wonder if he's smitten. But as for Bristol-merchants, Caro, there are a lot more men to choose from than *that*. In London you could snap your fingers and have half a hundred dashing young sparks, well-born and in the pink of fashion, fighting for the honour of carrying your fan.'

'Dear me, sir, you're talking nonsense again,' Caroline said, though her eyes were shining. 'I'm sure you will like Mr Pinner greatly, if you will join us. And – Mr Locke, I think, is of your party? If you would do us the honour also, sir?'

'Him? Aye, I'll answer for him,' the colonel grunted, 'as long as you don't let him near the brandy. I know these young ensigns.'

Misunderstanding, Mr Tiverton said to Fairfax, 'Oh, you are a military gentleman also, sir?'

'No, no,' Fairfax said. 'I am a tutor.'

Sir James's head went up. 'Good God! A schoolmaster? Well, that's Bath for you nowadays: no distinctions. I'd supposed you a gentleman, sir.'

Well, looked at in a certain way, that was a compliment, Fairfax thought: he could *pass* for a gentleman, in other words. He tried not to care but he was filled with black rage.

Before he could speak, however – and the words that sprang to his lips would certainly have ended his association with the Delaboles altogether – Mr Tiverton put in: 'A tutor, sir? I am glad to know you. I place the highest value upon education. Caroline had the best of governesses, and I was always tempted to the schoolroom myself, wasn't I, my dear? I was sent to apprentice as a youth, alas, and sorely missed knowledge. Please, join us this evening, Mr Fairfax. You will be more than welcome.'

Well, that was genuine enough – though of course he was also being used in the battle between Mr Tiverton and the colonel. 'Thank you,' he said, 'I shall be honoured.'

'As long as you don't talk Latin and Greek to us over the dinner-table, sir,' the colonel said, with an unpleasant smile.

'I assure you, Sir James, I shall endeavour to fit my conversation to your understanding.'

' 'Tis settled then. Sir James, Lady Delabole, Miss Selina, sirs: I shall see you this evening,' Mr Tiverton said. He had the look of a man who has just made himself swallow some nasty medicine. 'Caroline, are you ready?'

'Perhaps I shall hear you play tonight, my dear?' Sir James said, keeping hold of Caroline's hand. 'You are quite the musician, I understand. Ah, I have missed out on so much . . .! We have been estranged too long, Tiverton – really it is a damnable shame, eh? What say you?'

Fairfax saw Mr Tiverton's shoulders twitch, but all the old man said was: 'Aye, aye: let us just be easy.'

Delabole wants him to be bitterly hostile, Fairfax thought. Either that, or full of tearful forgiveness, because he is sentimental and self-dramatizing, and he must have the big scene. But old Mr Tiverton was too close, dry and careful for that. Which didn't mean he wasn't harbouring powerful feelings underneath that drab waistcoat. If Locke's account of their past was true, Fairfax thought, then the merchant had every right to hate his errant son-in-law with a lasting hate.

I certainly do, he reflected wryly, and he's nothing to me. A vain, vulgar, self-indulgent tyrant, probably with a streak of self-loathing because once he was a scandalous young rip and now he's a gouty old pillar of society fulminating about the times . . . but why should that bother me?

Perhaps it was because Delabole, in spite of everything, possessed the secret of attraction. Robert Fairfax had a strong sense of his own merits, but he knew that being irresistibly roguish, devilishly rascally, was not one of them. Men like Delabole drew handsome women to them, whilst he . . . Well, face it, he told himself, this is what it's all about, is it not? Still mooning over his lost love, Cordelia, who had chosen to go back to her careless bastard of a husband. Just thinking of it made him want another drink.

He couldn't have one, though, not if he was to be fit to face his pupils: it was past noon, time he was gone. Mr Tiverton had already hustled Caroline away, but Fairfax took his leave of the rest of the party. Sir James, with Locke still fussing courtier-like around him, all but ignored Fairfax's farewell, and Selina just pouted; but Lady Delabole, in her worn-out way, seemed to sigh wistfully in her goodbye – as if she wished she too could just walk away from the whole thing and be free.

Three

'*Maison*,' Fairfax repeated. '*La maison*. Come, say it with me.'

'Oh, Lord, I can't!' Miss Euphemia Bassett crammed her handkerchief into her mouth to stop the rising tide of giggles. 'I can't, indeed, sir, I shall die!'

'Miss Felicia, then?' Fairfax turned to her sister who, as ever, went lobster-red to the roots of her hair. 'Try it. *La maison.*'

Making noises as if she were going to explode, Miss Felicia shook her head.

'Oh, come now. Never shake thy gory locks at me. Try . . .' That was a mistake: when he 'talked in quotes', as the Misses Bassett called it, there was always a riot. He waited till the squeals, splutters, elbowings and heel-drummings had subsided. 'Now. Miss Aspasia, *you* try. *La maison.*'

'But what does it mean?' Aspasia Bassett, at thirteen the youngest of the girls, was also the one with the most command of herself, though that wasn't saying much. 'Is it a mason?'

'No. It means "house". But you can see, can't you, that the words are related, when you think of what a mason builds, and masonry, and—'

No good. Miss Euphemia was in fits.

'Oh! Oh, Papa, do come and listen! You'll never guess what they call a house! Oh, it's the queerest thing I ever heard!'

Mr Bassett came over, smiling quizzically. It was one of the oddities of Fairfax's employment here that, although the house the family had rented in the South Parade was a fine and spacious one, everything took place in this one back parlour. He gathered with the girls around a small table, and Mr and Mrs Bassett sat by the fire, he with a newspaper, she with her needlework, both benignly looking on. But he surmised that the Bassetts, who were wholesale haberdashers from Eastcheap and enjoying their first Bath season, found it more comfortable that way; and the terms of his employment did include, besides French for the girls, a short daily session with the elder Bassetts, for 'improving reading, polite conversation on elegant subjects, &c', as his written instructions had it. It was 'a fond relative' who had engaged him for the job, conducting the business anonymously in letters brought by a servant. All very strange – though not inexplicable. Plainly the relative was as much embarrassed as fond, and wanted the Bassetts quickly polished up; in the meantime Fairfax was to be utterly discreet about his task, speaking of it to no one, and entering the house by a rear door.

'Well, what is it now, my ducks?' Mr Bassett said genially, jingling the change in his fob.

'You'll never guess it, Papa,' Euphemia said, while Felicia puffed and fizzed beside her. 'What they call a house – it's the most monstrous peculiar thing you ever heard—'

'A mason!' shrieked Felicia. 'They call it a mason!'

'Do they now? Well, well, my poppets, it must be so if Mr Fairfax says it: he knows all about it, you know,' Mr Bassett said, benevolently smiling. 'Upon my soul, though, Mr

Fairfax, it is a curious thing. Why would they do that, now? These French?'

'Call a house a *maison*? Well, sir, in the French tongue that is the word for a house.'

'Ah. Mighty confusing, though, ain't it? Why not just call it a house?'

'Because . . .' Here it was again. The Bassetts were bright enough, and could easily have picked up French – but there was this baffled resistance to the very notion of there being other languages than English. 'Because the French language is different from ours. Through history, separate groups of people began to speak in different ways, and so we have separate tongues. Not just English – and not just French. In German, for example, a house –' Damn! Bad choice. 'Well, it is *haus*. But—'

'Ah!' said Mr Bassett with a significant nod. 'There, you see.'

'Well, but French is not all like that, Papa,' Aspasia chirped up. 'There is *table* – that's what they say for table, isn't it, Mr Fairfax? And so you see they've *nearly* got it right.'

'Very good, Spash, very good,' Mr Bassett said, impressed. 'Well, now, attend to Mr Fairfax, my ducks. It's all mighty curious, but he should know: remember he is half French himself.'

Fairfax wished he hadn't reminded them of that. When they had first learned it, the girls had spent half the afternoon staring at him, with occasional fascinated glances under the table at his legs, as if they were trying to discover which half was which. But they only giggled and goggled a little, and then Felicia surprised him by saying, out of the blue: '*Maissson.*'

'Very good. Let us just work on that *s* sound. It's more like

43

a *z*. Imagine . . . imagine there are some sprigs of may blossom here. And now—'

'It's unlucky to bring may into the house,' Aspasia confided.

'Very well, they are in the garden, set out on a bench – we'll pretend there is a bench,' he added, cutting Aspasia off. 'And you are to go out there, and put the sprigs of may in your hair, for a – for a picnic.'

'How pretty!' Euphemia said. 'Could we really do that?'

'Not in September, silly,' Felicia said. 'There's no may—'

'But imagine there is,' Fairfax said firmly. 'And your mama tells you to go and get ready. "Girls," she says, "go and put your *mays on*." Now. Repeat.'

They did, squealing with delight when they realized what they had done.

'Mama! Oh, Mama, guess what, you've been speaking French! Put your mays on!'

'You say it, Mama! It's a picnic, you see—'

'And you say it and it's French for house—'

'Not in the house though, because it's unlucky—'

'I don't know what you're talking about, my dears, but I'm sure it's all very clever,' said Mrs Bassett, a peaceable lady with the face of an untroubled madonna.

Well, it was progress of a sort, and Fairfax didn't much mind that it made the girls too over-excited to learn anything more. He let them chatter, rather than calling them sharply to order: the Bassetts were the tenderest-hearted people in the world, and if he so much as frowned they were full of anxious contrition. Once, when he actually sighed and held his head for a moment, Euphemia ran and fetched him a lavender bag and some comfits, Felicia cried and Aspasia stroked his hand. He thought, indeed, that the family were very well as they were, without the polish. But he needed the money, it was easy work in its bewildering way, and he had noticed that when he was teaching he did not, for once, want a drink.

Of course, he had one when he got back to his lodgings in Avon Street. But then he was going to dine at Mr Tiverton's and as that gentleman was an abstainer there might be no wine served, and so that was all right.

'Priming the pump, eh?' Ensign Locke said, walking in on him tippling. 'You needn't fear, though: I'll wager the old fellow keeps a cellar, even if he don't touch it himself. He doesn't strike me as a fanatical sort.'

'Your colonel will no doubt drink it dry, then,' Fairfax said, faintly annoyed at the interruption – and the wry glint in Locke's eye. 'I should think you'd need one yourself, if you've been with him all day.'

Locke gave his shout of laughter. 'Perfect gargoyle, ain't he?'

'Well, at least real gargoyles serve a purpose.'

The ensign only grinned, sitting down and propping his long legs up on the fender. 'Wasn't that piquant, when the old man turned up with his precious Caroline? In truth, this really is quite a step for the two old cusses. Tiverton's been not much more than frosty, and it looked chancy whether there would be any reconciling.'

'I confess I'm a little surprised, considering the way Delabole treated his daughter, that Mr Tiverton can invite the man to his table.'

'Well, time heals all wounds, and all that. Also – well, how would you say old Tiverton feels about his granddaughter?'

'I'd say he dotes on her.'

'Exactly. So much so that he surely couldn't refuse her anything. Even reconciliation with her scapegrace father.'

'Yes . . . But she seems an intelligent girl, thoughtful—'

'And quite a beauty too, ain't she? In a dreamy up-on-a-pedestal sort of way. Oh, I know what you mean. Can she really like that purple old devil? And there's another question on your lips, and that is: why do *I* truckle to him so nauseatingly? Ha! He amuses me, Fairfax, like I told you. And again like I told you, a fellow without prospects must know which side his bread's buttered. I keep in with my rich colonel, because he may do me some good. Apply the same to the lovely Caroline, and you've got it.'

'Is she so mercenary, do you think?'

'Oh, that's a needlessly hard word. Put yourself in her shoes. She'll come in for her grandfather's money, no doubt, which will be a respectable portion. But Sir James is worth a mint and, unlike Tiverton, who looks as if he'll outlive us all, the colonel's plainly on his last legs. He has no son, no entail on his estate: he can dispose of his property how he likes. Wouldn't you turn on the smiles, for the sake of that?'

'Well . . . not if I thought he had behaved abominably to my mother.'

Locke raised an eyebrow. 'The mother's dead and gone, no bringing her back. Whereas money . . . and not just money, neither: the world that goes with it. I reckon Caroline's had a pretty dull pottering sort of life with old sobersides Tiverton. Now comes her father to dazzle her: he's Pall-Mall and Rotten Row, he's the Court Calendar and Almack's and fashion and *bon ton*. See how she lights up when he talks of London. How can she not be tempted?'

'True enough. The colonel has it in mind, then, to introduce her to society?'

'He was talking of it again this afternoon. That's his notion:

take her with them when they go to London for the winter. All together – a family. Pretty, ain't it?'

'Hm. I wonder how it would have been if he'd come to see his long-lost daughter and found her a plain-faced hoyden.'

'I love it when you're dry! Ready to go?'

Mr Tiverton's house was in Orchard Street. In Bath's subtle index of status, it was more respectable than fashionable. How little its owner cared for fashion was revealed by the interior, which was all solid burgher comfort, with more oak than mahogany, and no sign at all of Chinese wallpapers, gilding, or tiny teacups too small to drink out of. No sign, either, of this Mr Pinner who was to be an honoured guest, though everyone else was there. Sir James Delabole, resplendently ugly in silver coat and red heels, was caustic.

'Perhaps the fellow's working late in his counting-house, Tiverton. Or got an awkward customer in the shop.'

'Mr Pinner keeps no shop,' Mr Tiverton said with a glance of displeasure. 'He is a dealer in the wine trade, as I was.'

'And don't tell me – he doesn't drink the stuff either.'

'As a matter of fact he does not. Well, we have had rain, and the Bristol road may be bad. We will wait dinner a while yet, Mrs Jessop, if you would be so good as to tell them in the kitchen.'

'Of course, sir.'

The woman Mr Tiverton addressed was something of a mystery. She had been sitting with them in the parlour like a member of the family, though silently: now she went off on the errand like a servant. She was plainly but respectably dressed: past forty but handsome, with lustrous black hair and an olive complexion, and buxom in figure – yet with something tight-laced and severe about her. Fairfax had a feeling of being studied when she was near: when he looked, however, her eyes were always cast down.

Sir James, frowning after her, said: 'Who is that woman, Tiverton? Your housekeeper?'

'Mrs Jessop keeps the house here, and serves as a companion-help to Caroline. Lacking a mother –' Mr Tiverton paused to take out his snuff-box, glancing darkly at Sir James – 'or any female relation, it seemed needful.'

'Aye, aye – but wouldn't a gentlewoman have done better? She looks like a village midwife – hard eyes and strong arms.' Sir James chuckled and looked round for appreciation: Locke obliged with a laugh. 'And God knows there are plenty of distressed gentlewomen in Bath, looking for a position.'

'Caroline had an excellent governess, and nothing was omitted in that regard. You may be sure, sir, that in the upbringing of my granddaughter I took every care: the more so, in that it appeared there was no one else who wished to interest themselves in the matter.' Mr Tiverton's tone was flinty.

'Come now, did you invite me here to reproach me with my sins, Tiverton?' Sir James said. 'If so, I'll bear it for your sake, my dear –' with a smile at Caroline – 'just so long as I know what I'm in for. Being abused plays havoc with my digestion, but there we are—'

'I spoke only in answer to your question, sir. I meant nothing more,' Mr Tiverton said, with a clenched look.

'Mrs Jessop is the kindest of women, sir, and our household would not have been the same without her,' Caroline Delabole said. 'I have been most happy in all respects. And now that we can all sit down to dinner together as friends, I shall consider my happiness complete.'

'Ah, that's well said, my dear.' Sir James beamed fondly. 'And there's only one thing that could make it better. If you would just say "Father" instead of "sir", that would complete *my* happiness. But there! I won't press. We'll say no more.' He patted her hand, then consulted his watch. 'Heyo! I hope your shopkeeper friend hasn't met with a highwayman, Tiverton. I'm hungry as a June crow.'

'Mr Pinner will be sorry to have kept the ladies waiting,' Mr Tiverton said with a stiff little bow at Lady Delabole and Selina, who were both got up very finely. The brocaded silks, flounces, jewels and feathers became Lady Delabole well enough, but Fairfax couldn't help thinking that they made Selina look like an overdressed doll, especially compared with Caroline, who wore a simple white gown without a hoop and looked angelically beautiful in it.

'Oh, you needn't fear on Selina's account,' Sir James scoffed. 'She eats like a bird. Something to do with this sensibility nonsense, no doubt. Or those damn novels she's always reading. Nobody ever eats in *them*, of course – they just sigh and languish and write each other endless letters with tears blotting the words.'

'Oh, sir, not all novels are silly,' Caroline said. 'Some perhaps. But I have read several that were instructive and elevating in their principles, as well as entertaining.'

'Ah, but plainly you have taste, my dear, and don't just gobble them up.'

Caroline turned to her half-sister. 'What are your favourites, Selina?'

'Probably the ones that you think are silly,' Selina said, with an airy shrug. 'But I don't care. It's of no consequence.'

Well, this is promising, Fairfax thought. At this rate we shall end up with a proper free-for-all fight over the soup-tureen.

'Here's Mr Pinner arrived, sir,' Mrs Jessop said coming

back. 'I've ordered dinner served directly.'

'Ah, my good friend, here's a welcome sight,' Mr Tiverton said jumping to his feet as a young man entered. 'I was beginning to fear you lost.'

'My apologies. There is such a press of business since my return – hardly enough hours in the day—'

'No need to apologize, my dear sir. My only distress is not to have seen you sooner. I spoke to your clerk last week, when you were expected back, and the news he told me was most disturbing. Apparently you had written him from France, and . . . Well, by and by. Let me introduce the company.'

Mr Tiverton did so, coming last to Sir James. 'Caroline's father,' was all he said, curtly. The young man who he introduced as Mr Edmund Pinner – slight, spare, wiry, nearer thirty than twenty, with a lined brow and such very pale blue eyes that they gave him a look of distant pain – was quietly polite in his greetings, but when he came to Sir James he visibly took the measure of the man, and said distinctly: 'Sir James. I've heard much of you.'

'Have you indeed?' Sir James said with a thin smile. 'Well, you have the advantage of me, as I don't know you from Adam.' Then, with that sudden transition to charm, he added, 'But I hope to, my dear sir: you must remedy the deficiency. Shall we go in now?'

'Yes, come,' Mr Tiverton said, his hand on Pinner's arm. 'And you can tell us what this extraordinary business is all about.'

'Oh – really, no great matter . . .' Pinner looked uncomfortable; but as soon as they were seated at table, in a dining-room so panelled and dark and beeswaxy that it was like being shut up in a big box, Mr Tiverton pressed him again.

'Well . . .' Pinner shrugged. 'It was nonsense of my clerk to talk of it.'

'He was concerned, as was I.' The first dishes were brought in by a maidservant. Mrs Jessop did not sit down with them: she stood by, making sure all was in order, and then left the room. It was noticeable that Edmund Pinner was given the place of honour opposite his host. At least, Fairfax noticed it, and he was pretty sure Sir James noticed it too, and was meant to. For the moment, however, the colonel was concentrating on the wine, which was there in abundance. 'He said they had detained you at Calais,' Mr Tiverton went on. 'Did he mean you had *been* detained? No, he said: they had arrested you.'

'Well, so it was. But all a misunderstanding, I assure you.' Pinner laughed self-consciously, his eyes straying to Caroline. They always were, Fairfax observed. He thought of the expression 'feasting on her face', but that wasn't right: Pinner's eyes constantly nibbled at the beautiful face of Caroline Delabole, like a man giving in to guilty temptation.

'Mr Pinner, you have not turned smuggler, I hope,' she said.

'Good Lord, no. No, no. Hardly. In my line of trade that would be – well, it would be undercutting my own interests, of course.'

Too serious, Fairfax thought, too serious by half. He remembered his own youthful courtships – the dreadful tendency to say too much, that anxious *presenting* of yourself.

'No,' Pinner said, 'it was a mere mistake – absurd really. I would have been released much sooner, but it needed the official word of the Calais governor and he was from home, so I had to cool my heels at his residence a couple of days. He was most obliging when at last he did see me, and apologized for my having missed my packet, which delayed me further of course, and – well, that was an end of it.'

'Surely not,' said Ensign Locke. 'Innocent Englishman arrested and imprisoned at Calais for no reason at all – trade and commerce of the nation interrupted – honour insulted – why, we have gone to war for far less. Sir James, you have influence: lay this before Parliament, and let's have war on the Frenchies at once. We have been at peace for too long anyway – two whole years, it ain't natural.'

Caroline laughed, but Pinner was very earnest.

'No, no – indeed, sir, you mustn't see it in that light. The French authorities thought they had reason—'

'What reason?' Mr Tiverton said indignantly.

'Well, they denounced me as a spy. Yes – yes, I know,' Pinner said as there were gasps around the table, 'quite ridiculous. The governor said so himself when he came to examine me. The fact is, I had passed the time while waiting for the tide in sketching. That's all. And Calais being of course fortified, and a port of some importance to the French nation, some over-zealous soldier saw me sketching and jumped to the wrong conclusions. It was very soon smoothed over. I was in France on legitimate business to do with the wine trade, as I had been before, and there were several reputable associates of mine who could vouch for me, and – well, there it is. I would have said nothing of it, but I thought I had better account to my people in Bristol for my delay. Indeed I had quite forgot about the whole thing, Mr Tiverton, until you reminded me.' Pinner coughed and sipped at a glass of water. Like many deliberate abstainers, he looked as if a drink would do him good, Fairfax thought.

'Well, without going so far as our young military friend here, I still think it was shabby treatment,' Mr Tiverton said.

'Only to be expected from the French,' Sir James pronounced. 'They have not forgiven us for besting 'em in the last bout. But you take this in a mighty meek spirit, it seems to me, sir. Any Englishman with fire in his belly would demand a formal apology.' His beady eye lit on Fairfax. 'What say you, sir? Would you swallow it?'

'You ask the wrong man, I fear, Sir James. My mother was French and I count myself quite a friend to that nation. Which does not mean that I am an enemy to this.'

' 'Od rot it, half a Frenchie! There's an uncommon thing to make a boast of,' the colonel cried. Fairfax was just preparing himself for more xenophobic idiocies when a strange look came over Sir James's face. For a moment Fairfax thought he must have seen a ghost.

Then, glancing over his shoulder, he saw that in a way he had. Directly behind him hung a small portrait on the panelled wall. A fair young woman, shyly smiling, with a kitten in her hands.

'My daughter Lydia, Mr Fairfax,' said Mr Tiverton, who missed nothing. 'Painted in her nineteenth year. Caroline's late mother.'

'She is very charming.'

'Was,' Mr Tiverton said, gently but emphatically. 'Was, indeed.'

'Quite a likeness,' said Sir James huskily, after a moment, and then applied himself to the wine.

'Mrs Jessop don't sit down with us, sir,' Locke put in. 'Have we offended?'

'It is her choice not to dine with company. She will join us in the drawing-room after,' Mr Tiverton said. 'We pursue our own quiet ways here, sir: we do not run after the fashion. I have not found that world congenial in the past.'

'Miss Delabole,' Pinner blurted, 'I – I have something for you. Some new music from London. It is – I forget, a sonata I think – but quite the newest thing.'

'That's kind of you, Mr Pinner,' Caroline said. 'You really should not go to such trouble on my account.'

'Oh, indeed it's no trouble, I assure you. You know I like to – to bring you things from London, as I always have.'

'Well, but that was when I was quite a girl. I blush to think of what a nuisance I was. Now I am grown, you really should not put yourself out.'

'A nuisance? Not at all! I was always very happy to . . . Do you recall when I brought you the canary-bird, and I was concerned because the creature would not sing? I feared there was something amiss with it, but no sooner did it see you than it started trilling away. And you took it on your finger to show it me, and it gave me a peck at once as if to say it was me it didn't care for—'

'I remember, of course. It was a pretty thing. Lady Delabole, are you fond of music?'

Wrong, wrong, Fairfax thought, while Lady Delabole murmured some dutiful commonplaces about music. She's twenty-one: the last thing she wants to be reminded of is her girlhood.

'So, Mr Pinner. You carry on your trade at Bristol, I think.' Sir James's florid face had turned yet darker from the wine he was drinking: he looked like a man choking to death. Which in a way he was, Fairfax thought: the colonel was certainly hastening his end by toping, when he was so inflamed with gout. 'Do you make a good thing of it? Only, as I say, your name is not known to me.'

'My business is solid, sir – perhaps not extensive.'

'Ah. But Bristol, now – when one says Bristol, one thinks

of the slave trade. There are fortunes to be made there, are there not?'

'Yes. That is, I suppose so.' Pinner seemed to have this awkward compulsion to qualify everything. 'For those who are prepared to undertake it. There is the question of conscience.'

'Oh, come, trade is trade. If a man will go grubbing in one sort of article, he may as well go grubbing in another.'

'I declare I cannot think of those poor blacks locked in irons without melting into tears,' Selina Delabole said.

'Pooh, girl, that don't stop you eating a pound of sugar every day,' her father said. 'And where do you suppose that comes from? Well, Mr Pinner, you may be in the right of it. For myself I know nothing of trade, thank heaven.'

It was a good dinner but plain – no fashionable fricasees or ragouts – and when it was time for the ladies to withdraw, while the men sat on over the port, Fairfax felt heavy and disinclined for any more drink. (There's a wonder, said a voice inside him.) Sir James showed no such reluctance, however.

'A good bite to this port, Tiverton. You're sure you won't be tempted to try it? Or you, Mr Pinner? Damme, a man must indulge a vice here and there, or else he's only half alive. Eh? *You* have vices, Locke, that I'm well aware of, you young dog; and you, Mr Fairfax, I'm sure, for all your grave airs. Now, don't look at me like that, Tiverton. Yon Jessop woman, now: don't tell me you keep her here just because she lays a nice table. You're a forty-years widower, and you're made of flesh and blood. Don't blame you in the slightest, sir, though I could wish she'd lighten that stony face of hers.'

Mr Tiverton, bristly brows tightly drawn, made an

impatient gesture. 'You must pardon me, I have no taste for these pleasantries.'

'Still starchy, eh? Oh, you know I mean no harm. But if we are to be reconciled, my dear fellow, we've no call to go on tiptoeing around one another like this. In case you haven't heard the gossip, Mr Fairfax – and you, Mr Pinner, though you seem so at home here I'm sure our friend has given you the whole tale – the matter is this. Twenty and more years ago, I met Lydia Tiverton. Only child of our friend here. Much beloved. Mighty lovable, indeed, for I fell for her, and would marry her. But our friend didn't approve of me, and wouldn't have it. So we eloped. 'Tis a tale of youthful folly, you see; and in the way of youth we fancied ourselves more in love than we were, and found that married life on nothing a year was more sour than sweet. So we quarrelled, and parted—'

'If you will talk of it,' Mr Tiverton said, his glare baleful, 'then have the goodness to be accurate, sir. It was hardly a *parting*. You abandoned my daughter. Left her alone and penniless in a foreign country, when she was heavily with child. Those are the facts,' he added, turning to Fairfax, as if he could not bear to look at the colonel any longer, 'not that there can be any benefit in digging them over.'

'Penniless, because you would give her nothing,' Sir James said. 'Come, man, admit that. You were still stubbornly determined to punish her for disobeying you. I'm a stubborn man myself, so I comprehend it. But let us be honest. As for Lydia, when we quarrelled she wanted none of me. Two people who have fallen out as we did simply can't stay together, not if they're made of flesh and blood. 'Tis a melancholy story, no doubt of it – but come, some good came of it in the end. Caroline. A delightful girl, and you've had the joy of her all these years, Tiverton.'

'A great joy. A greater joy would have been to have had her mother by me all these years also.'

'Oh come, man, I didn't kill her,' Sir James snorted, taking up the port bottle again.

'Lydia was not strong. The privations and sufferings you put her through hastened her early end, sir. You cannot doubt that. Why else, indeed, would you keep your distance from this household for so long, if not from a guilty conscience?'

Sir James sat back and looked at his host with airy perplexity. Then he shrugged. 'Well, well, I dare say you have been waiting a long time to say these things to me. If it relieves you to get 'em off your chest, then I suppose I shouldn't complain. But upon my soul, Tiverton, you must know I mean to make it up. What I intend to do for Caroline is no small thing. No doubt you'll see her comfortable, but I –' Sir James groped for his cane which leant by his chair, and made an enchanter's wave with it – 'why, I shall transform her prospects. She shall have such a life as – well, as the heiress of Sir James Delabole *should* have.'

Mr Tiverton looked uneasy. 'But you have another daughter, sir, after all, and—'

'Oh, Selina shall have her portion. But she must acknowledge that Caroline has the prior claim. Selina's a giddy chit, besides, and would most likely make foolish choices if she had the command of a fortune. Dear God, I shudder to think . . . But Caroline, I see, has her head firmly fixed on her shoulders. I say again, she's a credit to you, Tiverton. Now there, surely, is something we agree on: we both want the best for her. Eh?'

Mr Tiverton hesitated. He seemed to Fairfax about to say that there were different opinions on what was best for someone: certainly that was what went through his own mind. But instead he nodded briefly, then pushed back his chair.

'To be sure, that is the first consideration. And the bitterness of the past—'

'Is past,' said Sir James.

'Is not a fit subject for the dinner table, I was going to say. But there, enough. I think it is time we rejoined the ladies.'

Sir James seemed reluctant to leave the port, but his steps were already erratic as he made his way to the drawing-room, where Mrs Jessop was presiding over the making of tea. As she handed Sir James a cup, Fairfax saw unpleasant mischief in his glance.

'Ah, thank you, ma'am. We were just speaking of you – oh, in the most complimentary manner. I was remarking what a treasure Tiverton had found in you. A great comfort to a man lacking a wife.'

Impervious, Mrs Jessop said, 'Thank you, sir. I try to give satisfaction.'

'I'll wager you do, too!' Sir James said, grinning with delight. 'I'll wager you do, Mrs Jessop.'

'I hope the meat was dressed to your liking.'

'It was excellent. And the wine was excellent. And this tea is excellent – but still only tea.' With fumbling fingers Sir James unscrewed the silver head of his cane and poured the contents into his cup, winking at the housekeeper. 'This is my recipe for tea, ma'am. A measure of usquebaugh, and it's improved immensely. Know what that is?'

'A spirit, I think,' Mrs Jessop said, wrinkling her nose.

'And spirit is what it gives you. Don't take my word for it – try a sip.'

'No, I thank you, sir. I never touch liquor.'

'Another one! It is very curious to me, that so many people

have this prejudice against one of the most estimable creations on God's earth.'

'Pray, sir, don't bring the Lord's name into it, not in that connection,' she said sombrely, her eyes always avoiding his.

'Why, He wouldn't damn a man for enjoying his wine, surely?'

'I think you are joking, sir. But the bottle is the surest road to perdition, that's what my late husband always said. And I have seen the proof, with my own eyes, of what it may do.'

'Oh, my apologies, ma'am. You are a parson's widow, then?' Sir James glanced archly at her buxom figure.

'My husband was a farrier and horse-doctor. But he was a member of the Methodist connection—'

'Oho, I see. I see now.' Sir James was all amused scorn. 'A preaching horse-doctor.'

'Yes, sir. A good one. But many people felt the benefit of his ministrations also—'

'Aye, aye, he meddled with souls also, no doubt, instead of leaving it to the established Church. No, you must forgive me, ma'am, I have no truck with that sort of enthusiasm.' As if suddenly bored, he turned his back on her. 'Caroline, my dear, I've heard much of your playing. Will you put it to the proof, sweetling, and entertain us?'

Caroline, who had been talking quietly with Ensign Locke, smiled and rose. 'You make me tremble, sir. But I must obey.'

She need not have trembled: her playing at the harpsi-chord, Fairfax thought, was among the best he had heard. She had execution, taste, and command of expression – everything you might expect from this very elegant and self-possessed young woman. Listening, he watched the faces of the others. Sir James smiled wetly, rapturous, especially when the music was tender (in the difficult passages he fidgeted, vulgar sentimentalist that he was). Lady Delabole equipped herself with an attentive look. Selina looked both moved and envious. Locke basked like a cat, long legs out, narrowed eyes fixed on the player. Mrs Jessop sat with tightly folded hands, gazing at the wall, as if listening to a sermon. Mr Tiverton, grave, faintly troubled, kept his eyes cast down: was that a tear he put his hand up to brush away, or the rheum of age? Mr Edmund Pinner seemed most affected of all, perching on the edge of his seat, his whole nervous frame yearning towards the music. Or the musician.

When the applause broke out, Pinner jumped as if he had forgotten the others were there. He started forward to the harpsichord.

'Admirable! Admirable! See, here is the new music I brought. Perhaps next you would care to—'

'Oh, I look forward to studying it, and learning it,' Caroline said, 'but you know I cannot play it straight away at sight, Mr Pinner. The results would not be admirable at all.' She smiled.

'No . . . no, of course not. Might I request then – if you will play again, I'm sure you will – let it be "The Soldier's Lament".'

'Oh, sir, I must be excused.' She glanced at the company. 'It is quite a silly old air, and really a beginner's piece. Let us have something else.'

She had the most exquisite swan-like neck, Fairfax thought: but he wouldn't have liked to have it turned to him as she had just done to Pinner.

'A beginner's piece – yes, of course it is,' Pinner said. 'Of course, it was when you first learned to play. I used to sing it with you – try, that is. I have the most dreadful voice. Only—'

'You are no beginner, my dear, that I can tell,' Sir James said. Drink had made his voice overly loud. 'I may not know much, but by God I can tell you this – put you in a London salon, and you'd set them all tail-on-end. Damme, you'll make a stir, Caro. I've a mind to whisk you off tomorrow and prove myself right. What d'you say? You've been buried here long enough. Eh, Tiverton? 'Tis only giving the girl her just deserts, to take her into society. Come – you know you're stubborn, but you'll admit the truth of that, eh?'

'We must talk of these matters some other time,' Mr Tiverton said.

'Why so prim, man? We're not talking of state secrets – just of my taking my daughter to London for the season. It's not as if she'd lack a chaperone – you'll take her under your wing, won't you, my dear?'

'I should be happy, of course, to oblige Miss Delabole at any time,' Lady Delabole said, mustering up a limp smile, 'pending, of course, Miss Delabole's own choice, and her guardian's permission.'

Sir James shot her a glare. By Lady Delabole's standards, at least, that was pretty assertive.

'Of course Caro must do as she wants. But as for permission – why, where's the question? Do you mean to play dog-in-the-manger, Tiverton, and spoil her chances? Or do you doubt my true affection for her?'

'I do not doubt your affection, Sir James. Past experience, perhaps, might lead me to doubt its constancy. I should not be happy to see another member of my family taken away with great promises, and then left in the lurch.'

'What? Why, damn you, Tiverton! If you were a younger man I'd call you out for that!'

Caroline looked anxiously from one to the other. Caught between curmudgeons, Fairfax thought. 'Grandfather, sir, please . . .'

'That was not well said,' Mr Tiverton muttered. He was trembling. 'I – perhaps I should not have . . .'

'Well, damn it, it's out now. Any other insults you'd care to throw at me, man, while you're about it?' Sir James's face was a hideous damson hue. Spray came from his lips and a rattling noise from his throat: Fairfax started to jump up. The man must be choking . . .

Then he realized. Sir James was laughing. It came out as an awful barking and braying, but laughter it was.

'Oh – oh, cock's life, a fine pair we make! Two old crocks snarling at each other. These young ones must think we're only fit to be knocked on the head, I fear . . .'

'Not at all,' Locke said smoothly, joining in the laughter, 'and I hope I may have as much spirit in me when I am – rich in years.'

Mr Tiverton relaxed a little, though he did not laugh.

'You're a damned stubborn old stick, Tiverton – but I've a good bellyful of food and wine under my belt, and I'll not rise to your bait. Not now, anyhow. Flag of truce, eh?'

'Well, I don't know about the "Soldier's Lament", but *this* soldier is dying to hear you play again, Miss Delabole,' Locke said. 'Will you be so good?'

She gave him a grateful look, and did. They made a fair couple, Fairfax thought: both good-looking, confident, adept at greasing the social wheels. Of course, her position as heiress to Sir James would put her rather out of Locke's league. The same went for poor Mr Pinner who looked wretchedly on as Locke and Caroline traded more pleasantries, Locke leaning over her shoulder to sort her music-sheets for her.

'What is the matter, my dear?' Lady Delabole said, as Selina jumped to her feet, begged to be excused, and ran from the room. Her face was pink and raw.

'The matter? She's having a weeping-fit, that's all,' Sir James grunted. 'She's always weeping. Least thing sets her off.'

'I'll go with her,' Caroline said.

'No, my dear, let me,' said Mrs Jessop. 'The lady's a little high-strung, I fear.'

And feeling horribly pushed-out, Fairfax thought. He felt sorry for the girl, having to come back into the room. But as soon as she did, Lady Delabole, more motherly than he had given her credit for, went and kissed her tenderly, and took control.

'I fear we are all a little tired,' she said, 'and should not trespass on your hospitality any longer, Mr Tiverton.'

'So soon?' said Sir James, though he could hardly stand. 'Hey, well, you don't keep late hours, Tiverton, that I know.'

Interrupted in her playing, it was Caroline's turn to look put out. The lapse was only momentary, but Fairfax wondered if that was a spoilt miss he saw there before the serene smile returned.

Mr Tiverton sent a servant to call for chairs for the Delaboles. Fairfax and Locke said they would walk home.

'And Mr Pinner, where do you lodge?' Locke asked.

'Oh, he will lie the night here, will you not, Pinner?' Mr Tiverton said. 'Your usual room is ready.'

'Thank you.' For the first time that evening, Edmund Pinner's face broke into a broad smile. It not only made him look younger: it was as if a boy was standing there in place of the man.

There was triumph in the smile, of course. Enjoy it, Fairfax thought: I fear it's all the triumph you'll get. He was tired himself, and was glad to get the leave-takings over and stride out for home in the fresh night air.

Ensign Locke, who sometimes gave the impression that he could go on talking for ever, was unusually silent as he fell into step beside Fairfax. But they had only reached the corner of Stall Street when Locke stopped dead, slapping his own thigh with his glove.

' 'Od rot it, I shall have to step back. I left something there.'

'What?'

Locke looked at the glove in his hand. 'My other glove,' he said. 'Silly of me. You go on, Fairfax: I'll catch you up anon.'

Fairfax did as he was bid. He didn't know what Locke was after, but it certainly wasn't his other glove, for that was plainly sticking out of his coat pocket.

Nor did Locke catch him up. Fairfax was back in his rooms at Avon Street, had done his long-overdue unpacking, and begun undressing for bed when there was at last a tap on the door.

'Heyo, Fairfax. How goes it?' Locke put his head round the door.

'Did you get it?' Fairfax said.

'Eh? Oh – the glove, yes. Well, you're for bed, I see. Suppose I should too.' Locke gazed abstractedly at the candle-flame. 'Yes . . . Tell me, Fairfax, how can you tell if a woman speaks true?'

Fairfax was surprised by the flood of bitter replies that rose to his lips, and thankful that he didn't let them out. 'I don't know,' he said, and then, curiosity getting the better of him, 'Why do you ask?'

But Locke was already gone.

Four

Fairfax was up rather late, and felt odd. Not ill. Rather, he noticed the absence of certain bodily symptoms he had come to associate with mornings. Then he realized. He had not, for once, drunk too much last night. He wondered if the example of Sir James Delabole, gross and empurpled, tippling at his usquebaugh, had something to do with that.

There was no sign of Locke.

'Yon soldier fellow went out early,' Macleod the painter said, calling Fairfax into his room. 'About some mischief, I should think.'

'Mischief?'

'Why, what else does a young half-pay officer do, with time on his hands and no money? Mischief's his element. 'Tis written in his physiognomy. We write our stories in our faces, Mr Fairfax. Now, on that subject, tell me frankly. Niobe's expression.' He gestured at his painting. 'Do you see uttermost inconsolable grief? Or are the contours a little too softened towards pathos, resignation even?'

Fairfax was afraid Mr Macleod's Niobe looked as if she had a mild case of the gripes. But he nodded judiciously and said, 'Grief certainly. Agony, even . . .'

'Exactly. I used a green underpainting to create that pallor.

A fine touch, though I say it myself.'

'You are a lover of Shakespeare, I see,' Fairfax said, turning over a book on the table.

'A worshipper. Inspires and animates me. He's never out of my hands – well, except when I'm painting, of course, which is the pity of it. I had Locke read to me one evening while I was working, but the fool would keep putting on ridiculous voices, and I made him leave off.'

'I'd be happy to read for you some evening. No, really. It will keep *me* out of mischief.'

'Obliged to you, sir: we'll make a roaring dramatic night of it. I can't help declaiming out loud when it gets to a fine bit. You're going to your pupils, sir?'

'Not yet. I thought to go out for some breakfast.'

'Aye? I couldn't ask you . . .? No, 'tis an imposition . . . Well, I'm lacking charcoal. There's a little stationer's in Green Street that deals in artist's goods. If you'd be so good – only I'm all over paint, and I've to clean up and go to my pupil presently—'

'My pleasure.' Not having a hangover, Fairfax found, made you very good-natured.

'There's money on the table there if Locke hasn't had it. A thousand thanks to ye. The stationer's is a touch awkward to find – in a queer old house, up two pair of stairs, with a milliner's below.'

Fairfax would certainly not have found it without the milliner's shop to guide him. It was in an old peeling building with a leaded shell-hood. Behind the milliner's, some wormy stairs led up to a dim landing with several doors bearing hand-drawn signs, one unpromisingly reading *Children taught here*. At the stationer's neat little premises above, he made his purchase and debated buying letter-paper for himself before coming to the self-pitying conclusion that he had no one to write to.

On the way down, he peered at another of the signs, its ink faded with age. *Samuel Fry. Gentlemen's Tailoring. Bones set here.*

Curious combination. But he made a mental note of the place, as Ensign Locke had been seeking a bone-setter – though the young man seemed as fit as a flea. All very odd: as was his behaviour after the dinner at Mr Tiverton's last night. Fairfax wondered if Locke was intriguing with Caroline Delabole. He was fishing in some muddy waters if so, he thought.

The door of the tailor and bone-setter's opened, and a man came out. Fairfax recognized him: it was the man with the hook who had helped him with his trunk yesterday.

'Good day to you.'

The man had reached the top of the stairs before he glanced round, impatiently it seemed, at Fairfax's greeting.

'Sir?'

'You played the Samaritan to me yesterday.' As the man only frowned at him he added, 'You don't remember, perhaps. No matter—'

'Oh! Yes.' The man was looking at Fairfax, but not really seeing him, he felt. 'I – I cannot stay, sir.'

'Of course,' Fairfax said, gesturing for him to go on; and the American, pulling down his broad-brimmed hat, turned and went downstairs at an urgent clip. Well, whether he had just been tailored or bone-set, Fairfax thought, the experience seemed to have agitated him.

He had a late breakfast of apple tart from a cook-shop, stepped back to Avon Street to give Macleod his charcoal, and was taking the air in the pleasant space of Queen Square when he heard his name fairly screeched from the other side of the square. Ensign Locke came hurtling to him, nearly falling under the wheels of a phaeton, leaping over the bandaged legs of an old man in an invalid chair, and again proving himself highly athletic for a man with an ill-set break in his ankle.

'Fairfax! I need you!' Locke cried, seizing him by the shoulders.

'Flattering, but not, perhaps, a thing to be shouted so *very* loudly in the street.'

'What? Oh – nonsense.' Locke obliged with a brief laugh, but he looked wild. 'Fairfax, listen. I've just come from the colonel's—'

'How is the old humbug? I've just come from a place that may interest you, as a matter of fact. I found a bone-setter's in Green Street.'

Locke looked at him as if he were mad. Then he shook his head impatiently. 'Oh – that. Never mind, that doesn't matter now. I—'

'The ankle is not troubling you any more?'

'Damn the ankle. You must do me a favour.'

'Oh, of course I must. It is all I live for.'

'Rot you, will you do me a favour then? I'm a distressed creature, Fairfax, don't heap whatsname on thingmebob.'

'Ossa on Pelion?'

'Knew you'd know it. Look here, I need you to take a message to – well, into the colonel's house.'

'Why on earth . . .? I thought you were always welcome there. You said—'

'I know. I was. But now . . .' Locke winced. 'I ain't, not since this morning. Fact is, the colonel turfed me out. Go on now, have your laugh.' Locke dug his hands in his breeches pockets and kicked viciously at a stone.

'I'm more amazed than . . . Mind you, I have seen the colonel's temper for myself. What did you do, dare to disagree with him for once?'

'Unworthy of you, my dear fellow, unworthy . . . In truth, it's rather ticklish and delicate and all that. Now, as things stand I'm forbidden to enter that house – and the servants have even been instructed to turn me away, which is monstrous discommoding . . .'

'Dear me. You *have* offended.'

'Well, that's why I need someone to smuggle my message in. And who better than you? Quite natural that you should call on the Delaboles this morning. Renew delightful acquaintance of last evening, and all that—'

'It wasn't a delightful acquaintance. I think the man's a brute.'

'Never mind that. The message ain't to him. It's to Selina.'

'Indeed? Ah.'

Locke's face gave nothing away. 'Ticklish and delicate, like I say. And needing someone utterly disinterested and discreet, like you. Now don't say any more, Fairfax, except that you'll do it.'

'Oh, very well.' He liked Francis Locke without particularly trusting him; but he couldn't see any harm in this. 'What is the message?'

'A note. Just a note – only I haven't written it yet.' Locke fished a scrap of paper and a stub of pencil from his pocket. 'Turn about, won't you, my dear fellow?'

Fairfax did so: leaning the paper on his back, Locke scribbled away. Fairfax's curiosity was aroused and he found himself making a rather absurd effort to read through his shoulder-blades.

'Discreet,' Locke said when he had finished, folding the paper tight, 'that I know you are, Fairfax, and will respect this as a confidential communication—'

'All right, all right. I don't see how I'm to give it to Miss Selina, though. Not without its looking mighty strange.'

'I have the utmost faith in your resourcefulness,' Locke said, 'and I can't think what else to do. Come, I'll show you where it is.'

He led Fairfax up Gay Street, a steep incline made more difficult by refuse and horse-puddles. A pair of sedan-chairmen were having such a struggle carrying a fat frizzled matron, who rapped with her fan and complained at every jolt, that they looked ready to tip her out on the cobbles. Ahead was the Circus, newest and most fashionable of Bath addresses – a great ring of tall Palladian houses, regular, graceful, unimpeachably correct, surrounding a paved circle.

'I won't come any further,' Locke said. 'Best keep out of the way. There's the house – black door. Go in and win, Fairfax.'

'But – do I try and get an answer?'

'No need. Just be sure Selina gets that note. It's – it's most dreadfully important.' Locke clapped him on the shoulder. He looked white, drawn and haunted, for all the parade of cheer. 'I've a thirst needs quenching. Thousand thanks and all that.'

Fairfax went up the steps to the house feeling, now that it came to it, pretty reluctant about his errand. He didn't relish making small talk with the Delaboles, and how he would pass the note to Selina he couldn't imagine. Then, as he waited for an answer to his knock, he had an idea. There was a book in his pocket – a volume of Milton. He had just slipped the note inside the book when the door was flung open by Sir James Delabole himself.

'Stand away there, man, I'm in a hurry,' Sir James growled, stumping past Fairfax with a bare glance. 'Nolan! Where's that damned chair?'

'I'll go fetch one directly, sir.' A liveried manservant, a little crushed-looking, bow-legged man like a superannuated jockey, hurried down the steps ahead of his master and scuttled across the Circus.

Leaning heavily on the area railings, nursing his silver-headed cane, Sir James spat copiously and then turned a yellow cockerel eye up to Fairfax.

'You've come calling on me, sir?'

'Yes – that is, I came to present my compliments to the family, after our agreeable evening—'

'Jane!' Sir James bellowed back into the house. 'A gentle-man calls here: will you leave him on the step all day? Look alive, girl! Well, well, compliments, eh?' he said turning back to Fairfax. 'I wish you joy of 'em. For my part, I'm glad to quit this house this morning. An abode of fools, knaves and shrews.' He glowered up at the windows; then, as the manservant came panting back with a chair in attendance, spat heartily again. 'Nolan, if the lawyer comes while I'm out, have him wait. I'll make it worth his time.'

'Where away, sir?' the front chairman said as the colonel got in.

'Orchard Street. And if you go cheating me, calling it a mile and asking a shilling fare, I'll have the hides off your backs.'

Orchard Street: home of Mr Tiverton, and Caroline. And a lawyer . . . Not a happy family, then, he gathered: trouble in the air. None of his business, though – except for this damned errand Locke had inveigled him into. And what was this all about? Was Locke mixed up with the other Delabole girl as well? Murky waters indeed.

The chair took Sir James away, whilst a grey-faced maid took Fairfax into a lofty drawing-room that faced on to the Circus and was full of cold light reflecting off brand-new furniture. The house was rented for the season, of course: all the same, Fairfax felt he had never been in a place with so little of home about it.

'Mr Fairfax. Quite an unexpected pleasure, I'm sure.'

Lady Delabole came languidly in. She looked, as ever, as if she were just about to arrange some flowers or do something similarly ladylike and trifling. But there was a sharp line between her brows, and that scent he caught wasn't pomade, unless they had started putting brandy in pomade these days. How tiresome it was to be always right, he thought.

'Lady Delabole. I wished to take this opportunity of enquiring after your and Miss Delabole's health, after our so very pleasant evening.' Plausible enough, as it was correct form after an evening party to enquire after the ladies' health, and generally reassure yourself that they had not fallen down any holes or contracted scurvy in the meantime.

'Miss Delabole? That I can't say, sir.' Lady Delabole picked up some embroidery from a side-table and looked at it critically. 'Oh, but of course you must mean Selina. A forgivable mistake. I still make it myself. Selina has always been *the* Miss Delabole, you see, until lately. Now she has a senior who takes precedence, and so she must be called Miss Selina. All quite unimportant, no doubt.'

Not to you, Fairfax thought. Just then Selina herself rushed into the room. At the best of times her pretty, sulky face had an edge-of-tears look, and this was not the best of times: she had cried herself crimson.

'Mama! He should not have quarrelled with you like that! I don't care what the old brimstone beast does – he should not have treated you so, indeed he should not . . .'

Eyebrows soaring, Lady Delabole made a shushing sound and gracefully put her fingers to her lips. Selina stopped, saw Fairfax, and set her jaw. The looks he had had from her before were kindness itself compared to the glare she scorched him with now.

'My dear, these domestic trifles,' Lady Delabole sang, 'we must not trouble about them when we have a visitor. Mr Fairfax has most politely come to enquire after us.'

'Well, but it's true,' muttered Selina, turning her shoulder to him. '*I* don't mind it – I don't care what he said. I *glory* in it. But when he is such a beast to—'

'My dear Selina, Mr Fairfax comes to enquire, and we are quite remiss in our courtesies to him. How do you find yourself, Mr Fairfax? Will you have tea?'

'Thank you, I – I cannot stay.' Just let me out of here, he thought. 'I came indeed to enquire – also, Miss Selina, by your leave, to lend you that book of which we were speaking last evening.'

From the look she gave him, he might have said 'and also to pour pigswill all over you, with maggots'. Hastily he took the volume of Milton out of his pocket and proffered it to her, tweaking Locke's note so that it protruded from the pages. He fixed her eyes with his, willing her to comprehend. It was curious how people who made a boast of their sensibility were often so obtuse.

'The book . . .' she said hesitantly.

'Of which we were talking.' Though we hardly said a word to each other all evening, which in itself should give you some notion, so just *take* the book, damn it.

She did, at last, understand; her fingers deftly pushed the note back between the leaves as she took it. Fairfax had a moment of regret that he had been so staunch, and had not just opened the note and read it.

Still, none of his business; and now that such business as he had was concluded, he made haste to be gone. Selina, though, was not done. Having brought herself to speak to him, she was almost bold.

'Thank you for the book, Mr Fairfax. It was kind of you to remember. My father, sir, has gone out, I think? Did you see as you came in . . .?'

'Oh! Yes. Gone out.' He took a risk. 'Like a shot from a cannon, in fact.'

The flippancy was out of place, no doubt. Certainly Selina was not amused, though by the look of her she never was.

'You know nothing about the matter, sir,' she said, pressing the book to her breast, and walking stormily out. It was hard to walk stormily, but Selina Delabole managed it.

'Well, Lady Delabole. My compliments again, and I should go.'

'You need not, sir,' Lady Delabole said, still willowy and composed, looking out of the window at the Circus with amiable interest. Yet for a moment he had a strange surmise that she was about to look at him squarely, as one toper to another (they always knew each other, damn it), and suggest setting to work on the brandy-bottle together. Then she looked down at her hands and said, 'But we must not detain you, of course, from your employment. I hardly need add that as a gentleman you will carry away from this house no . . . impressions, I am sure: certainly none that you would care to speak of indiscreetly.'

He made a grave bow in answer, and left. He felt sorry for

Lady Delabole, but not that sorry – it had been her choice to marry Sir James, after all. A plague on both your houses! was his dismissive thought as he got away, and went to see his pupils in the South Parade.

There, with the Bassett girls gathered about the table full of unteachable eagerness, and the Bassett parents benign at the fireside, all was pleasant bewilderment as Fairfax approached the long-postponed task of instructing them in the gender of French nouns. 'Gender' meaning masculine or feminine – meaning sex. The girls were commendably sober about that, and only shrieked, fizzed, choked, and drummed their heels for about half an hour before they were quite collected. But probably he was unwise to bring up their old friend *maison* again. Yes, *maison* was *la* or *une*: it was feminine. The idea of a house being feminine was too much for them. Euphemia actually had to be plied with smelling-salts. In the end he quite entered into the spirit of the thing, making it a guessing-game. Table – masculine or feminine? Book? Hat? The last one made Aspasia, always the sharpest, quite indignant. A table was quite feminine, she supposed (wisely declining to specify), but a hat could be anything.

Mr Bassett was just ambling over, with a look as if to say 'Answer that, my friend!', when a maidservant came in with a sealed note which, she said, was for Mr Fairfax.

Fairfax took it, opened it, read it. He felt as if he had faded from the world for a moment, and when he came back he found the Bassetts watching him with genial curiosity.

He couldn't tell them what was in the note, however. The person it came from forbade that. The news it contained was that Colonel Sir James Delabole had been murdered.

Five

The gentleman was waiting for Fairfax in a closed carriage a dozen yards distant from the Bassett house. He was a sleek dapper man past fifty, powdered and immaculate, with a smooth bland face in which the mouth was a mere line – as if even to have lips was to commit himself more than he would like.

'Mr Fairfax. We have not met. But you recognize, perhaps, my handwriting.'

'You . . . must be the person who engaged me to tutor the Bassetts.'

The gentleman sighed and rapped on the carriage roof. 'The Bassetts,' he said as the carriage lurched into motion, 'are connections of mine. That is, they are relatives of my dear wife. Attaining wealth, they decided to seek fashion also. So they came to Bath, where I have long been established and, I think, eminent. I fancy I am not overstating the case when I say that there was, ahem, no stopping them.' He gave a faint shiver. 'That being the case, I judged it prudent to impart to the Bassetts – excellent people, I do not deny – a little polish. As much as may be, and quickly, as it were. Sir, my name is Goode, William Goode. A name that elicits the respectful nod anywhere in Bath society.'

Fairfax inclined his head, wondering if he had managed the respectful nod, or some other sort of nod altogether.

'You will readily understand then, Mr Fairfax, the pressing need for discretion in the matter of the Bassetts. It was my confident belief in your discretion that impelled me to hire you for the job, having noted your arrival at Bath, and then thoroughly investigated your credentials.'

'I'm glad, sir, you found me satisfactory. And I am most happily placed with the Bassetts. But you have summoned me here with – well, with news I can hardly believe. That is . . .' Well, was it so unbelievable? He had felt like killing the man himself once. 'What can this matter have to do with me?'

'You are disingenuous, Mr Fairfax. Those credentials I spoke of included tributes from Justice Fielding of Bow Street, among others whom you have assisted in criminal cases. I confess I did not anticipate using your services in this particular way – but so it is. I am, among other things, Justice of the Peace here. I turn to you, sir, because I think you will be the very one to help me – especially as you have acquaintance in that quarter.'

'You are well informed, Mr Goode,' Fairfax said with a lift of his eyebrows.

'I make it my business to know all that goes on in Bath,' Mr Goode said with complacency. 'I am, among other things, a close friend of the Master of Ceremonies. Loath as I am to take you away from your duties with my – with the Bassetts, I'm sure you will appreciate the pressing gravity of this matter. Our city is the foremost resort of society. Its genteel reputation, its prosperity—'

'Yes. Bath is supposed to cure you, not kill you.'

'You are pithy, sir,' Mr Goode said with a twitch of his

vinegary mouth. 'But you take my point. This unfortunate affair must not be allowed to blight our season. A swift resolution, rather than a prolonged scandal . . .'

'I do take your point. But what has happened? I saw Sir James just this morning. Is it certainly murder? He was in indifferent health . . .'

'There is no doubt. I have just spoken with the doctor who was summoned – though Sir James was quite beyond his help. Someone gave him poison. A strong dose of arsenic, the doctor concludes from his examination – of the late gentleman, and of the receptacle.'

'Receptacle?'

'Sir James was in the habit, I believe, of carrying a cane with a hollow head of silver, in which he kept a reviving spirit.'

'Yes, Scotch usquebaugh. Fiery stuff.'

'It would appear that someone tampered with this, placing the grains of arsenic in the spirit. Sir James's agonies were severe, though mercifully not prolonged.'

'Dear God.'

'Indeed – it is a most unhappy mischance – to such a very distinguished and well-connected gentleman, and when the town is so full of company . . . And a horrid crime, of course. A crime that I believe its perpetrator hoped to remain undetected. You mentioned Sir James's infirmity. First appearances might have suggested that this had simply caught up with him. He was returning to his home in the Circus by chair. When the chairmen stood down outside his house, they were surprised to find he did not get out. Opening the door of the chair, they found him insensible and in the deepest throes. They supposed a heart-stroke, and with some difficulty lifted him and carried him into the house. The cane was still gripped in his hand, but the top was not there, and they subsequently found it on the floor of the chair and brought it in, where the doctor who had been summoned had the wit to examine it. One of the chairmen recalled that when they picked him up at Orchard Street, Sir James, on first entering the chair, had unscrewed the top and begun taking a draught. So it appears that it was a man dying horribly that they carried home.'

'Orchard Street. Yes, he went there. To call on his daughter and father-in-law, no doubt. When I saw him earlier,' Fairfax said in answer to Mr Goode's enquiring look. 'It was at his house. He was just leaving to go to Orchard Street. Shortly after noon, I would think.'

Mr Goode inclined his head. 'It was around half-past one that he returned. For the last time.' Mr Goode coughed, and seemed to regret the melodrama of this. 'The doctor sent at once to me. And having taken the measure of the situation, I decided to enlist your services, Mr Fairfax.'

'I see.' Fairfax shifted a little irritably. The carriage shuddered and rattled as it made its laborious way up Gay Street.

'You are familiar, perhaps, with Sir James's family affairs—'

'Yes. I dined with him last evening, at Mr Tiverton's.'

'Ah. You are no doubt shocked. I am sorry indeed to be the bearer of this news—'

'No, no.' Shock, certainly . . . But he was shocked, too, at the response of his own mind. He shook his head. 'Sir, you speak of my services—'

'Indeed. We have a parish constable, of the usual sort. He is a good fishmonger when he is not drunk.' Mr Goode waved his hand dismissively. 'I mean to pursue this matter as a magistrate, of course. But there are my social obligations, among other things, and if you were to be my right hand—'

'Sir, excuse me . . . You did engage me as a tutor to the Misses Bassett and as such I am happy to earn my fee. But . . .' But what? But it didn't mean he was casually available for hire, like an old saddle-horse at a livery stable? Something like that, perhaps. The old prickly pride. Misplaced, though, wasn't it? Coming from a bottle-loving failure who had moved to Bath precisely because he needed to hire himself out to whoever would have him.

It was something else then, something equally bleak in its implications of what he had become. He thought of the investigations he had conducted before, and saw that what had animated him then was justice. Right and wrong: good and evil. But now there was a horrible whisper in his heart: what concern was this of his? What did it matter if this selfish, acquisitive, thoroughly reprehensible man, near the end of a misspent life, was quietly put out of the way?

He had framed the disturbing thought now, and pursued it. It was a wrong, yes. But there were wrongs aplenty. Even in decorous Bath you could find dingy streets by the river that offered every sort of crying evil: starveling rickety children, wives black with bruises, girls of eleven turned prostitute and already riddled with venereal disease. And those were wrongs he couldn't help. Was this so much greater?

'I shall be happy to continue with that arrangement,' Mr Goode said. 'I take it the renumeration is satisfactory?'

Fairfax stared at him. 'It is.'

'Good. I understand, of course, that you lack independent means, which makes that a matter of importance. Neccessity, even.'

So here was his choice. Help find Sir James's killer, or consider his employment at an end. Before he could frame a reply, however, the carriage stopped. He saw they were outside the Delabole house.

'You will want, at least, to convey your sympathies to the family,' Mr Goode said, eyeing him shrewdly. 'A widow, dear me, and a fatherless daughter. A dreadful affair. Come.'

Gnawing his lip, Fairfax stepped out after the magistrate.

That chill, lofty, unhomely house. The grim irony was, it seemed to have more *life* in it now. Servants were milling about the hall, eyes big with scandal: one, the manservant Nolan, was sitting with his little wizened head in his hands. A Chinese vase lay broken on the floor near the front door – knocked over, Fairfax surmised, in the struggle to carry the dying man indoors. Through the door to the rear parlour Fairfax saw the two chairmen, seated awkwardly on a sofa in their greatcoats and mud-spattered shoes. And through the door to the front drawing-room, above the back of another sofa, he saw the elegantly dressed heads of Lady Delabole and Selina, close together, like two flowers on a single stem.

'The late master has been . . . laid upstairs, my man?' Mr Goode said.

Nolan nodded. Tears in his eyes, Fairfax noted: eyes like a whipped but faithful dog. How utterly strange people were.

A plump-cheeked man in the full wig of a physician came out of the drawing-room.

'Dr Reed. This is Mr Fairfax. How are the ladies bearing up?' Mr Goode said.

'Bravely, bravely, under the circumstances. Intimate with the family, sir?'

'No, I . . . that is . . .' Fairfax frowned, looked away from Mr Goode's watchful face. 'Can I see him?'

God knew why. He didn't want to.

Sir James lay upstairs on a canopied bed, covered with a sheet. Fairfax saw that a fire had just been lit in the grate. As if to warm him. He was cold past warming, of course, and the sight beneath the sheet was about as horrible as Fairfax expected. Not expected, or at least forgotten, was the sense of intrusion, looking upon that helpless stare and grin: the end of everything included the end of privacy.

'The spasmodic appearance is characteristic of poison,' the doctor was saying in a comfortable yeasty voice. 'Though I understand the gentleman was visibly racked by his infirmity in any case. Not that he was my patient.'

Well, Fairfax thought as the sheet was replaced, he hadn't really needed to do this. Just the atmosphere of a house visited by death had done the job. Yet seeing the mortal husk of Colonel Sir James Delabole had helped clear his thoughts too. One's fellow man, common humanity, and all that, as Locke might say: but it went deeper than that. It occurred to his reluctant mind that he had disliked Sir James because he was reminded of himself. Grotesque! Yet the lineaments were there. Drink, and cynicism, and a sense of a life compromised and unsatisfactory, and sentimental maundering as a way out of it all. For hadn't he been bitterly, indulgently wallowing since the loss of his love, Cordelia? Wallowing, and pretending the contemptible world wasn't worth his attention. But the real contempt was for himself. All hatred was disabling – but self-hatred most of all.

And if this had happened to him – if his own life had been horribly snuffed out – wouldn't he hope that someone would seek justice on his behalf? That someone would see past the soured, self-despising creature he had become to the true man beneath, and consider him worth avenging?

He looked up at Mr Goode.

'I'll do all I can,' he said, shortly.

Mr Goode inclined his head. Fairfax had earned the respectful nod.

The doctor showed him the flask inside the silver head of the cane.

'Traces of white, see. A heavy dose, but the fiery quality of the liquor no doubt prevented him from knowing anything was amiss until it was down. The cane is his own, I take it?'

'Yes. He always carried it when he went about,' Fairfax said. 'It was his habit to take a peg of the usquebaugh to revive him.'

'It would only have inflamed such a gouty condition,' the doctor said with a shake of his head. 'However, that's by the by now.'

'The poison is not uncommon.'

'You could buy it at a dozen druggists' here. Bath is well supplied, of course, with such. And many people keep it in their medicine-chests. The curious thing about medicine is that what is bad for you is also good for you, in different proportions.'

'Not only medicine. I suppose Sir James cannot have taken the dose deliberately . . .'

The doctor shook his head. 'Tis highly unlikely. I gather he was not a man who seemed apt to put an end to himself. And the manner of it . . . He took a draught before beginning his journey home. Surely no man would furnish himself with the means of suicide, and then casually employ them at such a moment.'

'No . . . The only conclusion, then, is that someone put

the arsenic in the flask, unknown to him. Someone who knew about the cane and his habitual use of it. And that must have been – when? At some time this morning, I suppose. Depending upon when the flask was filled. I had better talk to the manservant.'

Mr Goode thanked the doctor and said they need trouble him no longer. Downstairs Fairfax stepped into the parlour to speak to the two chairmen. Their story was much as he had heard already. Chairmen of good repute, licensed to carry on their trade by the corporation of Bath: they had been plying for business in the Circus about noon when they were hailed over to this house by the manservant in the hall. Fairfax nodded: he was there. So, they picked up late gentleman and carried him as instructed to Orchard Street. No stops on the way. At Orchard Street, late gentleman went into a house, commanding them to wait. They waited, for near an hour: they were careful of that, on account of totting up. It was a sixpenny fare, and a ten-minute stop was allowed in the price of that, and any longer was charged at sixpence the half hour. Then late gentleman came out of the house and ordered them, rather snappish-like, to take him back to the Circus. Anyone else there, at the Orchard Street house? Only the servant, who had gone back in and shut the door: no one came out to take leave of the gentleman. Fairfax made a mental note of that. Late gentleman got into the chair, unscrewed the top of his cane and had a swig – a neat arrangement, the first chairman thought. They picked up the poles, and off. No stops on the way back here? No: smooth for home. Terrible sight when they drew up, and opened the door. Late gentleman unable to speak? Past that, the first chairman said, mopping his brow: past that, God save him.

Fairfax thanked them and sent them on their way. The first chairman hung back and asked awkwardly whether this would reflect badly at all, when it came to renewing their licence . . .

'No. You may be assured of that, my friend,' Mr Goode said. 'I am on good terms with the gentlemen of the corporation, among other things.'

The second chairman, having returned, gave the first a nudge.

'Is there something else?'

They hadn't been paid. Mr Goode dug in his pocket, nostrils pinched.

Fairfax fetched Nolan into the parlour. The little manservant looked at them as if they were the Inquisition, but also as if they could do their worst and he wouldn't care.

'Mr Nolan, you've been in Sir James's service a good while, I think?' Fairfax ventured.

'Fifteen years, sir,' Nolan said in a soft Irish brogue, blinking miserably about him. 'Fifteen years, and never a harsh word!'

Well, the man was upset, but that was too much. 'Never?' Fairfax asked incredulously.

'None as was meant. It was only the colonel's way, you know, sir. *I* never took any heed of it. He was a soldier, you see, and I'd been a soldier, and you get accustomed to a certain way. He used me very well, and – and it's a crying shame, that's all.'

'It was you who waited on the colonel, then, and assisted at his dressing and so on?'

'Me and no other, sir. 'Twas me who shaved him every morning. He liked it close, you know – that was his way. "Go in and win, Nolan," he'd say, "right under the nose! D'you think I fear a nick?" And I can say I never did nick him, sir. Never. Not above half a dozen times.'

'And the colonel's cane? Please, sit down, Mr Nolan.' Those tottering bow legs were getting too much for Fairfax. 'What about the flask in the top – was it part of your duties to fill that?'

'No, sir. I took it down and cleaned it every night, and polished the top, and the silver banding near the end. Then I'd place it in the hall-stand for the morning. Each day he'd fill it himself from the bottle. 'Twas the same wherever we lived. He kept the bottle locked in a bureau here. Not that he didn't trust the servants, mind . . . only 'twas rare stuff, you know, and hard to come by. His poor hands were getting shaky of late, but he'd still do it himself.'

'I see. And it was the same as usual this morning?'

'Yes, sir. At least – as far as that goes, it was the same.'

'So the cane stood in the hall, with its flask filled. Very well. What was not the same, Mr Nolan?'

'Why, pretty much everything, sir. I wouldn't want to be telling tales, mind . . .'

'Your master is murdered,' Fairfax said gently, 'and so I'm afraid the time for telling tales is here.'

Swallowing, Nolan edged his neck from his tight-wound stock, like a mournful tortoise. 'Heyo! Well, 'twas not a happy morning, from what I saw. First there was the young gentleman come calling early. I don't know what went on, but it seemed to put the colonel out of humour—'

'What young gentleman?'

'Why, the one as is sitting with the ladies now, sir. Pinker I think was the name—'

'Pinner?'

'You have it, sir. He came a-calling early, like I say, wanting

87

to see Sir James particular and confidential, and Sir James took him into his study upstairs, and sent me away. When he called me back a while later, Mr Pinner was gone, and Sir James was . . . well, not waxy, not in that way he gets sometimes. There was thunder in his face, but 'twas more sorrowful than anything. I asked him if there was anything amiss, but he just said no, and sat on there at his desk, brooding. That's what I'd call it. Brooding and staring at this paper. Head on his hand, like so.'

'A paper? Did you see what was written on it?'

Nolan scratched at his chin with a rasping sound. 'Well, I'm not a reading man, sir, not really. Missed out on my letters, on account of being raised poor. There's a few words I can piece out, from seeing 'em written up a lot. "God Save The King" I know straight off, for it's always on the bottom of notices, I reckon. And "Delabole" I'd know anywhere, from seeing it on our packing-cases a thousand times. Now that I can vouch for, on the top of this paper.'

'You're sure of this?'

'Aye, sir: my eye falls on that like an old friend. But as for reading, that's like a closed book to me. As you might say.'

'I see . . . What then?'

'Well, then Sir James says to me he wants a lawyer. Just like that. Go send the boy to fetch him: Mr Carson at Princes Street, he says, and tell him I want him here as soon as may be. So down I goes to the kitchen and sends the boy off, and then I come back to the study to tidy up.'

'Tidy up?'

'Yes, sir – there was a piece of chiney-ware broke, sir. Used to stand on his desk. He'd – well, mebbe knocked it off. Mebbe smashed it deliberate,' Nolan said with a wince. 'As I say, he was mighty black-looking, and I thought best not to ask. Well, the master had gone downstairs now, and when I come down there's voices shouting and doors slamming – a regular commotion. There's Miss Selina piping her eye – not that that's so very unusual: but the worst of it was, the master and my lady are having high words – terrible high words.'

'About what?'

'Oh, they were mortal high words. They had their disagreements like any married folks, but never like this . . . Well, I fancy my lady had asked what the boy's errand was, because she was crying out about a lawyer, and what did he mean by it, and how it wasn't fair . . . terrible high words. They called each other such names, sir – shocking!'

'And this was – not usual?'

'Well . . .' Nolan sucked his teeth. 'Only on the master's part, sir, if you take my meaning – oh, and 'twasn't often, no. And never like this. Then it goes quiet at last, and me and the other servants were in the kitchen asking each other what the matter could be, and then down comes the colonel looking in a terrible passion, and rounds on the maids something fearful. Tells them to mind their ways, and know he's the master in this house, and says they're to let no one in on the sly without his say-so. Meaning especially the young ensign, Mr Locke, he says. Well, that threw me into amaze, sir, for the young strip's been here ever and anon, and naught but a welcome before. Heyo! Then he tells me to get out and call him a chair. He wanted away from this house o' bedlam, he says.'

'And this would be about noon?'

'That's it, sir. When you came to the door. I hailed him the chair, and he got in it, and off he went . . . and that was the end of him!'

'And he took his cane from the hall-stand when he left the house.'

'That was his habit, sir.'

'Which is not to say,' Mr Goode put in heavily, 'that the cane had been tampered with at that point.'

'No indeed. There is another household concerned in this . . . Let us see this paper that Sir James was so occupied with. Lead the way, Mr Nolan.'

Mr Goode coughed and put a finger on Fairfax's arm. 'Is this quite appropriate, sir? A house of mourning – and to go roaming about it without a by-your-leave—'

'Is the very way to find what we seek. As opposed to announcing our intentions every step of the way so that the murderer may steal a march on us. I'm sorry, Mr Goode, but if I am to pursue this matter I must be allowed to do it in my own way. Let us be clear on that from the outset.'

He turned without waiting for an answer, and followed Nolan upstairs to Sir James's study.

'Well, it was here,' Nolan said. 'Here, right on the desk.'

'Sir James took it with him, perhaps,' Mr Goode suggested.

'No, sir: that I can engage for, because it was here when I came to sweep up the broken chiney. Right in the middle of the desk.'

'Then someone has put it away,' Fairfax said, 'or taken it away.'

The study did not look like a place that was much used, and in the desk drawers he found only a few tradesman's bills. Nolan shook his head when presented with those.

' 'Twas nothing of that sort, sir. There was Delabole in big writing at the top, and – well, I'd know it if I saw it, and it ain't them.'

Fairfax looked round at the study. Here, it seemed,

Sir James had sat brooding, struggling with contrary feelings, coming perhaps to a crucial decision, little knowing that the shadow of death was on him ... One felt that the furniture ought somehow to be impregnated with it, the air a-tingle. Yet it was just a room. What little impression even a forceful man like Sir James really made on the world.

Well, it was time to see those he left behind. Fairfax went down to the drawing-room.

Lady Delabole and Selina, tightly holding hands, their flower-like heads still close together, regarded him from the sofa with blank dry eyes.

'Mr Fairfax,' Lady Delabole said. 'It is good of you to come.'

'Ma'am. A great shock. I do not mean to intrude on your grief, only to—'

'To help find out who killed my husband. That is what it is, is it not? Someone poisoned him. He died rather horribly, Mr Fairfax.'

'I am indeed sorry, Lady Delabole.'

'Many people will be sorry,' she said. Her face was suddenly animated. 'People are very *good* in trouble, I find, don't you? Here is Mr Pinner come most kindly to offer his condolences. The first of many, I'm sure.'

Fairfax nodded at Edmund Pinner who was standing awkwardly by the window. The harsh light there made the young man look bleached, almost emaciated. 'Sir, you are ... very prompt.'

'I sent a servant to Mr Tiverton's house at once, as soon as – as soon as my husband was no more,' Lady Delabole said. 'It seemed imperative as he has close family there too. Miss Delabole has a claim to know as soon as we.'

Very good and typically proper of her, Fairfax thought. Fearfully self-possessed too.

'I elected to come on behalf of Caroline and her grandfather, to offer their respects and condolences,' Pinner said with, Fairfax noticed, sweat on his brow though the room was chill. 'Caroline was greatly shocked, and quite prostrated. I've never seen her so – in all the years I've known her.'

Still staking that claim, Fairfax thought. His eye lit on an elderly man in a bag-wig, bespectacled and beaky, who sat to one side, apparently disregarded.

'Carson, sir,' the man offered at once, jumping up, 'notary, of Princes Street. I thought it best to remain, as you were so good as to suggest –' with a writhing bow at Mr Goode – 'though truly I fear I am only in the way.'

'You are the lawyer Sir James sent for this morning.'

'Yes, sir. A boy came to me and, being desirous, of course, of being of service to the late gentleman, I came as soon as I could, a little past one o'clock. I found the late gentleman was from home, but apparently I was instructed to await his return here, so I did. I did not have to wait long – though, dear me, the unhappy result . . .'

'Of course. So, Mr Carson, had you any notion of what Sir James wished to speak to you about? You are his lawyer?'

'Oh, no, sir – that is, I am not the legal representative with whom Sir James customarily entrusts his affairs. A gentleman in London has that honour, I understand. But Sir James did come to speak with me last week, informally as it were, about a certain matter.'

'Which was?'

'Oh, sir – I'm not sure that I may disclose such confidential matters—'

'Nonsense,' Fairfax interrupted. 'Here's a man murdered, sir: we must have the truth.'

'Dear me – yes – well, the matter under discussion was the disposition of the late gentleman's property. His will, in short.'

Lady Delabole stirred. Fairfax saw her fingers whiten where they gripped her daughter's.

'What about his will?' he said.

'Oh, sir – an ailing gentleman, of good fortune, must think of such things,' the lawyer simpered. 'Very proper.'

'You drew up a new will for him?'

'Oh, no, sir. We simply discussed terms, should he wish to do so. I said I would be happy to act for him, pending notification of his usual representative in London. Professional courtesies, you know. He said he would call upon me when he had decided his arrangements. That is why I was not surprised to be summoned today. I supposed . . .' The lawyer looked timidly round. 'Dear me.'

'So there is no new will?'

'To my knowledge, Sir James's disposition of his affairs stands as it was. That is, his will is the one that is lodged with his London representative, and that was made some years ago, I understand. If Sir James drafted a new will, reflecting any, dear me, changed circumstances, then he did not inform me.'

But was he going to today, Fairfax wondered? And was that where the missing paper came in?

He thanked the lawyer who looked grateful to be able to scuttle off. Couldn't blame him for that: it must have been deadly uncomfortable, having to sit here with the blank-faced bereaved. The same went for Pinner who, if he had come to offer consolation, was not doing much offering: he looked, indeed, less capable than his hostess. Fairfax suggested it might be best if he returned to Mr Tiverton's.

'But a word first, if you will be so good,' he added and ushered Pinner into the back parlour. Mr Goode followed.

'I understand, Mr Pinner, that this is not your first call here today.'

'No. That is, I called earlier in – in quite a separate connection.' After a nervous glance at the chair, as if he feared it might explode under him, Pinner sat.

'You came to see Sir James?'

'Correct. Yes, quite so.' The young man's jaw worked convulsively. He was quite handsome in a gaunt way, but his face seldom stayed still long enough for one to see it.

'And how did he seem?'

That was plainly not the question Pinner had expected.

'Sir James? He seemed – let's see. Really, I can't think what – he was much as ever, I think—'

'Yet this was only your second meeting with him, I think,' Fairfax said. 'There was the dinner last evening, and now today.' He smiled gently. 'I simply mean it is difficult, surely, for you to say whether he was the same as ever or not. On such a slight acquaintance. And that is what puzzles me about your coming to call on him this morning. It was hardly, I think, as if you and Sir James struck up an immediate friendship last evening.'

'Social call,' Pinner said. 'Yes, a social call, and – well, you are wrong, Mr Fairfax, if you suppose I was not glad to make Sir James's acquaintance. That is, when I say wrong, I mean mistaken. I was most eager to make his acquaintance, as I have been intimate with his family – that is, a part of his family, for many years.'

'Ah, yes. Miss Caroline Delabole.'

'Quite so. Caroline. Oh – it is my habit to use her Christian name familiarly in that way, sir, from long and close association. It is not disrespectful. Far from it.'

'To anyone with eyes to see,' Fairfax said, genially, 'it is plain that you are a great admirer of that lady.'

'Long association – the innocent intimacy of youth, and my cordial relations with her grandfather . . .'

I do wish he wouldn't talk like that, Fairfax thought and, as if acceding to his wish, Pinner suddenly sat forward and nodded.

'Yes,' he said. 'I admire Caroline greatly. No secret there. She is . . . well, it is plain, as you say, sir, how I feel about her. Not that I have allowed my feelings to trespass on the borders of propriety. You do wrong to suppose it.'

'I suppose nothing, believe me. I wonder, Mr Pinner, whether you should take a drink of water or something—'

'No need for that. I am quite composed,' Pinner said, looking more wrought up than ever. 'We were talking of my relation with Caroline. I make no secret of my – my tender regard in that direction. It can hardly have any bearing on this business. At least . . . this terrible death.'

'Death of her father, whom you came to see early this morning. You speak of a social call, but it was only Sir James that you spoke with, not the ladies. According to his man-servant, you were closeted with Sir James in his study.'

'Oh, yes. Certainly. That was my intent – that is, I mean I sought an interview alone. Simply to speak with him and lay before him my situation. As there was little opportunity for that, you will allow, last evening. In company.'

'Your situation?'

'In regard to Caroline.' Pinner spread his hands and smiled painfully.

'Ah. There is some undertaking, then? Some arrangement?'

'No.' Pinner looked bleak for a moment. 'That is, there is nothing concrete. But my long-standing regard – I thought it best that Sir James be aware of it, as he is her father. Or rather, has resolved to play a father's part, at last. He is dead, now, of course,' he added with an awkward chuckle, 'so it doesn't apply. But this morning I was not to know that. After a night of reflection, and bearing in mind Sir James's plans for Caroline, I thought it best to – to—'

'To stake your claim?'

Eyes averted, Pinner nodded – but what he said was: 'No. There is no claim as such. It would be wrong of me, impudent of me, to say there is.'

'I see.' Talking to this man was like hacking your way through a thicket, Fairfax thought. 'Not a claim, then. To declare your interest. Is that a suitable way of putting it?'

'Well – yes.'

Fairfax caught Mr Goode's audible sigh of relief.

'These plans of Sir James's for his daughter,' Fairfax went on. 'I would imagine, from what you've told me, that you would not be happy with them. Taking her to London, introducing her to society, and so on.'

'Why so?'

'Because,' Fairfax said, summoning his patience, 'they would take Caroline out of your sphere, would they not?'

'The claim of a father is greater than that of a fond friend,' Pinner replied woodenly. 'I have no power over the matter. Besides – it is Caroline's choice. That is the crux of it – what she wants.'

But if Sir James is put out of the way, Fairfax thought, then there is no choice.

'So how did Sir James respond to your – your declaration of interest?'

'I don't understand.'

'Please, Mr Pinner, I am asking for your help here. A man is murdered, and I am trying to understand what happened on his last day alive. One of the things that happened was a private interview with you, sir. And I understand, from Sir James's manservant, that he was not in the best of humour after it. Now why should that be?'

'I can't say,' Pinner said, dabbing his brow with his handkerchief. 'You perplex me, sir. I stated my case, civilly, and he listened, civilly. That was all.'

Well, as the old saying went, Fairfax thought, *that's a lie with a lid on, and a brass handle to lift it with*. Sir James had made it quite plain, at Mr Tiverton's dinner, what he thought of a middling Bristol-merchant as a suitor for his daughter. And the very notion of Sir James Delabole 'listening civilly' was absurd.

'The gentleman was of a generally choleric temper,' Pinner said, and for the first time there was challenge in his pale eyes. 'Everyone knew that. If that temper showed itself today, then I'm sorry, but I wouldn't have thought it surprising.'

Lying, Fairfax thought, or at least not telling the whole truth about his interview with Sir James . . . But then, it *was* true about the man's temper. He had seen for himself – that incident in the street with the man from America. And it might be that whatever went on in that study had nothing to do with Sir James's behaviour afterwards.

For that, he would need to talk to Lady Delabole and Selina. And he had a feeling that they were going to be hard work too.

He rose, and Pinner sprang up at once.

'Thank you, Mr Pinner. If we need to speak to you again,

you are to be found at Mr Tiverton's house, I take it?'

'Oh, yes.' A hint of smugness there. 'That is, for the time being.'

'Very well. I dare say I shall be there shortly myself. It was very prompt of you, by the by – coming over here to offer the family's condolences. You must scarcely have waited a moment.'

'It was all I could do. Besides, I could not bear to – to witness Caroline's distress. I had to get away. I was glad to be able to . . . I would do anything . . .' Pinner swallowed, and got out in a hurry.

You would do anything for Caroline, Fairfax thought – even kill for her? Or rather, kill to keep her?

And this distress of Caroline's: what did it mean? Distress at the loss of a father she had only just met – or distress at the loss of a fortune? For it seemed, thus far at any rate, that Sir James had died before he could make arrangements to settle his property on Caroline: which meant, presumably, that Lady Delabole and her daughter inherited everything.

So it appeared. But there was still the matter of that document which had been on Sir James's desk, and was now nowhere to be seen.

He found Lady Delabole and Selina still sitting together dry-eyed and baleful; but a small addition had been made to their comfort in the shape of a tray with a decanter. Lady Delabole looked at him over her glass of brandy, and for a moment he almost thought she was going to raise it to him in an ironic toast. *Here's to tippling, openly and freely! Huzzah!*

He wished he could have one. And at the same time, a touch of that earlier doubt, black and cynical, returned to him. Was Lady Delabole's chief emotion at the death of her husband a feeling of liberation – and if it was, who could blame her?

But that depended, of course, on whether she had done the liberating. It was hard to picture her doing anything so unladylike, so *inappropriate* as murder; but he had to consider it, of course. As Selina Delabole knew: for he had hardly begun to present his apologies and commiserations before she burst out vehemently, 'Don't listen to him, Mama! Don't pay any heed – he's only thinking to catch who did it to Papa, and he's not sincere, not a bit.'

'I am indeed out to catch that person, Miss Selina, as Mr Goode here has asked me to assist in the matter,' Fairfax said. 'And I am most *sincerely* out to catch that person, believe me. You must surely feel the same, Miss Selina – the wish to see him or her brought to justice.'

Selina pouted. 'It will not bring Papa back.'

Now *that*, Fairfax thought, is insincerity.

'My dear, we must help Mr Fairfax all we can,' Lady Delabole said, setting down her glass. 'It is hard, I know, but we must put aside our feelings for now.'

'How *can* one put aside one's feelings?' Selina stamped her foot. 'That is sheer insensibility.'

'Sheer insensibility,' Lady Delabole replied, refilling her glass, 'is not such an undesirable state, my dear, as you'll find when you are older.'

Hear, hear, Fairfax thought. And he found himself hoping that Lady Delabole was not the killer of her husband, because there was a good deal about her that he liked very much.

That stamp of the foot had been revealing, at any rate – not so much regarding Selina's temper, as her footwear.

'I shall not trouble you with questions for long,' Fairfax said. 'All I need is—'

'An account of my husband's last hours,' Lady Delabole finished for him. 'Of course. Ask away, Mr Fairfax.'

'Well, I have a partial account. Sir James was visited by Mr Pinner this morning, and was closeted with him in his study. Did he say anything about this interview?'

'Nothing whatsoever,' Lady Delabole rapped out.

'I see. And your husband's manservant, Nolan, says that Sir James remained alone for some time in the study afterwards and seemed to be preoccupied with a document of some kind. Nolan is no reader, but says he recognized the name Delabole inscribed on it. That document does not seem to be in the study now, though Sir James left it there and did not take it with him when he left the house.'

'Indeed?' said Lady Delabole, absently benign, as if listening to an anecdote that had nothing to do with her.

'Yes. And I wonder what that document might have been, and where it has gone.'

'You may well wonder,' Lady Delabole said, 'if you do not know Nolan as I do. My husband was indulgently attached to him, on account of his military background, but I fear he is not the most reliable fellow, especially now that he is getting up in years. No reader, as you say, Mr Fairfax; and as he is often unsure even of what day it is, I would not place too much faith in anything he says.'

'I see. But either there was not a document, or there was. And as I see no reason why he should say there was when there wasn't, I still want to know about it.'

'You see, Mama,' cried Selina, 'he is just being monstrous and insinuating! It isn't fair we should have to sit here and—'

'Hush, my dear. Mr Fairfax, I know of no document so I cannot say where it has gone. Really, that is all.'

'Very well. But there is surely no doubting Nolan's other testimony – that Sir James ordered him to send for the lawyer – as the lawyer came.'

Lady Delabole inclined her head.

'Nor can I doubt what he told me about Sir James's actions when he came down from the study – that is, he went into a great rage, and there was a quarrel. I gathered as much myself, when I called here earlier.'

'It was not a peaceful morning, certainly,' Lady Delabole agreed.

'Ensign Locke also came here this morning, I understand – but was ordered to leave by Sir James. So he told me, at any rate. Very odd. Was that the occasion of the quarrel?'

'My husband was a man of capricious and changeable humour, I fear,' Lady Delabole said, while her daughter's eyes tugged at her. 'He has often been glad of Mr Locke's company, but today he declined it for some reason. I think there is no more to it than that.'

'And the note, Miss Selina? Locke asked me to give you a note. I'm sorry but the time for discretion is past, and I must ask you about it.'

Her lips tight, her look venomous, Selina muttered: 'It was nothing. Mere nonsense. He is – he is a great one for nonsense. I threw it away. It was nothing improper, if that's what you mean.'

He didn't mean that: he wanted to know what she and Locke were up to, but he was afraid she was not going to tell him. He glanced down.

'I see you have been out, Miss Selina. You wear overshoes, and they are muddied.'

Too late, she tucked her feet under her skirts.

'I went for a short walk. That is not so uncommon, surely.'

'Alone?'

Flushed, Selina said: 'I simply wanted to get out of the house for a space – clear my head. After all the quarrelling—'

'Yes, the quarrelling: what *was* it about?'

'Mr Fairfax,' Lady Delabole said, 'have you ever been married?'

Always that damn question. He tried not to stiffen. 'No, I have not.'

Lady Delabole smiled faintly. 'Well, there is a vast deal of stuff talked about matrimonial felicity. There is such a thing, of course, but like most things it is seldom found in a pure state. It is mostly mixed up with misunderstandings and disagreements and even quarrels. That's the way of it, I'm afraid.'

'One doesn't have to be married to know that,' Fairfax snapped, feeling himself patronised, 'but I think this was no ordinary quarrel. You were both upset: that I saw with my own eyes. Was it to do with Locke?' His eyes flicked to Selina, who would not look at him. 'Or even Mr Pinner's visit? Or was it this matter of sending for a lawyer? Lady Delabole? You were aware that your husband had sent for the lawyer – and in the present circumstances, that could surely mean only one thing.'

'It might mean any number of things,' Lady Delabole said blandly. 'And as for present circumstances—'

'Caroline,' Fairfax said. 'His first-born daughter. His reconciliation with her. Those are the circumstances to which I refer.'

'He's being horrible again, Mama. Don't listen to him, send him away—'

'Indeed I don't mean to be horrible, and this must seem very hard when the shock is still fresh upon you. But you surely cannot pretend this matter of Caroline has had no effect upon the family.'

'You speak as if some great secret has been suddenly revealed: I have always been aware of my husband's first marriage, and the child that survived it,' Lady Delabole drawled. 'It was quite natural that we should meet her at last, and I am glad we did. She is quite charming.'

'A little jealousy would be quite natural too, though, I think.' Fairfax said it as gently as he could – but Selina fired up at once.

'Mama, it's too monstrous! I can't bear it any more. Mr Goode, make him go away. Papa lies dead upstairs and all you can do is torment us!'

Mr Goode coughed. 'Perhaps, indeed, we should leave the ladies in peace for now, Mr Fairfax. It has, as you say, been a great shock.' He rose.

Reluctantly Fairfax followed suit. They weren't telling him everything, he was sure of that; but he was not certain why.

'Go and see *her*,' Selina hissed at him, clutching her mother's hand. 'Go on – go and torment *her*. She's the cuckoo in the nest. We were very well until she came along. And what could *she* feel for Papa? No, Mama, I shall say it. She never knew him. All he was to her was a fortune. Have you thought of *that*?'

He had, of course. A good deal hinged on the character of Caroline Delabole. If she was mercenary, was she mercenary enough to kill her own father? And yet that didn't wash because as things stood there was only Sir James's old will, made long before their reconciliation. If she were going to do away with him, it would only make sense to do it after he had changed his arrangements, and settled his property on her.

Unless there *had* been a change and only certain people

knew about it. His mind kept returning to that paper Sir James had been brooding over. If he could only lay his hands on that.

Yet it made more sense from the opposite angle: kill Sir James *before* he could change his will in Caroline's favour. Putting himself in Lady Delabole's shoes, that made perfect sense – as far as murder ever made sense. She was seeing her own daughter pushed out in favour of a young woman from her husband's past. That must be hard. And when the man was a brute who seemed to reserve all his care and affection for this newcomer . . .

Fairfax spoke of these things to Mr Goode as they left the house and got into the magistrate's carriage. He was really thinking aloud, and was startled to see the expression of perplexed distaste on Mr Goode's face.

'Dear me,' Mr Goode said, 'how very ghastly it all is.'

'Eh? Oh, yes, no doubt. A grim business. But one must think of these things—'

'Of course. And I am sure you are the very man for the job, Mr Fairfax. So much so that I see no necessity for my accompanying you further. You are going to Mr Tiverton's, I take it? Very well: I shall drop you there, and then you will forgive me if I take my leave. I have, among other things, many social obligations. I will arrange the inquest: the evidence of the doctor and the chairmen should suffice. Call on me at Queen Square if you have anything to report, and do make free with my name to facilitate your investigations. But – dear me – it is all very ghastly.'

'Human nature sometimes is, I'm afraid.'

'Oh, no doubt, no doubt. I am sure you have the measure of the case, Mr Fairfax: but, dear me, I would not have your mind for a thousand pound!'

Well, thought Fairfax, a little dumbfounded as he got down at Orchard Street, how the compliments fly today! The man wanted the crime solved, after all – and that, Fairfax well knew, meant suspecting the worst of everybody. It wasn't such a bad habit of mind to cultivate, anyway: it meant when people behaved well you were pleasantly surprised.

Six

'Prostrated with grief' was how Pinner had described Caroline Delabole's state. If so, she had recovered wonderfully. She looked grave, seemed collected, gave Fairfax a cool firm handshake. The more he thought about it, the more he thought it sensible of Caroline, and silly of Pinner. She had, after all, only recently met Sir James, who had never played a father's part to her. Surely the greatest loss was . . . well, those glittering prospects he had laid out before her?

'Of course, sir, I quite understand,' she said when Fairfax explained his mission and apologized for intruding. 'It is a horrid crime, and we must do all we can to see justice done. Please be seated.'

'How are things at Sir James's house?' Mr Tiverton asked. He looked stony and inflexible as ever – but also a little grey, Fairfax thought, like a man who has not slept. 'The ladies, I mean. They must be mighty shaken up.'

'They bear up – as no doubt Mr Pinner will have told you,' Fairfax said. Pinner was there, of course, his watery eyes as anxiously fixed on Caroline as if she were an invalid only just out of bed. He didn't know, but he imagined it would be rather wearing to be the object of such dogged attention. Mrs Jessop was there too, with needlework on her lap, but her hands were idle. She was putting everything into a look of penetrating hostility – at Fairfax – which he couldn't imagine he'd deserved.

'Sir James called here about noon, I believe,' Fairfax said. 'How did he appear to you?'

Mr Tiverton started to speak, but his granddaughter cut him off. 'Oh! I'm afraid it's not much use asking me that, sir. I hardly saw him. He was closeted with my grandfather most of the time.'

She shot Mr Tiverton a glance that was decidedly cool. Hullo, Fairfax thought.

'Yes,' Mr Tiverton said heavily, 'we spoke in my private office. We had much to talk of.' He avoided Caroline's eyes.

'That is so,' Mrs Jessop put in. 'I went in to ask the gentlemen if they would take a dish of tea. The late gentleman, of course, was one for strong liquors, so he declined. But Mr Tiverton and the late gentleman did talk in the private office, that I can vouch for, sir.' She picked up her needle and fiercely jabbed it into her sewing. 'I hope my word's good enough for you.'

'Indeed, I have no doubt—'

'Don't you? Well, I hope not. You must pardon me, sir, but I don't hold with this prying and poking and – treating this household as if it were a thieves' kitchen. 'T'as always been most respectable. And this is all a very sad business I'm sure, but the sooner we can lay it to rest and put it behind us the better.'

Mr Tiverton waved a hand. 'Mrs Jessop, please! Mr Fairfax is charged with this task, and we must submit. The fact is that Sir James met his death after coming here: no getting away from that.'

'Why, you can't mean there's any suspicion on this

household,' Mrs Jessop said, with a glare, before Mr Tiverton hushed her again. Yes, there is, thought Fairfax; and that, madam, includes you. In fact if there was anyone who had manifested an open antipathy to Sir James Delabole, it was her. There had been quite a clash between them last evening over the matter of drink and the devil's works generally. And it was Sir James's portable liquor that had been poisoned, too – which had a touch of poetic justice about it. But was disapproval a motive to kill a man? Of course, Sir James had thrown out those crude hints about the relationship between his host and the housekeeper being more than professional . . . Could she have taken murderous umbrage at that?

Murderous umbrage. There was a new one for the statute books. He collected his thoughts.

'You had matters to discuss, you said, Mr Tiverton.'

'Of course. Sir, you are not unaware of our situation – our history. It was Sir James's intention to achieve a reconciliation. With his daughter –' Mr Tiverton pursed his lips – 'and with me. I acceded. At your wish, my dear,' he said pointedly to Caroline. 'At your wish only.'

'It went hard with you, sir?' Fairfax said.

'Let me be plain, Mr Fairfax. I am shocked at this news; but I would be a liar if I said I felt any love for Sir James, or even any degree of warm regard. His treatment of my daughter Lydia is not something that even the passage of twenty years can expunge in my memory. Nor could this late repentance, if such it was, incline me to repose in him a confidence that his early career did so little to warrant.' The creak of emotion in the merchant's dry, rusty voice was faint but perceptible. 'For Caroline's sake I was civil. That is all.'

'You felt, then, that you still could not trust Sir James?'

'I said something – something hasty to that effect last evening, I know. And I do not deny there were hasty words between us again today.'

'You were quarrelling, Grandfather,' Caroline put in quietly. 'I could hear raised voices. And when my father left—'

'Not a quarrel – not a quarrel as such. Sir James was of an inflammable temper – you know that, sir. With the matters we had to discuss, we both grew heated, I dare say. But that is hardly surprising, in view of our history, and in view of his – his ideas. Ideas that touched very nearly on all that is dearest to me.'

He was tremulous, imploring even, as he looked across at his granddaughter. But Caroline only said crisply, 'Ideas: that is all they were. Nothing was settled. I never meant to do anything that would displease you, Grandfather; please don't suggest that I would.'

'Sir James wanted you to go with him to London,' Fairfax said.

'It was in the air. A notion. That's all. It can hardly – there is no sense in talking of it, as all is finished now.' Caroline got up, with barely restrained pettishness, and went to stir the fire.

'He was too precipitate,' Mr Tiverton said, watching her sombrely. 'Too impetuous. That was why – that was where we could not agree. You must understand, Mr Fairfax, that I have had the sole charge of Caroline these twenty years. She is no less dear to me than a daughter. Indeed, after the daughter I lost . . . Well, you take my meaning. And so there were some high words between us.'

Natural enough, Fairfax supposed: the one thing Mr

Tiverton and his late son-in-law had in common was stubbornness. He had to wonder, though, if there was anyone Sir James had *not* quarrelled with today.

'Did Sir James speak of any other intentions, Mr Tiverton? To do with his property, for example?'

At the fireplace, Caroline's shoulders went rigid.

'That was a matter for his discretion,' Mr Tiverton said, at his most stony. 'I had no power over that. He had, of course, spoken freely of what he meant to do for Caroline.'

'This is most unfair of you, Mr Fairfax,' Caroline said, straightening and coming back to her seat very coolly. 'Unfair and disappointing. My father is dead – horribly killed – and because he was rich, and there is an inheritance at stake, you begin putting two and two together in the most cold-blooded way. Please don't trouble to deny it. It is something that has exercised the tongues of the gossips ever since he came to Bath, I dare say: will that new-found daughter of his get the money? Oh, yes, I know what people think. I am supposed to be all a-dangle for these riches. It is rather hard, as no one can possibly know what my feelings are towards this father I never knew, and whom I have now lost, unless they are uncommonly clairvoyant. They might be surprised,' she said with a sudden, harsh, beautiful smile. 'But to be condemned out of hand as a mercenary minx is surely a little unjust.'

Or is it? thought Fairfax, but he did feel slightly abashed. Then Mrs Jessop spoke up, surprising him.

'All very well, my dear. But you know how the world wags. The love of money is the root of all evil – that's scripture. And the gentleman's in the right of it – people will want to know about the will, when a rich man's done to death.'

'We did not speak of his will,' Mr Tiverton said testily. 'As I said, that was his affair, it didn't concern me—'

'Pardon me,' Fairfax said, 'but it must have. Being Sir James Delabole's heiress would have made such a vast difference to your granddaughter's way of living. So much would have changed—'

'You say *would have*, Mr Fairfax,' Caroline put in, 'as if it were known that it is not so. But *do* we know? What arrangements had my father made? There, you see, I can speak of it quite calmly, without drooling in anticipation.'

'I suppose we don't know. The only known will left by Sir James is one deposited some years ago with his London lawyer, which – well, which reflects his previous situation. It is precisely the question of whether he made a new one that I am trying to answer.'

'We did not speak of it,' Mr Tiverton said. 'I know nothing of that matter, sir.'

Fairfax looked at Caroline.

'Me? Oh, I know nothing, Mr Fairfax. I am, you must remember, just the person who is talked *about* in all this, not talked *to*. Rather like a prize heifer at a stock-fair.'

She smiled but there was real hurt in her tone, Fairfax thought; and some truth in the protest. All the same, he was getting an increasing sense of will from this young woman, like a metallic tang.

'All I have done, I have done from care of you, Caroline,' said Mr Tiverton. 'And that care did not stop just because your father suddenly took it into his head—'

'Grandfather, I am a woman grown, and not a fool. I had no illusions about my father's character. But your quarrels are your own. It was dismaying, to say the least, to have him speak to me the way he did today.'

Fairfax's ears pricked up. 'Which was . . .?'

'Unexpected. There, Mr Fairfax, you are doing it again.

You see a falling-out, aha, that throws suspicion on me. It was simply this: when my father came out of my grandfather's office at last, I hastened downstairs to give him my respects, and he looked in my face, and said: "Well, miss, you must shift for yourself: I've done with you." And out he went with a face like thunder.'

'Caroline,' Mr Tiverton said wincing, 'you don't understand—'

'Oh, I do, Grandfather. You were angry with him, which I can quite understand; and he, being the man he was, got angry in turn, which I can quite understand also; and when he saw me, the cause of it all, he took out his anger on me. And that too I can quite understand. It is just a pity that was the last I saw of my father – that's all.'

And did she feel her grandfather had ruined her chances of being made Sir James's heir? Was that the real source of the grief in those great pellucid eyes?

Pinner was on his feet. 'Really, sir, this is too bad. You are upsetting Caroline – digging over this ground. She has just lost her father. There can be no justification—'

'Sir James is not *lost*,' Fairfax insisted. 'Someone killed him with poison, and he died in agony. That is justification enough. That poison was put into his cane-flask at some time this morning and, aside from his home, the only place he was at was this house. Now, on that subject, Mr Tiverton, can I ask which of your servants is responsible for answering the door?'

'That would be the maid, Beth,' Mr Tiverton replied, ringing the bell. 'I keep no footmen, sir: I am a plain man, and don't hold with that flummery.'

Beth was elderly and grim-jawed, and answered Fairfax's questions without hesitation. Yes, she had let Sir James in earlier: yes, she remembered the silver-headed cane. She had taken it along with his hat and placed them on a side-table in the hall. Then Mr Tiverton had invited Sir James to step into his private office, and in they went and stayed there. No, she had not been summoned to show Sir James out: he must have left of his own accord.

'I should say, sir,' Pinner put in, after Fairfax had thanked the maid and said she could go, 'that I was not in the house at this time. I had matters to attend to in the town, and I only returned here shortly after Sir James had left.'

'Indeed,' Fairfax said, 'but you did call on Sir James earlier this morning, Mr Pinner, which is the salient point.' He saw Caroline dart a curious glance at Pinner from under her beautifully lowered eyelids. How would she feel to know that Pinner had been 'staking his claim' upon her that morning? He thought he knew . . . but he *could* be wrong. Perhaps she was as much in love with Pinner as he was with her. It was a mighty good disguise, if so, and he couldn't think of a reason for it.

'Sir,' Mrs Jessop said suddenly to Mr Tiverton, 'I'm sorry, we must be quite truthful. You weren't closeted with the gentleman the *whole* time. I was seeing to the linen-cupboard when you came by. To use the close-stool, I think.' Her severe face dimpled with a curious embarrassment. 'If you'll forgive me mentioning it, Mr Fairfax.'

Having attended gentlemen's supper-parties where the chamber-pot was used freely at the side of the dining-table, some gentlemen not even interrupting their conversation while they noisily relieved themselves, Fairfax found the mention quite forgivable. More interesting was why Mrs Jessop had mentioned it. Certainly it established that Mr Tiverton had also had an opportunity to tamper with the cane. Did she have suspicions of her own? Of course, she was the relic of a Methodist and had made a point of her strait-laced morality. Perhaps she was simply preoccupied with truthfulness.

'Yes. That is so.' Mr Tiverton swivelled his big fleshy head at Fairfax. 'Well, sir? You are angling to find who could have administered the poison, and plainly enough we are all under suspicion. What more? You wish to know whether there would be poison in the house? There is a well-stocked medicine cabinet downstairs, and no doubt there is arsenic in it. And, of course, you know that any of us might have bought the grains from a druggist, in a twist of paper. What more? Did I hate Sir James Delabole? I suppose in a way I did; and I think I had reason to. Now if—'

'Grandfather, please.' Caroline was weeping: Fairfax saw that the lace handkerchief she was twisting in her large fair hands was torn. 'Please, no more. I apologize, Mr Fairfax . . . Far from my habit to have the vapours, I assure you . . . Pride myself on never playing the miss – but really, I can't bear . . .' She got up: even in distress she was regally tall and self-possessed and, as her firm rejection of Pinner's eager hand showed, quite able to stand on her own feet. 'You must excuse me. No doubt in your shrewd way you will suspect me of harbouring a guilty secret, Mr Fairfax, but the plain fact is I must be alone for a space. You see, I never had a father, and then at last I had one – and now he is taken away. It seems hard – like a punishment which I can't think I deserve . . .'

'Of course,' Fairfax said, bowing and going to open the door for her; but he paused, keeping it shut, and added: 'If I might just ask one question, Miss Delabole: did Mr Locke find his glove last evening?'

'What?' She was startled, and Pinner was all terrible alertness.

'Oh, it was after we left here. Locke said he had left a glove behind, and came back to fetch it.'

After a moment, Caroline shrugged. 'I saw nothing of him. You must be mistaken.'

'Or the young man was jesting, or some such,' Mrs Jessop put in. 'He seemed a light-minded sort. There was no glove here, sir, that I can vouch for: I would have known it.'

'I see.' He didn't, though: he didn't know what to make of it, except that someone was lying again.

'Sir?' Caroline's look, despite the veil of tears, was peremptory. 'May I pass?'

'Oh – I'm sorry.' Fairfax opened the door. Pinner showed strong signs of wanting to go after her, which of course he couldn't do. There was surely no worse position for a hopeful lover than intimate friend of the family.

'You would not, I trust, wish to trouble us much longer,' said Mr Tiverton, who was gazing mournfully after his granddaughter as if she were dwindling into an unreachable distance. 'Our peace has already been grievously disturbed, and I fear for the effect on Caroline's health. Yes, she looks strong,' he added, reading Fairfax's thought, 'but her mother was consumptive, and I have always feared a recurrence.'

'She'll do well, sir, never fear,' Mrs Jessop said. 'She feels she has lost a father – but what sort of father was he, in truth? No father at all. When she sees that, she'll see there was no loss.' Her face was dour and scornful as she jabbed at her sewing and added, 'No great loss to the world, neither.'

That was so close to Fairfax's own earlier thoughts that he had to take her up.

'Not the loss of a life created by God, Mrs Jessop?'

'Oh, I know nothing about that, sir. Do you?'

He smiled. 'I am no theologian. I just supposed, from

what you were saying of your late husband—'

'A rare, good man. Honest and hard-working and with true godliness in his nature, that was plain to all. He made me into a better woman, I know that.'

How so? Fairfax wondered. Methodism often saved people from drink: could that be the reason Mrs Jessop was so severe on liquorish habits – the zeal of the reformed?

'But as for his preaching, that was his own affair. I could never quite follow the business of being saved, and that making everything all right. Surely our sins don't go away so easy?' She looked at him questioningly, as if expecting some definite answer. 'But there, I don't know: I'm an ordinary woman, and never had any learning.'

Ordinary was not what he would call her: the stiff-backed housekeeper put him in mind of a poker that looked as if it had cooled but would burn you if you tried to grasp it. Again, he wondered whether Sir James had hit the mark when he made those crude hints about the relationship between Mrs Jessop and her employer.

Not a thing he could ask, or at any rate expect an answer to; and besides, it was a private matter with no bearing on the case. Except . . . if you added love to loyalty, that gave her a pretty good motive to be covering up for Mr Tiverton.

For if Sir James Delabole's murder was indeed a matter of his sins catching him up, then who was more likely to have stolen the divine prerogative than Gilbert Tiverton? He had good reason to feel that Sir James had robbed him of his daughter: now the old prodigal seemed about to rob him of his granddaughter too. Long-postponed revenge was a concept Fairfax found difficult to believe in – to commit murder, he believed, a person had to be subject to an immediate, pressing emotion. But Sir James *had* followed up that long-ago wrong with a new one, which gave Mr Tiverton motive enough. And yet in that case, why consent to the reconciliation in the first place? He could have turned down Sir James's first approaches – it must have been plain where they would lead.

Of course, that was to leave aside the wishes of Caroline herself, and it was plain that her grandfather could refuse her nothing. It was also becoming plain that Caroline Delabole was quite a strong character in her own right. And whether that meant she was spoilt, wilful and ambitious, or simply independent-minded, forthright and hungry for life, he still could not decide. Leaving the house in Orchard Street, he turned to look back at it. Dim and shady, its narrow windows filmed with dirt and muffled with heavy drapes . . . Wouldn't an intelligent woman want to escape?

There was one other person implicated in the day's events, and he rather dreaded interviewing him for the simple reason that he liked him: Ensign Locke.

It occurred to him that Locke would not even know that Sir James was dead. Supposing him innocent, of course – which he could not do, for Locke's being at the Delabole house gave him the opportunity to have poisoned the usquebaugh. And there was, besides, the strange affair of the note to Selina, and the fact that at some time after it she had undoubtedly gone out. Where? A clandestine meeting? An intrigue? That did not necessarily mean a murderous intrigue, of course. But there was no doubt that Locke was up to something – or, given that business of the glove that wasn't missing, up to several somethings. And friendship would have to be put aside if Fairfax was to get it out of him.

But where *was* Locke? Not at their lodgings in Avon Street: Fairfax looked into his rooms, and found them undisturbed

– or rather, the unholy mess of dirty linen, empty bottles, unwashed dishes and torn playing-cards was the same as ever.

Fairfax went to see the painter, Macleod, and found him lying on his bed with legs up against the wall.

'Forgive the strange position, Mr Fairfax. I have worked myself into a state of exhaustion, and only putting the legs above the head relieves me. I fancy it redistributes the animal spirits. Be so good as to look at Niobe there, and tell me – first glance, no reflection – *is* her arm out of proportion?'

Macleod's Niobe was so well-developed that, if the bottom had dropped out of the mythological-heroine market, she might easily have become a coal-heaver. Fairfax contented himself with saying: 'I think there is a quite appropriate grandeur in the modelling of her limbs . . . Mr Macleod, have you seen Francis Locke since this morning?'

'Aye, damn him, and I wish I hadn't. Oh, 'twas just the usual – wanting to borrow money from me. Take it, take my last damn shillings, says I, for I was just in the fiery heat of moulding Niobe's brow – now that, you'll allow, is a damn fine passage, is it not, sir? – and so I gave in, as I might not have if I'd been fully in possession of myself, for he's had a mint of me already, damn his eyes.'

'Did he say what he wanted the money for?'

'Gambling – drink – whores – powder to titivate him-damn-self – take your pick, sir, for I'll wager 'twas one or all of 'em.'

'How did he seem?'

Macleod pinched the bridge of his nose, thinking. 'Excitable. Aye, that's what I'd call it: in a taking. Which suggests that it was whores after all. Ah, I'm hard on him. There's no harm in him: just wholly a young fool and half a rogue.'

'You've no notion where he is now?'

'Not I. What, has he picked your pockets too, Mr Fairfax?'

'No. Nothing like that. Thank you, Mr Macleod.'

He was tired and hungry, and stepped out to buy some broiled chops from a cook-shop nearby, wrapping them in a handkerchief and spiriting them back up to his rooms as swiftly as he could: he was used to the prohibitions of landladies on cooked food in rented rooms. ('It burrows into the curtains' was how one had memorably put it.) He ate and then, after a grudgingly met request for a basin of hot water, washed, listening out for Locke's return all the while.

There was still no sign of him when it was time to light the candles. Stepping out again, Fairfax found a link-boy and sent him with a message to the Delabole house, asking if Ensign Locke had called there. The boy came back with a negative answer: Lady Delabole's compliments, but no. Well, he supposed she could be lying, but there was surely no reason to; and it was still a mystery that Locke had not come home. He had spoken of going to the Assembly tonight, Fairfax recalled. Of course, that was before he had fallen from Sir James's favour. And what *had* that been about?

Only Locke could tell him. But as the evening wore on, Fairfax was forced to conclude that Ensign Francis Locke had disappeared.

And if that was a coincidence, it was a very unhappy one indeed.

Seven

Fairfax had a strong suspicion that, late as the hour was, he would not be greatly welcome at Mr Goode's house in Queen Square. A sharp cry of 'What?', audible from the ante-room in which the footman had left him, confirmed it. Well, damn it, reflected Fairfax – reflecting also in a gilded pier-glass that showed him to be as weary and shabby as he felt – damn it all, *he* wanted me to do the job.

An irritable click of heels announced the entrance of Mr Goode.

'Mr Fairfax, you have something material to report to me, I hope? You require a warrant for an arrest, perhaps.'

'Er – no, sir. Nothing so definite.' Fairfax took a moment to recover from the shock of the magistrate's appearance. Mr Goode was all fashion: silk breeches, jewelled shoe-buckles, embroidered waistcoat and gold-frogged coat, tightly curled wig, even patches on his face.

'I see.' Mr Goode looked his displeasure. 'In that case you will forgive me a little impatience, sir. I am about to go out to the Assembly, with company who are doing me the honour of staying here tonight. There is, among others, a relative of mine from Gloucester who is connected by marriage to the Duke of Kingston.' Mr Goode stalked back to the door, listened to the voices beyond for a moment with an anguished expression, then closed it to.

That was one relative he didn't mind acknowledging, then . . . 'In that case, I'll be brief. I have no definite discoveries because there are a number of people who could have committed the crime. They can be reduced, however, to the households of Mr Tiverton and of Sir James himself – with one exception. Ensign Locke, who had been quite an intimate of Sir James's circle until there was an apparent breach this morning. I'm troubled about this, because Locke appears to have vanished.'

'Ah!'

'He has not returned to his lodgings which are next to my own, and, as far as I know, he had no connections here in Bath – no one who might help us locate him. It is very strange . . .'

'Strange and, one must say, suspicious,' Mr Goode said, and then darted to the door again as there was the sound of loud laughter from beyond. Grimacing, he put his ear to the crack, then shook his head. 'I swear that must have been a *bon mot* of the Duke's, and now I have missed it . . . Well, my dear sir, I would earnestly suggest that finding this young soldier must be our highest priority. I fear we do not have enough to put out a warrant on him – unless you have some further grounds for suspicion against him?'

'I suspect him of some involvement with one of the colonel's daughters – or even both—'

'Dear me!'

'And his behaviour today was certainly odd . . . But as for firm grounds for an arrest, no.'

'A pity. In that case, our resources are few. Something might be done with posted notices, if the magistrates meeting in session should agree – but I fear that is premature. This young man is not a missing child, after all, and may yet reappear.' Mr Goode hesitated, fingering his lace stock. 'But come. Tell me, Mr Fairfax, your feeling – your intuition. You must have a particular suspicion, I think.'

'It looks bad for Locke, as it stands,' Fairfax mused, 'and yet for a man to commit murder, and then make himself so conspicuously absent – that is surely diverting attention *on* to himself. My prime difficulty, Mr Goode, is that the late Sir James was very much disliked by a number of people, and they could all be conceived of as wishing him out of the way. A melancholy reflection on a man's life, is it not? Even . . . well, now that I think of it, that man cannot be under suspicion, as he could not have put the poison in the flask – but I was just thinking of a man from America I happened to meet, and who Sir James nearly came to blows with simply over an encounter in the street. Sir James had, I fear, a gift for antagonism.'

Mr Goode nodded, distracted by another gale of laughter. 'Dear me . . . Well, if that is all you have to report—'

'And there is the matter of the missing will – if it *was* a will. Sir James was certainly preoccupied with some species of document, which has now vanished. But short of searching the houses of everyone concerned . . .'

'It would require stronger evidence before one could authorize anything of that kind, Mr Fairfax. This is not France. The domestic privacy of the Englishman is still sacrosanct, thank heaven. Of course, if . . .' A foxy look came over Mr Goode's face. 'I'm sure I can leave this to your discretion – but if one creates a healthy fear in those suspected that they may be searched, then there may be interesting results. Guilt is like an itch, sir, it demands to be scratched. Witness the murderers in Shakespeare – Lady Macbeth, King Claudius. Guilty consciences: just prick them in the right place, and . . .' He darted to the door at another eruption of laughter. 'I must rejoin my company. Press on, my dear sir: don't fear making a nuisance of yourself, invoke my name all you like. Squeeze them, sir, squeeze them and something is sure to – leak out.' Mr Goode seemed to regret this expression as soon as it was out, but the *bon mots* of the Duke were calling him, and with a shrug and a bow he was gone.

Fairfax walked back to his lodgings. There were a lot of sedan-chairs about and even a few carriages negotiating the awkward streets: society was heading for the assembly-rooms. He was glad, he told himself, that he wasn't. Hours of stifling boredom, stiff ceremony, stiff minuets. Smoking candles and greasy pomade. Yet he felt a little wistful somewhere inside.

He had a thought, though – to do with that American. He pursued it over a bottle of sack that he had been hiding from himself in the bottom of his trunk. (It made his dingy rooms look better – that was excuse enough.) The man said he was from the American colonies. That might mean he was a free-born American – or something else.

Convicted felons were transported to America for terms of seven, fourteen or twenty-one years. What if that burly man were one of them? It might account for that certain reserve in his manner . . . and it might account for something else. Fairfax was sure that Sir James, like most propertied gentlemen, must have served as a Justice of the Peace at some time, probably at his Hampshire estate. Transported felons were forbidden, on penalty of death, to return to England before their sentence was served. Any who did had to run the risk of being recognized and turned over to the law. Well, what if the burly man was a transported felon who had been committed by Sir James on the bench, and had illegally returned? And what if Sir James – not at first, no, but gradually – had recognized him? After their quarrel in the street, perhaps. A dawning realization in Sir James's mind; and in the man from America's too, filling him with desperate fear . . .

It was so very neat and ingenious. Pity it made no sense at all.

First, transportation was surely, like hanging, a punishment only dealt out by professional judges at the assize courts – not by local magistrates meeting at petty or quarter sessions. So that wouldn't wash. And then, most importantly, the American had not been in either the Delabole house or Mr Tiverton's; and Fairfax was certain that those were the only places in which the cane could have been tampered with. The American was a curiosity, a minor mystery perhaps, but he was not a murder suspect.

Neither, he felt, were the servants at either house. There had to be a compelling reason for someone to poison Sir James, and that simply didn't exist. Unless the kitchens harboured a maniac maid who had suddenly discovered the joy of random slaying, he could discount them, and he was inclined, too, to discount Nolan, Sir James's manservant, who had plainly adored his master. No, he had the people he suspected in his mind's eye, which the wine had sharpened (this was the stage he loved – knowing that soon enough there would be fog and heaviness and regret).

Lady Delabole. Quarrelling with her overbearing husband, seeing him turn away from his family to the sweet fruits of a former love, fearing even that he would cut them out altogether. A strong shadow of suspicion there. And yet she had put up with Sir James's ways for nearly twenty years. She must have great powers of accomodation. Could they have been so unequal to this crisis – leaving her no resort but murder?

Selina. A giddy creature: surely too frail-minded . . . And yet a follower of that growing fashion, sensibility, which decreed that whatever you sincerely *felt* must be right. She seemed devoted to her mother – was apparently outraged at Sir James's treatment of her today. Surely jealous too of Caroline – and of what Caroline might inherit? And then there was that note from Locke . . . No, she could not be ruled out.

Neither could Mr Edmund Pinner. There were several things about that respectable young man of business that did not add up. The curious affair of being taken for a spy at Calais was the most peculiar – and, Fairfax had to admit, the most difficult to fit into this case. Could he have made up such a story, and for what purpose? But then, he had seemed rather eager not to have it brought up: it was his overseer who had mentioned it to Mr Tiverton. No, Fairfax could do nothing with it. More suspicious, he thought, was Pinner's behaviour today. Calling on Sir James to 'declare his interest' in Caroline? It was possible, he supposed, but he couldn't imagine the fire-eating Sir James politely listening to such an avowal. The colonel had been no more than mildly insulting to Pinner at the dinner the day before, but he had made it plain that he thought the young man very small beer, and as for a suitor for Caroline . . . And then there was Pinner's odd promptness in hurrying over to the Delabole house as soon as Sir James's death was known. The act of a guilty man, impelled to make sure that it was true, that his scheme had worked? Possible again. If Pinner saw Sir James as a threat, the one who would take Caroline away from him far more effectively than any love-rival, then he certainly had a motive.

And then there was Caroline Delabole herself. He pictured her, with her luminous beauty, her graceful and guarded manner, her self-possession that skirted the edge of self-satisfaction – or did it cross it? – and realized how little he knew. For instance, he assumed that Pinner's devotion was more of an annoyance than a gratification to her. But what if it wasn't? Surely part of the reason why Sir James had seen her as ready for an entrance into society was her careful absence of spontaneity: the girl was a perfect actress. So she might well be concealing her real relation with Edmund Pinner – even conspiring with him . . .? Yet there was surely no reason for her to want her father dead – except his money. And that, to put it crudely, was not yet in the bag. He hadn't changed his will – unless, of course, she knew better. Again that question: if he had, then where was it now? That polished manner might be concealing something else too – something to do with Francis Locke. The young ensign had been mighty attentive to her and she had seemed to like it; and when she said that Locke hadn't come back to the house last night, Fairfax simply didn't believe her. Suppose there was a romance between them, and Sir James had got wind of it, and sent Locke packing because of it? Might she not have resorted to murder to keep her love? Still, her grief today had seemed genuine; and even if the tears were mainly for the loss of a fortune, he supposed that was only human. He couldn't rule her out; but he reminded himself that if a woman was beautiful and clever, people were often rather too ready to believe she must be nasty underneath.

Mr Tiverton. A promising suspect. Almost too promising – for the old man made absolutely no bones about his dislike of Sir James, his mistrust of his intentions, his jealous possessiveness towards his granddaughter . . . And as with Lady Delabole, one would have to believe that there was no other resource left for Mr Tiverton but murder. But of course, that was leaving pure, explosive hate out of the question; and certainly something incendiary must have been said between Mr Tiverton and his son-in-law at their last meeting, something that made Sir James storm out without even a kind word for Caroline herself. Somehow Fairfax would have to penetrate the old man's oysterlike shell and find out his real feelings.

And that might include his real feelings for Mrs Jessop. If he was an oyster, then she, Fairfax thought, was an odd fish. More importantly, he suspected that she could be fearsome – perhaps even fearsome enough to kill? There was certainly something unruly beneath that matronly bosom: anyone who laced themselves that tightly, Fairfax believed, was trying to keep something in. So, if she did share Mr Tiverton's bed, had she feared that Sir James with his shrewd eye and careless tongue was about to expose it? That seemed tenuous – but Fairfax had a more convincing notion. Whatever the sleeping arrangements, Mrs Jessop had a very comfortable place there, especially for a woman of thoroughly humble origins. And she kept it because a female companion was needed for the motherless Caroline. But now came Sir James, threatening to take the girl away, embed her in his own family. Where would that leave Mrs Jessop? Killing to keep your comfortable place must entail a monstrous selfishness – but that, alas, was no rarity in humankind.

And then, of course, there was Locke. Fairfax turned his mind to the young ensign with reluctance, simply because the suspicion on him was so glaring; and he even got up and went to check Locke's rooms again, though he had heard no one come in, just in case . . . But no: no sign of him.

And yet wherever Locke had gone, he had not taken his possessions with him. And that reinforced Fairfax's earlier objection. If you were going to murder someone, why abscond immediately afterwards, and make yourself such an obvious object of suspicion? Failure of nerve, perhaps? Or perhaps he didn't care if it was known: he had achieved his object with Sir James's death and simply meant to go on the run . . . Oh, but that made no sense. Where was the advantage? Another bleak reflection, no doubt, but people did not kill unless they hoped for some advantage. Even killing in revenge meant seeking peace of mind, a restitution of order in your world. So this disappearance of Locke's was decidedly rum: it was the greatest argument both for his guilt and for his innocence. Even leaving that aside, Locke's position was ambiguous. He seemed to be one of the few people who got along famously with Sir James; and yet there had been such a spectacular fall from grace that he had been banned from the colonel's house. Fairfax would have to find out what that was about. Locke had candidly attached himself to Sir James because he was a man of influence; and if Sir James could do him good, then he could probably also ruin him, or threaten to. If that had been the drift of their quarrel, then it looked bad again for Francis Locke.

Soon after that, Fairfax's thoughts grew less lucid. He had a memory of attempting to play his flute, laughing at his own efforts, and crawling heavily into bed full of self-loathing.

The next thing he knew, he was trying to see through eyes that felt like twin wounds being mercilessly opened, and someone was knocking repeatedly at his door.

'Come in,' he moaned, mainly because he wanted the noise to stop. Some part of his fuddled brain also suggested that it might be Locke come back. But the person who entered, just as he was swinging his nerveless legs out of the bed, was Selina Delabole.

'Good God!'

'Oh – it's you . . .' She started to retreat, but her hooped skirts impeded her.

'Pardon me,' he said, grabbing his coat and wrapping that around him, to rather grotesque effect, 'but I had no idea—'

'Really, sir –' Selina, still wedged in the doorway, gave a hitch of her chin – 'it doesn't signify. I have seen a man in a nightshirt before.'

Where? thought Fairfax, looking round for his breeches.

'My apologies, at any rate,' Selina said, at last gathering up her hoop and squeezing it through the door. 'I have the wrong place. I thought . . . no matter.'

She was gone.

'Wait! Miss Selina!'

Fairfax hopped and lunged into his clothes and went after her. He caught her up on the steps outside. He was aware of his landlady's face rising like a disapproving moon at the area window.

'Miss Selina – wait! If you weren't looking for me, then – then I think you must have been looking for Francis Locke. Yes? His rooms are opposite mine. He told you the address, perhaps.'

Selina's lips made a resentful pouch. But she did not deny it.

'He's not here. At least, unless he came back in the night. I've been looking for him myself. Come, we'll make sure. And then perhaps we might have a talk.'

'It would hardly be proper for me to be in your rooms, sir.'

'Oh, well, you've seen me in my nightshirt, so it can make little difference.'

She did not smile. She would never like him, he decided. His age. Not old enough to be a mere pitiable half-dead elder, but too old to understand her feverish dreadfully-important youthful world. If only she knew.

Locke's rooms were unchanged. Fairfax saw her give the manly mess such a yearning look that he hardly needed to ask his first question.

Not that she would answer it. Reluctantly taking the edge of a chair in his own rooms, she turned crimson when he said: 'Are you in love with Francis Locke?' and rose to an affronted vertical.

'I cannot endure this. Good day to you, sir.'

'Miss Selina – please. It is surely quite plain, when you come here alone to call on him. And the note he sent you—'

'You know nothing of the matter, sir.'

'I do.'

That brought her up sharp.

'He . . . Francis told me of it,' he said, all earnestness. It was a risk, this, and a trifle unfair. But it was the only way he could see to draw her out: he would have to speak her language. He would have to get down there and wallow in the sickly waters of sensibility.

'He told you . . .?' The look she gave him was full of disdain, but at least she turned back. 'I don't believe it. He would never—'

'He would never carelessly betray so sacred a confidence,'

131

Fairfax said, nodding. 'That is so. But I think you must know, Miss Selina, the pressures of an overburdened heart which, when charged with the most exalted feelings, must be relieved, or even joy may be tuned to a pitch of torment . . .' This was hard to keep up when you were feeling a little queasy to start with. 'In short, he confided in excess of emotion, as a brimming cup spills over.' Or a slop-bucket, he thought. 'I received the precious trust with humble gratitude, and would never have alluded to it had I not perceived your distress at not finding him here.'

Selina sat down slowly. 'I – I thought he might have returned.'

'Do you know where he has gone?'

A touch too eager, that: her eyes narrowed at him.

'I am concerned for him,' he said, swallowing. 'When I saw him last – yesterday, when he charged me with bringing you that note – he seemed quite distracted.'

'No wonder, when he had been so shamefully abused!' Selina burst out.

Ah. Fairfax was careful not to press: he just arranged his features in what he hoped was an expression of tender sensibility. Something like a constipated lap-dog, he guessed.

'You will know, sir,' she went on, palpitating, 'if Francis has revealed to you that consecrated secret, that ours is an attachment of the most pure, exalted and uncommon kind – that it is a sincere union of hearts – a flame springing unbidden from the twin depths of being. It is no ordinary love.'

It never is, thought Fairfax unkindly.

'From the moment he joined us at Marlborough – when I felt as if struck by a thunderbolt – I have lived in the most rarefied state. Agonizing at first – but the anguish was made delicious when Francis confessed to me that he was – in short, that he felt as I did. I must emphasize, sir, that this has been no lurking clandestine matter. If it has been secret, that is because it is the holiest of affections, quite separate from the petty concerns of the workaday world.'

'Indeed, indeed. And yet – believe me, I tremble to trespass upon these painful associations – and yet your late father banished Francis from the house yesterday, did he not?'

Selina put her hands to her cheeks. 'It was horrible – monstrous. Not only the forcible separation from he whom I may with tremulous but leaping heart call *mine*. That was bad enough; but the vile, the vulgar aspersions my father cast upon us . . . I know I should not speak ill of the dead, but what of *his* ill words? Could there be anything more blasphemously cruel?'

Fairfax was seeing it clearly now. 'Your father discovered your – your hallowed secret.'

She nodded – looking genuinely miserable enough, in all conscience. 'Francis came calling yesterday morning. Our maid has grown discreet enough of late to show him, when my father is not about, into the back parlour where we can be confidential. So it was yesterday; but I fear I did not go to Francis in the delight of an open heart. I was disposed to be vexed with him, because – well, because I was jealous. In the sweet folly of love, I was absurd enough to think that he had been too attentive to that pert creature Caroline, at Mr Tiverton's dinner the day before. I fancied – well, all sorts of nonsense; and being utterly unable to constrain my emotions for very long, I taxed him with it. I had slept not a wink, I believe, and had drenched my pillow – but you know, it was worth those agonies to see the melting eagerness with which he met my reproaches. Oh, he was ready to do some violence to himself, I believe, in the very wretchedness of having given me a moment's uneasiness. He was a picture of torment; and though his tears would have pleaded his innocence with a far sterner judge than I, he was prepared to go away and foreswear my company as a just punishment for having even unwittingly put me to that pain. Between the tears, there was a kind of hysterical laughter at the very notion that he could admire that conceited miss –' here Selina looked momentarily very unpleasant – 'and, in short, he was so plainly the true purehearted Francis that my soul knew him to be, that I could not have remained vexed with him for a thousand pound. And so – well, I have no shame in this, I glory in it – we fell into one another's arms. If you have ever known what it is to love, Mr Fairfax –' Selina said this indulgently, but with a look as if she thought it hugely improbable – 'then you will know that the excess of tender feeling on making up a quarrel, is such as to overcome even the scruples of those who would preserve the flame free of the baser elements of common passion. In short—'

'Your father came into the back parlour and found you in each other's arms,' Fairfax said, adding hastily, 'Oh, dear God! Unlucky fate!'

'So it was.' Selina closed her eyes, doing some dramatic breathing. 'I thank heaven that both of us, I believe, maintained our dignity, even while my father so grossly abandoned his, along with all delicacy and decency. I will not repeat the expressions he used to characterize what he saw as our illicit relation. I will only say that he accused both of us of deliberately deceiving him. Me he called a little fool, for falling for the blandishments of a young rogue; and Francis he called a villain, for abusing his trust and hospitality. When Francis tried, respectfully, to put the true state of the case, to defend my honour and that of our attachment, my father grew even more abominable.' There was real disgust on her face now, Fairfax noted. 'He said that idiot as I was, I was his daughter still, and he wouldn't see me disgrace myself with some fortune-hunting popinjay. To hear Francis's intentions so hideously traduced was dreadful . . . Well, with many more crude and violent expressions, he ordered Francis out of the house, and warned him that if he still thought to steal me away, then I would get not a penny. And he laughed most horribly and said that was sure to cool Francis's ardour, if nothing else would.'

Fairfax had a pang of real sympathy. Cruel of the colonel, without doubt; and, given his past, thoroughly hypocritical.

And yet, when he called Locke a fortune-hunter, was he right? Fairfax hoped not.

'An unhappy story,' he said. 'So, that was why Locke was forbidden from the house. And, I take it, why I found such a melancholy atmosphere when I called yesterday. But what of your mother? She seemed to have been at odds with your father also.'

'That is because she is the best of mothers,' Selina said with decision.

'She took your part?'

'She always does, as far as she is able. At least – well, that is changed now.'

'Your father was an overbearing man, I think. Even unfeeling?'

'He was the most unfeeling man that ever lived. I do not say that lightly, Mr Fairfax. I used to suppose that it was a fault in me, finding him so. I supposed, indeed, that all men must be in the same mould. But with my Francis, I found it was not true. I found there could be delicacy of sentiment along with uprightness and candour. The more I see, the more I think there was something *missing* about my father. Why, even *you*, Mr Fairfax, have shown yourself capable of tender feeling. Even that oddity Mr Pinner, when he came to offer condolences to us yesterday, showed that he had a feeling heart: he was so much affected by our shocking state that he was obliged to go out of the room and was, I think, quite overcome for a time.'

'Indeed . . .' Now that, Fairfax thought, was curious – and highly suspicious. 'So, that would seem to explain Francis's agitation when I saw him – and the note he gave to me, of course.'

Her look of suspicion was back.

'Well, as I observed yesterday, you had overshoes on and plainly had gone out at some time after your father left the house. Francis had asked you to meet him, I think?' He made an effort. 'I say this only because the ardour of love acting upon the wounded heart would surely dictate—'

'Yes. Yes, I see no shame – he did ask me to meet him, outside the Abbey. And so I went. I will not say what was said between us, Mr Fairfax – only that there were tears of joy as well as grief, and mutual avowal. Suffice it to say that the stars would dim before he would give me up, or I him.'

'I see. But – what did you intend to do? I think your father was not a man who easily changed his mind.'

'It was enough,' Selina said grandly, 'that we knew each other's constancy. Before that, mountains might crumble.'

'Of course. But I must urgently ask you – where has Francis gone? Do you know?'

Selina sprang up. 'Now you are trying to trap me.'

'Indeed I'm not . . . but if you will call it that, then I can only conclude you must have something to hide. Come, if you love Francis as you say –' Damn: that was a thumping mistake. She glared as if he had spat on her skirts – 'as indeed it is plain that you do – then you would not wish to see him under a cloud of suspicion. And so he is, unless he can be traced—'

'I don't know where he is.'

She said it so disconsolately that he was inclined to believe her.

'Did he not say—?'

'I have the greatest trust and faith in him. He said he would communicate with me as soon as he was able. That's all I know – no, it isn't, because I *know* he has not run away, sir, as you are insinuating.'

'And yet you came here to try and find him.'

'That was because I . . . I could not bear not seeing him.'

'Miss Selina, do you have any notion where Francis Locke might have gone?'

She stamped her foot. A gesture, he gathered, that some men actually found charming. 'I've told you I do not. Would you call me a liar, sir?'

'No. But I fear you have, as it were, held back the truth. Yesterday you told me nothing of this – of your father's prohibition, the reasons for the quarrel—'

'Of course not. Because you would at once think it a reason for me to have poisoned my father. Wouldn't you? Well, I have been frank because I supposed you sincere in your feelings. But I see you are only sniffing about for something discreditable. You have imposed on me, sir.' She stalked to the door.

'Miss Selina, don't you care who killed your father?'

She gave him an unfathomable look. 'Probably about as much as you do,' she said, going out.

Well, well. She didn't tell him, because he would think it a reason for her to have poisoned her father . . . But then, it *was* a pretty powerful reason. Her father stood between her and her love. A true love, he supposed: just because someone talked about their feelings all the time didn't necessarily mean they didn't have any.

As for Locke . . . well, Fairfax didn't know what to think. It was an index of how enigmatic the young ensign was, for all his *bonhomie*, that he might easily have been a sincere lover or a conniving fortune-hunter: Fairfax wouldn't have been surprised by either. And the trouble was, in either case he would have a motive to murder Sir James. The lover, in resentful passion, disposing of the cruel father who would destroy his love: the fortune-hunter, working his way into an impressionable girl's heart and then coldly disposing of the man who seemed about to change his will and make the girl a less lucrative prey.

And yet there was still the suspicion that Selina was not the only string to Locke's bow. A suspicion that Selina herself had obviously felt. Was Locke playing a double game with Caroline? Was he waiting, perhaps, to see which daughter Sir James would favour with his golden approval? If so, then murder would make no sense . . . unless Locke knew something about Sir James's decision that he didn't. Again, it came down to that damn will.

'What you need,' Fairfax told himself in the mottled looking-glass, 'is a shave, some coffee and a hot roll.' What he really needed, he thought as he studied his haggard eyes and doughy complexion, was not to have drunk so much the night before, but no matter.

At least he had some new information. And Edmund Pinner, with his strange compulsion to go out of the room, was the man who could give him more.

Eight

'Mr Pinner left for Bristol early this morning, sir.'

It was Mrs Jessop who answered the door to him at the Tiverton house, and gave him the unwelcome news.

'I see. I wonder—'

'He has business to attend to, you see.'

'Yes. Tell me, where can I find his house in—'

'That I don't know, sir.' She was very abrupt this morning and had planted her sturdy figure in his way. Glancing down at her hands, Fairfax saw they were covered in grease. 'Pardon me, but I'm busy in the kitchen. We are dipping rushes, and I don't want to let the fat go cool.'

'The maids' job, surely.'

'I like to oversee everything myself. Pardon me again, sir, but I think we've had enough upset in this house, and so—'

'Is that Mr Fairfax there?'

It was Mr Tiverton's voice, coming from a room beside the staircase. The old man appeared in the doorway.

'I was hoping to find Mr Pinner, but it appears he has gone. Pray, tell me where I can find him there, and—'

'His house is hard by the quay. Oh, but anyone in Bristol would direct you. Like his late father, he is a much respected man there. Step in, sir, step in, if you would be so good.'

The room was Mr Tiverton's office. There was a desk, a couple of straight-backed studded chairs that must have been old in Queen Anne's day, some pewter hanging above the cold fireplace: the room was dark-panelled and gloomy. It struck Fairfax, though, that the whole house seemed steeped in dusty shade, though it was a bright, fresh autumn day outside. Did Mr Tiverton carry his long sorrow and bitterness about with him, infecting the very walls?

Or was he, in fact, something of a miser? Sir James seemed to have held that view and he was not necessarily wrong. Certainly dipping rushes to make rushlights was rather penny-pinching in a household that could plainly afford good wax candles. Fairfax hated rushlights. They were economical, all right. You couldn't see anything by them and they smelled so bad there was nothing to do but put them out and go to bed.

'I interrupt your accounting, I think,' Fairfax said, with a glance at the great calf-bound ledgers on the desk.

'No, no, my accounting days are done. Sit, sit, sir. No, these are my old account-books, from when I traded in the City. I have preserved them, and I like to read them over now and then.' Mr Tiverton turned a crackling page.

Fairfax tried, but he couldn't imagine anything more tedious than reading old account-books. It must have shown on his face: Mr Tiverton gave a rare chuckle.

'They bring back memories. I have heard women say, you know, that they can remember moments from the past by recalling what clothes they were wearing at the time. With me, recollection comes from the state of my business affairs. The fall of Madras, now: that I recall because I had a half share in a brig called *Madeleine*, and we were sure that she was lost too, foundered off Finisterre as was thought, but she came into port at last . . .' Mr Tiverton took snuff messily, gave an old man's rich sneeze.

'And personal recollections too?' Fairfax said.

'Oh, they hardly need prompting.' Mr Tiverton gave a spectral sort of smile. 'But I am not in thrall to the past, Mr Fairfax. I am not a man of imagination, for one thing. You, I think, are. And you perhaps fancy me brooding here, year after year, over the wrong Delabole did me, until I was a monstrous heap of resentment inside. Is that something like? I repeat, I am without imagination: I read no books and see no plays; that is simply how I suppose it would be seen, from an imaginative point of view.'

'Well, you have told me quite openly of how you hated Sir James – or rather, hated what he did.'

'A theologian's distinction. The sin not the sinner.' Mr Tiverton gave the ghostly smile again. 'Well, perhaps.'

'And yet it is not a life conditioned by hate that I see here. Love, rather, I would say. The love you have lavished on Caroline—'

'Ah, yes! So I have, so I have. I wonder if I have been right to do so.'

'I don't understand.'

'Oh . . . just that it may have given her the impression that the world is other than it really is. She has been very protected. But one cannot keep the wolves away for ever.'

'Surely she is intelligent and strong-minded – and well able to spot an approaching wolf at a fair distance.'

'That may be.' Now Mr Tiverton did not smile. 'But the darkness in men's hearts – what can she know of that? *I* know of it – none better. And I am a quiet old body without imagination . . . But yes, Caroline is as you say, sir. And that is also a precise description of how Lydia was – her mother –

twenty-odd years ago, just before she met James Delabole.'
Mr Tiverton wrapped his old snuff-brown coat about himself.
'Angry – yes, I was angry at the time. And that is why some
were ready to say I behaved like an unreasonable tyrant.
Certainly that's what *he* poured into her ear . . . But Lydia
was *not* a fool. I knew that. I was never one of those men who
don't know their own children, sir. Lydia's mother died in
childbed, and so it had always been the two of us – and *close*,
close simply in an open and straightforward and truthful
way. I knew her. She was sensible. And when this – this man
appeared, this rakish captain, I did not even conceive that
she could be taken in. When at last she confessed her
attachment, I was as dumbfounded as if – well, as if some
hard-headed merchant had come up to me on 'Change and
said he had put all his money into a scheme to grow bank-
notes on rose-bushes.'

The old man was breathing hard. Fairfax suggested
tentatively: 'And yet Sir James – at least, the younger man –
was surely not without attractions?'

Mr Tiverton made an impatient gesture. 'The sort of
attractions that turn the heads of silly chits. A regimental
coat, a deal of swagger. There are two types of people in the
world, Mr Fairfax – those who are fools, and those who
aren't. I could not believe that Lydia had fallen on the wrong
side. Disbelief – yes, that was what I felt when she ignored all
my reasoned advice, deceived me, and defied me at last. Yes,
I forbade the attachment. Does that make me a tyrant, when
I was only looking out for her interests? And yes, I was angry.
I suppose I was angry too that Delabole took *me* for one of
the fools. He reckoned that once he had stolen away my
daughter and inveigled her into marrying him, I would have
to accept the situation. I would relent. I would give in, and so

he would have won. He was wrong about me, sir, quite wrong, as he would have known if he had looked beyond his own conceit for a moment.'

'They went abroad, I understand.'

Mr Tiverton seemed to be gazing into a deep tunnel of abstraction. 'Hm? Oh, yes. He had no money and I would give them none, and so he dragged her across to France, where he supposed he could live cheaply. So there she was, cut off from all her friends and connections – with nothing but a husband who, it must have been plainer every day, had married her merely in the hope of a tidy little fortune.'

'She had made her bed, and . . .'

'You must not presume, sir, to guess what I was feeling at that time. If I was angry, I was also – bereft. That is the only word for it . . . But, yes, if you will: she had made her bed, and now she must lie on it. And then when she wrote me that they had quarrelled and parted, and that she was with child, I – I felt no satisfaction, sir. You must be clear on that. I did not think: There, I told you so! Nothing like it. I was detached. Because nothing had changed, not really. She had made her choice, and now she was pursuing the consequences of that choice; that was nothing to do with me. There was no crossing back from folly to wisdom. The world doesn't wag that way.' Mr Tiverton tapped his snuffbox. 'You think me hard.'

'I . . . think it an unhappy story.'

'That means nothing,' the old man said with a scowl. 'No matter. I know very well that I was called a hard, flint-hearted old beast, and more. Well, I don't mind it: my shoulders are broad. Far more galling was how little blame attached to Delabole. Oh, there was a scandal, and folk clucked their tongues over him for a while. But that didn't last and eventually there was nothing to prevent him taking his place in society again. A "youthful indiscretion" – how I detest those words! And in the meantime, my Lydia was dead.'

Mr Tiverton made no sound other than a little grunt, but all at once tears were streaming down his face. Taken aback, Fairfax said: 'These are painful memories, sir, and—'

'Of course they are. But it was my choice to speak of them, Mr Fairfax.' The old man mopped his face with his handkerchief. 'There, all over. You will have heard the gossips' version of the rest, sir. I dare say it is substantially correct. Lydia gave birth alone, in France, attended only by some starveling maid and some brutish Parisian midwife. No devoted husband at her side: no family to cheer her . . . And when she was well enough, she made her own way back to England with her child.'

'Seeking you.'

'Yes . . . there was no one else,' Mr Tiverton said, shading his eyes with his hand. 'Such money as that rogue had left her was very soon exhausted, and she was forced to take up a very mean lodging in a poor quarter near Gray's Inn Lane, and . . . Well, there I came to her at last and fetched her home.' He fixed Fairfax with a stare that was almost accusing. 'Yes, at last. For a time I remained obdurate: I confess it. But I gathered her into my arms at last, sir; and you should know that even then, living in friendless poverty as she was, she was anxious lest she miss a letter from *him*. She had written him still, and must have kept a shred of hope for a reconciliation. Well, well. He had no intention of that, of course. And as for me, I could only consider him as – as one dead. Gone, finished, not to be spoken of. And we did not speak of him, Lydia and I, in the short time that was left to her in this world. For she was dead within the year. Distress and privation had weakened her. And who is to blame for that?'

All at once the deathly smile was back, though Mr Tiverton's eyes still leaked tears. 'You choose, sir. You choose. But consider, meanwhile, why I am so protective of Caroline, who is all that remains of my daughter's short existence.'

'A man must be insensitive indeed who does not understand . . . I think, sir, you favour Mr Pinner as a suitor for your granddaughter.'

'It would . . . not be unwelcome to me, certainly. I have often spoken in his favour. I have known him, as I knew his father, for many years; and it is that *knowing* that counts for much.'

So, he was trying to dictate Caroline's inclinations as he had her mother's, Fairfax thought. Oh, it was a tragic story, right enough, but a tragedy of pig-headedness – among other things, as Mr Goode would say. Had Mr Tiverton never considered that telling a young woman that a certain man was no good for her was an infallible way of driving her into that man's arms?

And as for knowing Mr Pinner – did he, really? The one thing Fairfax was sure about, with regard to Edmund Pinner, was that he had something to hide.

He came out of these thoughts as a sweet scent stole over him. For a moment he had a superstitious notion that Mr Tiverton's tale had evoked the sad ghost of Lydia . . . Then he turned and found that Caroline had come noiselessly into the room, and was looking with gentle dismay at the tearstains on Mr Tiverton's face.

'Grandfather . . .?'

'All's well, my dear.' He got up, patting her arm and giving her a noisy trembling kiss. 'We have been telling over old stories, but it don't signify.'

'My mother.' Caroline sat down, giving Fairfax a straight

look. 'What news, Mr Fairfax? Is my father's murderer found?'

'Not yet. I am still—'

'Still burrowing about for deadly secrets. Well, here is one for you, or a peculiar mystery at least. I speak flippantly because I am in truth rather frightened by it.' Caroline did look hollow about the eyes, as if she had not slept. 'I think there has been someone watching me – or us.'

'My dear,' Mr Tiverton gasped, 'what is this?'

'Perhaps nothing. My chamber window, Mr Fairfax, overlooks the rear yard. Being unable to sleep last night, I got up and sat there with the curtain a little parted for air; and down below in the yard I saw a man.'

'Some thief prowling about,' Mr Tiverton said. 'Don't fear, my dear: we have stout locks, and I shall set the boy to watching tonight, in case—'

'If he was a thief, he was a very strange one. Because he made no attempt to conceal himself. He just – stood there, looking up at the house.'

'What sort of man?' Fairfax said.

'Big, stout, not young. I would know him again, because – well, this is the thing that I found unaccountably sinister – he seemed to lack his left hand. I fancy there may have been a hook there, but certainly there was no hand.'

The man from America, Fairfax thought, surely. But why on earth . . .? 'What time was this, Miss Delabole?'

'A little after midnight.'

'And it was light enough to see . . .?'

'It was, because there was a light still burning at the back of the house. I *think* –' she shrugged with a perplexed smile – 'that it must have been Mrs Jessop's pantry. And then, as I thought that, I heard a faint noise, and the light went out, and so did the man – out of the yard, I mean.'

Mr Tiverton said: 'You're sure you weren't having a nightmare, my dear?'

'It depends what you mean, Grandfather. This – what has happened lately *seems* like a nightmare. And I can only feel that this apparition was part of it. If the man was not a housebreaker then he must have had some other reason to be studying our house. And, as my father has just been horribly killed – I can't help feeling fearful. Nonsense, perhaps, but there it is.'

'But this man . . .' Fairfax nearly said *from America*, but he decided to keep what knowledge he had to himself, for now. 'This man can have had nothing to do with your father's death, Miss Delabole. That much we have established.'

'Not directly, perhaps. And indeed I cannot account for what I feel . . . Except to say again, someone wanted my father killed, and that does not dispose me to see such a thing as this as entirely innocent.'

Mr Tiverton went to the door and called for Mrs Jessop.

She must have been near at hand for she came at once, which was worth noting, Fairfax thought . . . or worth nothing? The woman was a companion-help: it was practically her duty to linger about being nosy. He bore in mind, though, that she had been far from eager to let him into the house just now. And he watched her carefully as Mr Tiverton asked her about the stranger in the yard.

'Yes, sir: I was awake at the time. I generally am, you know.'

'And were you aware of any disturbance?'

It wasn't that she avoided anyone's eyes, Fairfax thought. She just somehow distributed her gaze so that it fixed on no one.

'Not a disturbance, sir. I should hope not.'

'Then you saw nothing of this man?'

'Oh, yes, him? I saw him. Some vagrant, you can be sure. There's any amount of 'em. They tramp over from Wales in the season, you know, looking out for what they can get.'

'What did you do when you saw him?' Fairfax asked.

'Why, I opened my pantry window a little, and shooed him away. And off he went.'

'You did not think to say anything of this, Mrs Jessop?' Fairfax said.

'No, sir, not special. I believe we've had enough trouble in the house lately.' She allowed her inclusive gaze to dwell balefully on him for a moment, as if he were the cause of it.

'Have you seen this man before?'

'Not to my recollection. But 'tis as I say, there's any amount of 'em, and he could have been anybody.'

'But he lacked a hand, which was distinctive.'

'I dare say. I don't think anything of that, sir. That sort'll maim themselves, sometimes, for begging. I was brought up in a poor sort of place, and I've known it done, I'm afraid: I know what I'm talking about.'

'I see. Well, I wouldn't be too alarmed, Miss Delabole,' Fairfax said. 'Mr Tiverton says the house is quite secure. But if you should see anything more of this man—'

'I doubt that, sir,' Mrs Jessop said. 'I saw him off. They move on, as a rule.'

'Yes. Well, I should do likewise. Thank you, Mr Tiverton, for the information.'

Mrs Jessop saw him out: indeed, he felt her large presence practically propelling him out of the door.

He turned. 'You have been long widowed, Mrs Jessop?'

'Ten years, sir.'

'Your speech is not local, I think.'

'No, sir. I'm London-born. I came here with Mr Jessop. I was not sorry.'

'You knew the poorer quarters of the city, I take it?'

'Yes, sir. Places around St Giles, and Gray's Inn Lane – places I shan't forget. London isn't a happy or healthy place. Not unless you're rich, and not even then, I'd venture.'

'True enough . . . I think you don't consider me welcome here, Mrs Jessop.'

For a moment her implacable look softened: she even seemed troubled. 'There's naught personal in it, sir. Pray don't think that. 'Tis just that this has always been a happy home. The happiest I think I have ever seen. And it grieves me to see it spoiled. It's a crying shame.'

A happy home? Comfortable and safe, of course, but so dim and shadowy and airless. Still, he supposed . . . 'I suppose death has not touched it before.'

She looked blankly at him for a second. 'Oh – not just that. It was when *he* turned up in the first place. That so-called father.'

'So-called? But Sir James *is* her father.'

Mrs Jessop frowned. 'I speak of true parental feeling, sir. I may not know much, but I know about that, and—'

'Do you? You have been a mother?'

She looked away. 'Yes. I had a child many years ago, but it did not live. Yes, I understand true feeling, sir. Not like him. That was the start of the trouble, him coming here. And now I want an end of it.'

Very proprietorial: almost as if she were the owner of the house. He bowed, and went out into stabbing autumn sunlight that made him blink and squint.

Mentally, he did the same at the strange notion that was

invading his mind. The man from America – lingering about the Tiverton house . . . Did it have some sinister import? Or was the truth more shabby? He was still conjuring with his earlier thought that the man might be a transportee returned before his time. And now Mrs Jessop's curious evasiveness about the whole business – 'I saw him off'? – had started a wild hare of speculation. What if the late Mr Jessop wasn't late at all? What if, ten years ago, he had not been gathered to his rest, but convicted of a crime, and sent away on a prison transport for a fifteen-year term? Mrs Jessop would not be the first person to wash their hands of such a spouse and prefer the polite fiction of bereavement.

But of course, though it was a fair bet that that would be the last you would see of them, sometimes transportees did come back; sometimes, indeed, illegally, before their time. And if such a one should seek out a wife, now comfortably and respectably situated – well, he doubted there would be much of a welcome.

It was, admittedly, wild. And Mrs Jessop had been at pains to portray her husband as a rare good man, of Methodist principles, well-thought-of . . . but then that didn't mean anything. Still, even if this outlandish theory were right, what light did it throw on the mystery of Sir James's death? Well, just suppose that Sir James somehow had recognized the American for what he was, and somehow had threatened exposure, and Mrs Jessop had somehow got to know of it, and so had removed him . . .

He felt as if he were trying to draw together the ends of a belt that was simply, undeniably too small to go round. It might have helped if he could question the man from America himself but he had no idea where to find him: the man had said nothing of where he lived. It was notable, in fact, how little he had said about himself all round.

Fairfax did take something tangible away from the shadowy house in Orchard Street, though: a new perspective on Caroline.

It was all in the way she had said those words: 'My mother.' So deadpan, so unreadable. What *did* she think about her mother? She would have been too young when Lydia died to remember her; but that did not necessarily entail indifference to her fate. It might be quite the reverse. He had grown used to the Selina version of Caroline, as it were: the ambitious girl only too happy to kiss and make up with a scapegrace father who'd come bearing gifts.

And so she still might be. It was worth considering, though, another version of Caroline Delabole: one who saw only the callous deserter who had robbed her of her mother; a man who now added to that injury the insult of supposing he might buy an easy forgiveness. For that Caroline, reconciliation might only be a cloak for the ultimate revenge.

To go to Bristol, a dozen miles distant, he would have to hire a saddle-horse; but it was not only for that reason that he postponed it for a time. (Reason enough, though – between Robert Fairfax and horses there was a great gulf of misunderstanding.) No, first he wanted to call at the Delabole house, specifically to ask about Mr Pinner and his highly unpredictable movements.

He seized an early opportunity: the footman who admitted him to the chill tall house in the Circus showed a blessed willingness to gossip.

'Morning, sir. Any news? Of course, you can't speak of it – I understand that. Well, a proper to-ing and fro-ing there's been this morning. Not just the undertakers, I mean – they always give me the shivers, don't they you, sir? Pleasant men, right enough, but just something about 'em. No, company I mean – anybody who's anybody in Bath, calling to pay their respects. Never saw so many carriages – more than one of 'em crested, sir. Mind you, there's some, not many, as comes just to be ghoulish, I reckon. You can see 'em stretching their necks as if to see where it happened.'

'On that subject,' Fairfax said, 'do you recall Mr Pinner – the young man who came here yesterday, very soon after Sir James's death?'

'Pinner, yes I do; gentleman who came on behalf of Miss Delabole – t'other Miss Delabole I mean, "the new one" we call her. Well, that's what he said he came for – offering condolences and all – more likely one of the ghoulish ones, I reckon. Just sat there saying never a word. Next thing, he's wandering about upstairs.'

'Really?' Fairfax said, thinking *aha*.

'Really. I'd come up to fetch the doctor's gloves as he'd left behind, and I bumps into Mr Pinner on the landing outside the master's study. Said he was looking for the privy. He knew full well it wasn't there, because he'd called on the master early that very morning, and talked with him in that very study. Mind you, he did look green about the gills – which makes me think he was one of the ghoulish sort, who just have to take a peep at a dead man. Lord, unless you reckon he was up to something else, sir? I mean to say – the master *was* proper dead then, wasn't he? Couldn't be a case of the murderer going to finish him off? Brrr . . . Mind you, the doctor had pronounced him by then, of course he had. Just a thought.'

'Please confine your thoughts to the kitchens, Lucas,' said Lady Delabole, appearing from the drawing-room. 'Mr

Fairfax, how do you do? I'm sorry if the man has been bothering you. There is quite enough ill-informed speculation about already, I think.'

'No, Lady Delabole, it was I who was questioning him. I was curious about Mr Pinner's visit yesterday afternoon.'

'It was very good of him,' Lady Delabole said, floating ahead of him into the drawing-room. She wore a sack gown of dove-grey, with grey ribbons in her cap. Half mourning? he thought. 'Though I fear we were in no state to convey anything to him at the time. Selina, I fear, is no better. She had an airing this morning, but I think her strength was unequal to it: she has retired to her room again.'

Just as well, Fairfax thought: if she were here he might fall into some dreadful flippancy like 'Ah, we meet again, with clothes on.' And he preferred to keep what she had told him to himself for now.

'We have had many callers. I have been quite overwhelmed. Everyone has been kind – so kind.'

Lady Delabole gave a benevolent wave of her hand which seemed to include him; and he bristled a little. He wasn't here socially, after all, he was investigating a murder for which she was one of the suspects. He recalled Mr Goode's advice, and decided to be bullish.

'I'm sure they have, ma'am. But there is someone around whose intentions are less than kind, and the magistrate means to have that person caught. Now there are several things I have been told that simply do not add up, and it would be quite wrong to suppose I'm just going to drop them. There remains, for instance, this document that Nolan saw in your husband's study. If it is not found, I can only conclude that someone has concealed it or destroyed it.' He had an idea who, now, and *he* was not here; but he pressed on. 'Now if your husband was making a new will, I fancy you would know something about it, at least. In short, if you're not being frank with me, Lady Delabole, then I shall have to draw some unhappy conclusions about that.'

Damn. This wasn't his style at all. But it was done now.

'Mr Fairfax, I am a little cross with you.' Lady Delabole sat, all languorous dignity; but her eyes were hard. Plainly she had been Lady Delabole long enough to expect a cringe. 'These aspersions, even if they had the slightest of foundations, would be difficult to bear. When they are based on nothing more substantial than the dubious word of a servant, they are intolerable. Indeed, if you only give credence to what servants tell you, as appears to be the case, I don't see why you trouble me with these interviews at all.'

'And I don't see why Nolan should say he saw this document that engrossed your husband, if he did not. Is he an habitual liar and fantasist? Is that what you're saying? He didn't strike me as such.'

'He was my husband's manservant. He barbered him, saw to his clothes and boots, assisted with his dressing. He was not his *clerk*, sir. The man is unlettered. That is why I cannot believe—'

'He knows enough to recognize a document when he sees one. And also the name Delabole.'

'That might have been anything.'

'Really? Forgive me, but your husband's is not a *studious* study. He was not a man to concern himself with papers, I think: unless I have him very wrong, and he was in the habit of writing lyric verse in his spare time.'

He shrugged off the haughty look she gave him. The man was a boor and a clothes-horse and she knew it, so why pretend?

'I see very well the drift of your suspicions, sir. You suppose my husband made a will which . . . reflected his new tenderness for his first-born child. And you assume that I wanted it suppressed. Well, if that's what you choose to think, I cannot prevent you. But as for Nolan, I don't believe he would know a page of writing from a curl-paper. You are too credulous, Mr Fairfax.'

'Well, that's easily determined. May I trouble you for pen and ink and writing-paper, please? This bureau here? And ring for Nolan, if you please. We shall try an experiment.'

Lady Delabole did not look pleased, but she consented. While they waited for Nolan, Fairfax rapidly wrote out a sheet of nonsense – the alphabet, scraps of Latin, part of Hamlet's soliloquy, names that came into his head (*Cordelia* was one, written before he could stop himself.) In the middle, he wrote the name *Delabole*.

Nolan, with his habitual look of a man who had just been beaten up, sighed and scratched his chin and looked askance at Lady Delabole when Fairfax told him what he wanted him to do. But he took the paper and dutifully looked at it. He looked at it so long that at last Fairfax said: 'Well, Mr Nolan, can you point it out?'

Nolan smiled apologetically. 'Perhaps it's not there, sir,' he suggested.

'You don't recognize this word?' Fairfax said, pointing to *Delabole*.

'I can't say I do.'

'Well,' Lady Delabole said, her chin up, 'I think that's all, is it not, Mr Fairfax?'

'Didn't you say you could recognize the name Delabole, Mr Nolan?'

'Oh! Delabole, yes, sir, that I can do for you,' Nolan said

more cheerfully. ' 'Tis written on all the packing-cases, like I told you, so it's plain to me, after all these years. Show me Delabole, sir, and I'm your man.'

Fairfax thought a moment. Then he turned the paper over and wrote the word again – but this time, in block capitals. He surrounded it by a few lines of the Lord's Prayer, in capitals likewise, to be sure.

'There it is!' Nolan said delightedly, pointing to the word at once. 'Aye, I'd know it anywhere. Clear as day. Begging your pardon, sir, but I think there was something amiss with the other side.'

'Yes . . . And this is what you saw at the top of that document in the master's study?'

'That's it, sir. As for the rest of it, I couldn't say – only that it looked more like this –' Nolan indicated the capitals – 'than that other side. To my eyes, anyway.'

When he had gone Lady Delabole took up the paper between finger and thumb and looked at it as if it were a pornographic print. 'And now, I am supposed to be convinced, sir?'

'He can't recognize script,' Fairfax said, hardly listening. 'Only block letters. I should have thought, packing-cases are likely to be stamped or embossed in capitals . . .'

'And so this document – the existence of which is still very doubtful, sir – was inscribed in capital letters. Very curious. My husband was, as you suggest, no scholar, Mr Fairfax – but I can assure you he wrote a fair hand, and was not in the habit of forming his letters like a child's spelling-book.'

Fairfax was silent. He felt, if not defeated, at least baffled. Whatever that document was, it certainly didn't sound like a will. A man making out a will, even a draft, would write in his accustomed hand. 'Witness this my hand' – that was a frequent phrase. This business of capital letters made no sense that he could see.

With irritation, he became aware of Lady Delabole watching him. 'Curious, as you say, madam. It might mean any number of things.' He hoped she wouldn't ask him to name one. 'Well, I won't trouble you further just now. But please bear this in mind, Lady Delabole: though there may be things you would rather not speak of, the law has no place for such delicacy.'

She didn't look contemptuous, not quite: only very bored with him. He fumed a little as he left, aware that such *rapport* as he had managed with her was gone. Probably, he grumbled to himself, there had never really been any: she was Lady Delabole, and he was, as her look just now had made clear, only an underling. A hireling. Anything diminutive ending with *ling*, in fact.

Like a duckling? That cheered him. So did the knowledge that, for all her airs, Lady Delabole was wary of him. She had proved that by being less than truthful again. She knew about Selina's intimacy with Ensign Locke: it had triggered the row yesterday, and yet still she said nothing of it.

Well, the whole set of them seemed determined to lie, conceal, and obfuscate. Let them: he was quite as determined to surprise them into truth, starting with that alleged spy and definite liar, Mr Edmund Pinner.

Nine

It was inconvenient of Pinner to take himself back to Bristol today, Fairfax thought: really he should have insisted that the man stay in Bath whilst the investigation went on. Now here he was, faced with a twelve-mile ride and, though it was mild for autumn, there was a gusty tang in the air, and a veil over the western hills, that threatened rain on the way. Not to mention the expense of hiring a saddle-horse from the White Hart in Stall Street, where they drove a hard bargain. In fact he charged the cost of the hire to the account of Mr Goode – but the principle was the same.

The high road to Bristol was in fair condition, at any rate, and his mount seemed no more inclined to shy and toss its head and roll its eyes at him than horses generally did. And in the course of the journey, Fairfax even found he did some lucid thinking to do with that document, Pinner's behaviour at the Delabole house, and the curious business of his arrest for spying at Calais. And though his conclusions were tentative, he had a notion that visiting Pinner at home was actually the best way of putting them to the test.

It was strange to be in Bristol after Bath. The great port had a moderately fashionable spa of its own, the Hotwell, and at Clifton elegant new squares of the Bath sort were going up; but the old city itself was a very different place. Bath, where nothing more commercial than the sale of tea-cakes went on, was a place where money was displayed, flaunted, spent, and lusted after: Bristol was where money was made. The very air seemed sharper, as if it hummed with speculation. Threading his way down Corn Street and dismounting at last before the grand pilasters of the Exchange, Fairfax could almost suppose himself in London from the noise and bustle, the rumble of wheeled traffic, the hawkers and pedlars, sailors and bumboat-women, the hooped and corseted ladies attended by pages with armfuls of parcels, the sleek-bellied merchants hurrying to the Grand Coffee Room for the shipping news or conferring earnestly with marine captains on cobbled street-corners. What marked the place as unmistakable Bristol, to him at any rate, was the presence of Negro people, mostly in livery. Those were the lucky ones, retained as servants or even freed. For most, Bristol was the fountainhead of misery. Fairfax wondered how many of those handsome ships beyond the quay were slavers, plundering their human cargo from Africa, carrying it in bestial squalor and brutality across to the West Indies, and returning to this prosperous waterfront with that most innocent of substances, sugar.

Edmund Pinner, he recalled, had spoken out against the trade to Sir James. That did him credit, anyway. Alas, Sir James had probably been right when he said that was where the fortunes were to be made. When he found Pinner's house in Denmark Street, after stabling his mount at an inn by the Exchange, Fairfax saw at once that he was not one of Bristol's greatest citizens, whatever Mr Tiverton might say. It was not insubstantial, but it was old and lopsided, with bulging bow-windows and wormy timbers, and a blank-walled warehouse reared up on one side of it. Home to a merchant of the middling sort, in fact – just the sort to elicit a sneer from a Court-Calendar snob like Colonel Sir James Delabole.

A very young maid with flour on her hands let him in, and alerted the master of the house to the visitor's presence by yelling down the passage, 'Mr Pinner! There's somebody to see 'ee!' before going away whistling.

'Who is it, Nancy?'

Fairfax followed the voice. He came to a wainscotted parlour: its low beams and latticed window projecting over the quay made him think of a ship's cabin. There was nothing shipshape about the room, however. Furniture was piled up in disorder at one end, and the floor was covered in sawdust and shavings.

'Mr Fairfax.' Pinner, in shirt sleeves, straightened up from behind a large object by the window. The flush on his face might have been simply from stooping. 'How did you find me?'

'I asked where you were to be found.'

'Of course,' Pinner said with a faintly annoyed laugh, as if Fairfax had said something stupid. He dusted his hands. 'Well, what do you think? I was just making sure it was level. The instrument, that is. Unfortunately the floor is not. That is the chief difficulty.'

The instrument, Fairfax saw, was a spinet, brand new and probably just unpacked.

'Very handsome.'

'I ordered it some time ago,' Pinner said, giving Fairfax a narrow look as if he had accused him of something. 'From London, of course. It came by water. The safest way – still I'm not sure it hasn't taken some harm. What do you think?'

He pressed a single key. 'Does that sound out of tune to you?'

'I can't tell from one note.'

'Oh. I thought you musical.'

'I would have to hear two notes, to mark the relation between them.'

'Oh, well . . .' Pinner made a dismissive gesture. 'I don't know about that. I don't play, myself. I have purchased the instrument for . . .' He paused and extracted a fragment of sawdust from his lips. For Caroline, Fairfax thought. 'For the purposes of entertaining. That is, I think it is time I entertained here. Since my father died I have been wholly wrapped up in business, and this has just been a roof over my head. I never even *thought* of entertaining.' He said this dogmatically, as if Fairfax had claimed he had. 'But now that I am a little settled . . . The house is solid, if not fashionable, and this room I think might be nicely fitted up. What think you? The spinet here – there will be light to read music by, from the window. In the daytime, that is. There, a sofa. Ignore those old chairs, they will be gone. And a screen for the fire – embroidered or japan-work. That should complete it, I think. What do you say?'

'I think it will look very well.' Fairfax's eye fell on two cheap unframed prints that hung above the mantel.

'What?' Pinner was alert. 'The walls? I think to leave them as they are. I thought of Chinese wallpaper, but it is a great extravagance and will hardly suit the room, I think. Oh, the prints – I dare say I shall get around to framing them.'

The prints were engravings from Hogarth's *Harlot's Progress*. 'I am a great admirer of Mr Hogarth,' Fairfax said carefully. 'In an elegant drawing-room, though, as this will surely be, some people may not like them. I don't know why, classical scenes seem to be preferred.'

'Oh, I know nothing of pictures in that way,' Pinner said airily. 'All a great fuss, I think. I had a practical education, Mr Fairfax. I wish my company to be comfortable, sir, that's my chief concern: comfortable and social and easy. People count, not things. I've no patience with this mania for fashion.'

'Indeed. But a man's eye for pictures, I think, often speaks volumes for him—'

'Oh, not I. Pardon me, but to me that's all affectation and flummery. Give me an honest man, not some coxcomb forever puffing his own taste—'

'And yet when you were at Calais, you were engaged in making sketches of the town, were you not?' Fairfax said amiably. 'I thought that's what you said, at any rate – and that was the reason for your mistaken arrest. Isn't that so?'

'Oh, that! Merely to pass the time. Yes, that was – Calais, you know, is a damned dreary town to be detained in. God, yes.'

Fairfax had never heard him swear before. 'All the same, I should be interested in seeing your sketches. I have often wished I had a talent that way myself.'

'Oh, but I have no talent. That is – they were the merest—'

'Well, let me see, and judge for myself.' Fairfax smiled. 'Or – well, perhaps the French authorities confiscated them.'

'So they did,' Pinner said shrugging. 'Such nonsense—'

'Nonsense, indeed! Mr Pinner, you said the governor at Calais released you, and exonerated you of all charges, when he realized the true state of the case. So why was there any reason for him to keep your sketches? But perhaps you destroyed them yourself—'

'Yes, they were mere rubbish, as I said—'

'You just said they were confiscated. Mr Pinner, I don't

suspect you in the least of being a spy in France. But I strongly suspect that you have been up to no good here – or rather, in Bath. Please consider, sir, I am not Nemesis or an avenging angel: I am employed to look into the murder of Sir James Delabole, and as such I am afraid I must notice everything, and go into it, and never let it go.' Fairfax took out his handkerchief, dusted the seat of a windsor chair, and sat down. As the chair was stacked on top of a bench, it made him feel rather as if he were mounting a throne. 'You had a private interview with Sir James early yesterday morning. Afterwards Sir James was seen conning a certain strange paper on his desk, and was generally in a discomposed state. By the afternoon, he was dead; and as soon as news of his death reached Mr Tiverton's house, you hurried straight over to the Circus, supposedly to offer condolences to the family on behalf of Mr Tiverton and Caroline. But in between condoling, as it were, you slipped out of the Delaboles' drawing-room, and were found wandering about upstairs in the vicinity of Sir James's study. The very room where a servant saw that paper earlier, left on the desk . . . and now there is no sign of that paper. I thought at first it must be a will, but now I'm sure it was not, as I'm sure it was not sketches of scenery you brought back from France. And I'm sure, moreover, that you slipped up to Sir James's study to retrieve that paper, because you felt its presence would incriminate you. If I'm wrong, please explain how.' Feeling his throne wobble, Fairfax shifted gingerly. 'Unless you would prefer to explain to the magistrate, of course.'

'You can't,' Pinner said, swallowing, 'you can't come here and accuse me like this . . .'

'Why not?' There was something about a throne, Fairfax thought, that really did make you feel powerful, also unscrupulous. 'The servant is prepared to testify that he saw you coming out of that study yesterday afternoon. As for the authorities at Calais, it would take some time, of course, but I'm sure they would be willing to tell us just what you were doing that made them suspect you of spying.'

'You are an unfeeling man, Mr Fairfax.'

It was the second time today he had been reproached for that, so it didn't trouble him.

'It isn't – it isn't what you think.' Pinner turned and stood before the spinet, head bowed, as if it were an altar. 'I – you should understand something first, sir. Caroline Delabole and I . . . there is a strong attachment between us.'

'A mutual attachment?'

Pinner winced. 'We have known each other many years. Her grandfather has always shown great favour towards me, and in their house I have been almost one of the family. On Caroline's side, I do believe, there is esteem – easy familiarity – even affection. On my side, those same sentiments have ripened into a regard that is both tender and exalted. That is – love.'

'I had supposed it so.'

'Did you?' Pinner's pale eyes flashed at him. 'But I have always striven to be discreet in my conduct – to avoid embarrassing her by over-familiarity and presumption . . .'

'I am not quite an unfeeling man, sir.' Fairfax hesitated. 'Nor am I a stranger to the sentiments you describe. Or the pain they can cause.'

'Oh, there is no pain, sir. You are quite wrong there. Caroline has never given me pain. That is . . . she has always been considerate. But circumstances have somewhat conspired against the maturing of an attachment which, I have every reason to believe, is more than welcome to her grandfather – indeed I think he hopes for it almost as devoutly as I. Those circumstances could not have been predicted. Of course, I knew Caroline's melancholy history – that is, her mother's history – and that there was a father somewhere. I did not anticipate his suddenly appearing as he did. No more, I think, did Mr Tiverton. I remember asking him once if he thought Caroline's father would ever seek to acknowledge her. Bitterly, he said, "Only if there were some advantage in it for him." And so when he told me, last month, that Sir James was coming to Bath, and that he had agreed to see him, I hardly knew what to think. That is – I thought it a very ill proceeding. Very ill.'

'Yet wasn't this –' Fairfax decided not to say *none of your business* – 'a somewhat hasty judging, Mr Pinner?'

'Was it? I think I was right from the beginning. It has not been a happy turn of events. I took the trouble to find out about Sir James Delabole before his arrival. I was not much pleased with what I found. And when I heard from Mr Tiverton that they had met at last, and that Sir James was pronouncing himself mightily pleased with his daughter, and talked of doing great things for her, and so on . . . well, my heart misgave me.'

'You were not pleased for Caroline?'

Pinner frowned. 'How could I be?'

'Well, she had a father at last. The wounds of the past were, perhaps, to be healed. And she was to have wealth and consequence.'

'You have a very wrong estimate of me, sir, if you think I care for such things. Wealth and consequence – what are they beside true feeling, domestic virtues, honest contentment? Those are the things that last.'

'That's your feeling. Not necessarily Caroline's.'

'Caroline is . . . younger. She has, very properly, not seen the world.' Pinner carefully dusted the lid of the spinet with his sleeve. 'And faced with the glittering promises held out by a man like Sir James Delabole, she might be – well, a little dazzled. And from what I heard, it seemed she was, initially. I think one cannot expect a young woman, reared in gentle seclusion, to know her own mind.'

Pinner looked so smug as he said this that Fairfax felt a little disgusted. 'And so you decided to know it for her.'

'I . . .' It was not much of a rebuke: but all at once, to Fairfax's surprise, Pinner's voice faltered and there were tears in his eyes. Curiously Fairfax felt a certain relief. It was as if one had been waiting all this time for those hurt watery eyes to go on and weep. 'I feared losing her, damn it. Wouldn't you? I am respectably set up here, through hard work and application to business. But I have a competence, not a fortune. My talk is that of the Exchange and excise, not town tattle. I – how can I compete with what her father had to offer her? He was already speaking of taking her to London, introducing her to society . . . I longed to go over to Bath at once, see for myself – yet some part of me was afraid of what I would see.' Pinner wiped his eyes hastily. 'Well, there was a promised trip to France, on wine-shipping business, that I could not forego: my father had worked hard to forge those links. So I went, though my mind was hardly on what I was doing. And on my return journey, I had to wait at Calais for a favourable wind. It was, I repeat, deadly dull. I put up at the Silver Lion. There were some rowdy young gentlemen there who had been on the Grand Tour, and were always drinking wine and shouting crude things about the foreigners they had met – the women, particularly. I passed the time as best I could, walking about the town, but there was very little to see: a bleak, damp place. I took to going beyond the gates and there, a little way out of the town, I came upon an old convent, with near at hand a graveyard. There was a little corner set aside for those not of the Catholic faith – mainly English travellers who had the misfortune to die abroad, I surmise – and I beguiled the idle hour by looking at the inscriptions.' Pinner gave a shudder. 'God, I almost wish now I had not . . .'

'Why? What did you see?'

'A grave.' Pinner absently struck the keyboard with his fingers. By chance he produced the chord of C minor, appropriately sombre. 'Much overgrown. But the inscription on the headstone was plain enough, and in English. The words were these. *Maria Delabole. Born at Paris December fourth, 1744. Died at Calais December twenty-second, 1744, in the first month of her life. Beloved daughter of James and Lydia Delabole. Entrusted to God.*'

Pinner struck the keyboard again, this time producing a horrible jangle – but again apt for the confusion in Fairfax's mind.

'So – that would be twenty-one years ago . . .'

'Do you see?' Pinner smiled thinly. 'Do you see as *I* saw, in fact? You must know the Delabole history. How he eloped with Mr Tiverton's daughter Lydia, and they went abroad; and at Paris he deserted her when she was bearing his child. So she gave birth alone, and made her wretched way back to England with her child, and was finally taken back by her father, shortly before she died. And now look at this. 'Forty-four was the very year: December the fourth, indeed, is Caroline's birthday. Or rather, that is when it has always been celebrated. But you see my conclusion, the only conclusion I could draw. The child of Sir James and Lydia

Delabole's marriage had not survived: the babe had died within a few weeks of birth, her mother had buried her at Calais, and so come home to her father, bereft of husband and child. A terrible story . . . But not the story the world had been told.'

There was a faintly dramatic satisfaction on Pinner's face. Fairfax stared and at last found his voice.

'You are sure of this? There can be no – no error, no confusion—'

'Delabole is an uncommon name, sir. It surely stretches belief that there was another English couple named James and Lydia Delabole who had a child in France in 1744.'

'Indeed . . . Then who the devil is Caroline Delabole?'

'We think alike, sir . . . But you must understand something: I did not, do not care *who* she is, in that way. Whether the heiress of Sir James Delabole, or someone quite different: it is the living breathing woman I value and cherish, not the wordly appurtenances that go with her. You think me talking a lot of sentimental cant, I dare say.'

'No. No, I do not, as it happens. But this discovery . . . I don't understand. Mr Tiverton has brought up Caroline as his granddaughter – as the child of that marriage. And yet she can't be . . .'

'So it would seem. Believe me, I could not sleep the whole of that night, back at my inn: my mind turned it over and over. But my conclusions were inescapable. The girl I knew as Caroline Delabole was not the person she was claimed to be. What strange deception lay behind it I could not tell. I could only assume that Sir James, having deserted his wife and utterly parted from her, did not know the child had died; and that when she returned to her father in England, the death was known only to them – and Lydia of course did not long survive her return. My suspicions . . . I regret that they were unworthy, applied to a man as excellent as Mr Tiverton. But I could not help wondering whether Caroline, whom he called his granddaughter, was actually his daughter. Not legitimately, of course, for his wife was long dead. Rather, a by-blow.' Pinner's cheeks glowed pink. 'Mr Tiverton is flesh and blood, of course, and – such things are far from unknown. Raising her as his granddaughter would be a way of making her name respectable. It seemed plausible.'

'Yes . . . and the mother?' Even as he said it, Fairfax thought of Mrs Jessop. 'Or was she not far to seek?'

'Indeed, that occurred to me. Sarah Jessop has always seemed on oddly comfortable terms with Mr Tiverton for a paid companion. And yet she only joined his household ten years ago, when she was widowed, so that did not fit. Of course, it was still possible there was some former association between them, which was renewed . . . Yet I must emphasize, sir, I did not care about that part. My esteem for Mr Tiverton was not to be altered by such thoughts: nor my love for Caroline, far from it. All I could think was – with this knowledge I could utterly destroy Sir James's claim upon her. And that would not be – *wrong*, necessarily. It would only be making him aware of the truth.'

'A moment – when Sir James proposed a reconciliation, Mr Tiverton returned a favourable answer. He was willing for Sir James to meet this – this daughter who wasn't. Why would he carry on such a deception?'

Pinner shrugged. 'Perhaps, having begun it, he saw no other way but to continue. Perhaps he wanted to see what Sir James would do for his child, or what he thought was his child. Those were my notions, anyway.' He sighed. 'They turned out to be irrelevant. Sir, what I did – it was driven by love. Or fear of losing love. Or fear of losing my chance . . .'

'And what did you do?'

'I resolved that on my return to England, I would confront Sir James Delabole with my discovery. And so that I might have tangible proof to show him, I had the idea of taking a rubbing from that headstone. The next morning I procured paper and a piece of charcoal, and returned to the graveyard, and laid the paper against the headstone. My first attempt was unsuccessful: I rubbed too hard, and it smudged. But with care, I managed to produce a very clear and legible rubbing of the inscription. There could hardly be a better proof, I thought.'

'And the inscription was – of course, it was in capital letters. Funerary inscriptions always are.'

'Just so. What I could not have expected was that some meddlesome Frenchman – I believe it was one of those monks who are always begging for alms at Calais, and whom I had refused – saw my trips to the graveyard, my painstaking and, admittedly, secret labours with paper and charcoal, and reported me as a suspicious character. And so I was arrested. It was absurd, of course, but alarming too. As the days of my detention went by, and I waited for the governor's return, I had to beg leave to write a letter to my overseer here in England, who would be wondering what had become of me. I had some fear, moreover, that I would have to seek help from home, a testimonial to my character or something . . . Well, they let me send a letter by the packet-boat – the very one that had been waiting for the tide and that I should have been on, damn it – but first, of course, they studied the letter, with some wretched priest who understood English translating it. It was lucky that I had written in temperate terms. I didn't feel temperate: I fear it is true what they say about

France, riddled with priests, tyrannised by police and in-
formers . . . Well, I saw the governor at last. He was a rational
man. I explained – that is, I told him I had taken a rubbing of
an English grave, to take as a memento to relatives of the
deceased, and showed him the paper. He was profusely
apologetic, and condemned the zeal of his subordinates. He
said he was afraid they would believe any evil of an Englishman. So I was released, and after another wait for a packet, I
came home. My overseer, meanwhile, had received my letter,
and unhappily he had told Mr Tiverton about it – and so the
matter was brought up at that dinner the other evening,
when I could have wished it forgotten . . . I have offered you
nothing, sir. I do not keep liquor – that is, in my private
dwelling. I have cordials—'

'Nothing, thank you.'

'You fear drinking something that comes from my hand?'
Pinner said, with something like a snigger. 'You need not, sir.
I am only a venial sinner. Not even that . . . When I arrived
back at Bristol, I was still not wholly decided upon making
use of my discovery, even though I had been through a good
deal to preserve it. When Mr Tiverton had word of my return,
and asked me to come and dine and meet Sir James Delabole
into the bargain, I thought: well, let's see. Everything I knew
inclined me against him. But I wanted to see him for myself
first. Well, I did, of course: found him much as I expected, if
not a little worse—'

'And found him very eager to whisk Caroline away from
you.'

Pinner pouted. 'Just so.'

'But tell me, did you not consider Caroline's own wishes
in that regard?'

'She could hardly know what she truly wanted, in the

confusion of this sudden change . . . And besides, I had the proof, as I thought, that he was not her father anyway. There was no real claim. Surely it was best for everyone if the truth was established . . . and yes, all right, best for me above all.'

'But would it? After all, if you told Sir James your discovery, then he'd be sure to confront Mr Tiverton with it – demand to know why he had been deceived in this way. And Caroline in turn would know about it: indeed the whole thing would be horribly public. She would hardly thank you for that.'

'I know . . . But it might not happen that way. Sir James might just have it out with Mr Tiverton, and take himself off, and Caroline needn't know what it was all about. But even if she did – well, I still thought it was better, if it separated her from Sir James. That seemed to me – urgent.'

About to say something, Fairfax stopped. Pinner was only following a common lover's formula, after all: *I don't want to make you happy – I want to make you mine.*

'Well, perhaps I didn't deserve to succeed. Perhaps there was justice in what happened . . . I went to Sir James, early the next morning, and saw him alone in his study. I produced the paper, with the rubbing from the child's grave. I thought for a moment he was going to strike me. And then he began laughing. Which in a way was more horrible. He laughed . . . and asked why I was bringing him this old news.'

'He knew?'

Pinner nodded, pale and baleful. 'He knew. Oh, and he knew what I was trying to do, of course. "You thought you could turn me away from my daughter, did you, you puppy? So you could keep her walled up amongst your damn tradesman's books?" Those were his words. He was uncommonly insulting. Well, I had made a fool of myself, and he told me how. Yes, the child buried in that grave at Calais was his daughter: and so is Caroline. Because when Lydia was brought to bed in Paris on December the fourth, 1744, she gave birth not to one child but two. Twins: twin girls, whom she named Maria and Caroline.'

Fairfax stared. Pinner smiled.

'That is pretty much how I looked, I think, when he told me. He was still fearfully angry, by the way – his eyes were like stones. To be forced to speak of these things to a puppy like me, he said, was very bitter: but as I had begun it, let it be finished. Lydia, when the babies were born, had written him to tell him so. Though they had parted, she still wrote him. He reckoned she wanted a reconciliation: whether that's just his vanity, or the truth, I don't know. I think perhaps she did still love him: she gave up a great deal for him, at any rate. But he did not go to see her and the children. "We had parted on the worst of terms," he said, "and the marriage was at an end." Just that. Privately I still thought it inhumanly cold of him . . . Well, Lydia must have felt she could not stay alone in France with two babes, and so decided to return to England and throw herself on her father's mercy. As soon as she was well enough, she travelled to Calais, to make the crossing. But there the first-born of the twins, Maria, grew sickly and would not nurse, and very soon died. She was buried in that grave that I had seen. And Lydia had finally crossed to England – in God knows what state of grief and wretchedness – with her surviving child, Caroline, and was taken in at last by Mr Tiverton. Again, she had written her estranged husband the unhappy news. And it was he who went to Calais afterwards, he said, and saw the rude cross that the monks had erected for the grave, and had a mason carve a proper headstone instead. Yes: he had paid for that very headstone that I had taken a rubbing of. "So this," he said, and he waved the paper in my face, "is very familiar to me, sir." And then he proceeded to abuse me for a while. He said I was a two-faced rogue. He said I must have been an ungrateful dog to Mr Tiverton, who had been so good to me, if I had suspected him of some deception about Caroline. He said I had come trying to make mischief, and had trespassed upon family matters that were none of my business, and – well, if he were a younger man he would horsewhip me.' Pinner dug his hands in his pockets and aimed a moody kick into a clump of sawdust. 'And damn it all, I felt afraid of him. And I felt a fool, and a rogue, and – all the things he said. And I just wanted to get out of there. So I did – leaving that paper on his desk.'

'I see. And did you fear Sir James would tell all this to Mr Tiverton?'

'I suppose . . . though everything seemed such a miserable mess anyhow, it could hardly be worse. In truth, though, I have been so accustomed to Mr Tiverton's good opinion of me that I – well, I thought I could talk him round, if it came to it.'

Really? thought Fairfax. Or did you fear that you had wrecked your chances with Mr Tiverton and Caroline, and panic, and conclude that Sir James must be put out of the way?

'I can tell what you're thinking,' Pinner said sourly. 'You share Sir James's opinion. You think me a low, conniving intriguer—'

'A hasty conclusion,' Fairfax said. 'You have frankly told me of your feeling for Caroline. And you did what you did because you feared losing her, and saw a way of preventing it. Isn't that so? An unhappy story – but human. But at least this matter of the mysterious document is cleared up – or partly.

The paper that Nolan saw Sir James brooding over, and in which he recognized the word "Delabole", was a rubbing from his child's gravestone. Certainly an object liable to give him dark thoughts. The question remains, where is that paper now?'

Pinner shook his head. 'That I don't know.'

'Oh, come, sir. There's no need for concealment now. When news came to Mr Tiverton's house of Sir James's death, you ran over to the Delabole house at once, and made your peculiar sortie upstairs, supposedly in search of a privy. You wanted to get that paper back, did you not?'

'No – yes, I mean, damn it – I was afraid. Here was Sir James killed; and if that paper was found on his desk, it would be examined, and probably traced to me, and they would want to know what I was up to . . . If I could just get it back, I thought, there would be no need for me to be involved any more: it would all be kept quiet. But when I went into Sir James's study, the paper wasn't there any more. I even opened the drawers, and hunted about, as quietly as I could – but I couldn't find it. And then I heard the footman coming, so I got out quickly, and pretended I was looking for the privy. I swear to you, Mr Fairfax, I don't have that paper. I wish I had, for my peace of mind. I don't know where it's gone: I gather nothing of the sort was found on Sir James's body . . .?'

'No. All very curious. And so, Mr Pinner, what did you think when you heard that Sir James was murdered? Apart from fear that you might be incriminated, that is. Was it not – well, something of a blessing? A deliverance?' As Pinner only glared at him, jaw working, Fairfax went on: 'I'm just trying to put myself in your shoes. You wanted to sever the link between Sir James and Caroline: well, now it was done. It's a good look-out for you now, is it not? All this – the spinet, your improvements – they suggest you are looking forward to a hopeful future. Is it, though? After all, when Sir James left his house after his unhappy interview with you, it was Mr Tiverton he went to see. And *theirs* was not an amicable meeting, it seems. Were you talked of? I shall find out from Mr Tiverton himself, but you may as well tell me. I'm sure you know.'

'Mr Tiverton and I,' Pinner said with a pompous sniff, 'have long been on the most confidential terms, sir. I believe I can call him friend rather than patron. And yes, he took me aside last night, and said he understood that I had been – finding things out about the Delabole family history. Yes, Sir James had spoken to him of it, in his usual violent terms. Mr Tiverton said the matter of Lydia's twin babies was a thing he preferred to keep quiet. Old and sad things, he said. It was unfortunate that I had happened on it in France, and doubly unfortunate that I had gone to Sir James with the information. He didn't know what erroneous conclusions I had drawn, he said, and he didn't want to know . . . This was as close to a reproach as I got but I felt my shame keenly, believe me. Especially when he added that he always preferred to keep the knowledge from Caroline, who had suffered enough in losing her mother – and my rash action might have brought the tale to her ears. Fortunately Sir James had not wanted her to know about her dead twin either. I think Mr Tiverton was . . . well, disappointed in me. But then he has been quite open about his dislike for Sir James, and his feeling that he is a malign influence – and that, however misguidedly, was what I sought to remove.'

Fairfax looked at him sceptically. 'Hm. Still, very forgiving of the old gentleman, I think.'

'That's as may be.' Pinner was curt. 'But he has a great

esteem for me, sir, one that I have worked hard to deserve; and it is not easily destroyed. For that I am grateful. Indeed, now that I have spoken out, I find I am not disposed to think so very badly of myself. If you had come upon the evidence of that gravestone, would you not have come to the same conclusion? I could not know there were twins. I thought I was merely pursuing the truth. Even when I sought to recover that paper, I was not *stealing* anything. What do you say, Mr Fairfax? Have I committed a crime?'

'Not as far as I can see.'

'Excellent. And I have told you everything there is to tell. Then there is no need, surely, for me to be bothered in this way any more.' Pinner dusted his hands with hearty finality, and walked to the door. 'You will appreciate I have much to do.'

Fairfax got down from his throne, more awkwardly than he would have liked. His mind was thrumming like a stirred hive with what he had learned. But he wouldn't be dismissed so easily.

'I thank you for your frankness, Mr Pinner. You've answered some important questions. Alas, there are others. What has become of this paper, for example.'

'I've told you, I don't know. Perhaps someone threw it away. It can't be important, as you know what it contained—'

'No. You have told me, but that is not quite the same as seeing it for myself. There is something else I am trying to clear up: the whereabouts of Ensign Locke. You have seen nothing of him, by any chance?'

Pinner's lips went thin. 'That is hardly likely.'

'You didn't take to him, I think.'

'I really have no thought for that gentleman one way or another. Now, if you don't mind, sir—'

'And there is, of course, one other matter outstanding. Who poisoned Sir James Delabole?'

'I've told you, I—'

'It wasn't you, yes, certainly. But again, Mr Pinner, that is something I shall need to see for myself.' Fairfax took up his hat and went to the door.

'Oh, and sir, would you be so good as not to leave Bristol, as you left Bath, without informing the magistrates? It has a bad appearance.'

Ten

'These old memories,' Mr Tiverton said heavily, staring into the fire, 'are painful to touch upon. One learns to let them be.'

'All the same, it might have been better if you had spoken of this, sir. You knew what Mr Pinner had been up to. I gather it was the cause of high words between you and Sir James in this very office – is that not so?'

Mr Tiverton sighed. 'Aye, aye. He spoke of it. He was very fierce against Mr Pinner. Called him all manner of names and said he thought poorly of my judgement in favouring such a man.'

'And you, sir? What did you think?'

The old man shifted uneasily. 'I thought it a great shame. I said as much to Mr Pinner last night.'

'Only a shame? Pinner came back to England believing that Caroline was not Sir James's daughter, and that you must have been involved in some deception to present her as such. That suggests, at the least, a lack of trust, even disloyalty.'

'As I have said, I thought it a great shame. I believe I told Mr Pinner I was disappointed in him. But you must consider, Mr Fairfax, that on the evidence he had found in Calais, that *did* seem the likely conclusion. He didn't know the whole facts, and it's a pity he learned them as he did. He remains a young man of sterling qualities, and I am not disposed to banish him for this mistake.'

'I see . . . Your daughter's story is indeed a tragic one.'

'It is. If I did not care to let the world know just how tragic . . . then that is because I felt there had been enough unhappy scandal. The death of one of her little girls left her shattered; and when she herself died, I preferred to keep the matter secret from the surviving one – from Caroline. The history behind her birth was already melancholy enough. Even Sir James was agreed on keeping that private – though in his case I think it was guilt that was the prime motive. My constant aim has been to protect Caroline, sir. To shield her from the ills of the world as I –' Mr Tiverton gave a faint shudder – 'as her mother was not shielded.'

'A hard task.'

'I have not found it so, till now. And I can only ask you, Mr Fairfax, to say nothing of this to Caroline. I understand you have a job to do – but there is surely nothing to be gained by telling her.'

'Certainly, it is not my place to do that . . . This, then, was the substance of your quarrel with Sir James, at your last meeting? The behaviour of Mr Pinner?'

The old man's pouchy eyes wandered, a little vaguely, about the sombre panelled room. 'Yes,' he said. 'Yes, that was the occasion of it.'

'But you spoke of other things. Of Caroline's future, I think you said, and Sir James's plans for her.'

'Yes.' Mr Tiverton gave a drab smile. 'Come, Mr Fairfax. Do you suppose two men who disliked each other as much as we did, and who had so many bones to pick, could sit here long without quarrelling?'

Probably not, Fairfax thought, but it was an evasive answer all the same.

'Well, the question remains of where this paper has gone. Mr Pinner admits he foolishly tried to retrieve it from Sir James's study, without success. Which means someone else has it: or if they have destroyed it, they know what it said.'

'Maybe so. I can only repeat, I do not want it coming to Caroline's ears. She is – she is already in low spirits, and our peace is thoroughly disturbed.'

'Does Mrs Jessop know?'

Mr Tiverton looked up quickly. 'No. You know what her place is here, sir. She does not step outside it.'

'Of course. Did you know the late Mr Jessop, by the by?'

'I knew of him. A respectable tradesman, I think. But Sarah – Mrs Jessop only came to us after she was widowed.'

Mr Tiverton had got to his feet. Fairfax took the hint. He was tired in any case after the ride back from Bristol, during which the clouds had fulfilled their promise and delivered a fine soft western rain that had soaked him in no time. Still he found himself glancing back once again at the shadowy house in Orchard Street. *Our peace is thoroughly disturbed*, Mr Tiverton had said: but Fairfax thought *What peace?*

A peace of shadows. A peace built on buried resentment, bitterness, and tragedy: like a house built on a graveyard. Guilt, too, in the very foundations. Mr Tiverton had spoken of Sir James's guilt: he might equally, Fairfax thought, have spoken of his own. It was at least partly because of his intransigence that his daughter had given birth alone in a foreign land, and alone had to bury one of her children – almost as if she were a fugitive in some barbaric war rather than a married lady in a civilized society. All the way back from Bristol he had been picturing Lydia, that pretty young woman in the portrait in Mr Tiverton's dining-room, standing by the little grave at Calais with her surviving baby in her arms. The image saddened him beyond words. She must have felt her father had certainly punished her disobedience in full measure.

Fairfax returned to Avon Street for clean clothes. Above the serried rooftops of Bath the clouds had cleared and there was a curiously beautiful apple-green in the sky, suspended between afternoon and twilight. Going upstairs, he saw with a jolt that Locke's door stood open.

Not Locke, though. It was the landlady. The young officer owed her rent, she said, and as he continued to make himself scarce she had no alternative but to take something of his for a pledge. Fairfax didn't think she could rightfully do that but decided not to argue the point. She would have a job to find anything of value amongst the clutter, at any rate.

Still the sight dismayed him. If Locke had packed up his things and flitted, that would have been one thing; but this mysterious absence was quite another, and it was hard to find a hopeful explanation for it. Changing into his last clean shirt, Fairfax for the first time posed himself the question: what if something had happened to Locke?

He drank a swift brandy. And what did he mean by *happened to*? Did he mean, was Locke alive or dead? Fairfax shuddered. He supposed he did mean that. Very well, in that case, where was the body?

The last he knew of Locke, indirectly, was when Selina had gone out to meet him yesterday in response to his smuggled note. Sir James had just discovered them in each other's arms and thrown Locke out: the liaison, presumably, had been of the standard, young-lovers sort. Nothing will stand in our way, be strong my dear, and all that. And then . . .

Then what, damn it? The only notion that came to mind was of Locke going off to procure a marriage-licence. But that was not as easy as the romances made out – and besides, Selina wasn't of age.

And besides again, what *were* Locke's motives? Did he love Selina, or her fortune? If the latter, then they were treading once more in the murky waters of Sir James's murder, and the question of his will. Sir James had seemed to be about to settle his property on Caroline. If Locke wanted to marry money, he would have to . . .

Act quickly. Put Sir James out of the way. He kept coming back to that depressing conclusion. Or, of course, the young ensign could transfer his attentions to the other daughter. Did Caroline know where Locke was? It seemed so unlikely. And yet she was a subtle young woman, didn't wear her heart on her sleeve: Fairfax could imagine her keeping a secret very capably.

He simply didn't know. A second brandy produced no vivid flares of inspiration or insight: he just felt stupid and stuck. He realized he ought to go and see Mr Goode – inform him of his progress. Well, that shouldn't take too long, he thought. The only progress he had made was of a negative kind. The mysterious document was not a will after all – though it had mysteriously disappeared. Beyond that, he had only unanswered questions.

In fact, as he took a chair to Queen Square, Fairfax had it in his mind to tell Mr Goode that he could not complete this task. Very sorry, great pity, but no go. Yes, it would be a declaration of failure: yes, he would probably lose his pupils, the Bassetts, as a result. Well, no matter, he told himself. I'll get by. Oh, yes. I'll sit in my rooms, and live on credit, and drink at my leisure – good unhurried drinking, really concentrating on the job, appreciating each transcendent stage of it: the first glow, the rising spirits, the cheerful plateau, the oblivious fog, the stumbling slope down – and there I'll be when the bailiffs come, and none of it will matter.

He pictured himself thus, dispassionately. It was grim. He knew now that in pursuing this investigation, there was a kind of salvation for him. To give it up was to be lost. Still, he felt the temptation tugging at him. What finally tipped the balance was the fact that Mr Goode was not at home.

He had left a scribbled message: *I have the greatest trust in your diligence, Mr Fairfax, and if I am greatly needed I can be found at Prior Park. Yours, &c.* And that was it. Mr Goode, J.P., who had, among other things, many social obligations, did not wish to be troubled by anything short of a successful conclusion. It really was, Fairfax realized, up to him alone.

The thought of his pupils made him realize something else: he rather missed them. No doubt Mr Goode had informed them that he might be otherwise occupied, but he decided on the spur of the moment to go and see the Bassetts and present his compliments.

A touch unconventional, and the hour was late for calling – but the amiable family didn't mind a bit, and he felt he would have got the same welcome if it had been midnight.

'We have missed you, Mr Fairfax – it hasn't been the same!' Mr Bassett boomed. 'The girls have been very good, mind: they sat down this afternoon, and applied themselves to their French books as best they could. Not that poor Spash has been able to fix her mind on it too well – have you, my dear? She's took hurt, poor creature.'

'Miss Aspasia, I'm sorry to hear this – what has happened?'

'Oh, she's turned her ankle – poor Spash! – and it's swelled up so,' put in Euphemia, while her sister reclined in a chair, woefully giggling. 'She was practising her dance steps, well we all were, on account of going to the Assembly—'

'But it was mostly country-dances we were doing,' said Felicia, 'because they're the most entertaining, you know, not the minuets, everyone's glad when they're over, at least I'm sure I am—'

'And we were going at it so vigorously, and then Spash gives a scream—'

'Not a scream,' Aspasia corrected her, 'I didn't scream, you know, Phemie, it was more of a – an exclamation.'

'Well, she exclamated then – and next thing she was on the floor, and we had to help her up, and all she could do was hobble—'

'Limp,' put in Aspasia.

'Well, limp – only it *looked* like a hobble, Spash – and it hurts like anything, poor dear, and so we couldn't go to the Assembly after all.'

'Well, they might have, you know,' said Mrs Bassett, beaming at her family, 'if Spash had stayed home: I would have stayed with her and the other girls could have gone, but they wouldn't hear of it. "If Spash can't go," they said, "we won't, because it ain't fair." '

'Well, it ain't – isn't,' Felicia said. 'We don't want to go if Spash can't – there wouldn't be any fun – it would just feel horrible.'

'We'll all go when she's better,' Euphemia said. 'Poor Spash! When she screamed – or made that noise, I mean – I thought I would faint.'

'I don't know where they learned, Mr Fairfax, to be such good creatures,' Mrs Bassett chuckled, 'but I'm proud of 'em, at any rate.'

'You have every reason to be, ma'am. Miss Aspasia, I am

most concerned for you: I turned faint myself at the news.' That got them shrieking and fizzing, as he knew it would. 'Have you been examined by a doctor?'

'Aye, we had a sawbones in,' Mr Bassett said, 'the best that money could buy – but he only talked a lot of high words, and said she must strap the ankle up. A sprain, he says – or mebbe a dislocation. Well, which, says I? Too soon to tell, says he. All very rum I reckon it. He had a great physical wig and a cane and gold lace on his hat, so I suppose he must know his business. For my part I'd put my trust in a horse-doctor sooner.'

'Oh, Pa, I'm no horse!'

'No, no, my dear. I didn't mean you are. But I've known horse-doctors and farriers do wonderful things with sprains and wrenches. 'Tis all in the hands, you know, all in the feel. There was an old fellow kept a stable at Southwark when I was a younker – he was a marvel. Men would go to him bent double and come out walking tall and straight as dragoons.'

'Oh, Pa, I don't want to be wrenched by a horse-doctor!'

'Well, my dear, I'm only talking. You shall rest up, and no doubt you'll be good as new soon enough. Now, Mr Fairfax, what say you stay to supper? We have cutlets, and fowls, and all manner of things, and you're most welcome, you know – truly welcome.'

'Yes, do, Mr Fairfax,' Aspasia cried, 'because I can't go out, so I don't see anybody, and we can talk French—'

'And we promise not to be silly, and laugh,' Felicia said, very grave, 'because we do do that, I know, sometimes.'

'Thank you – I shall be very happy to accept your invitation,' Fairfax said, 'but only on condition, ladies, that you *do* laugh and be silly, because that's what I like best in the world.' Which sent the girls off into such red-faced squeakings and hissings, and hitting each other with cushions, that it really seemed they would never recover.

It was the pleasantest evening he had spent, and the best meal he had eaten, since coming to Bath; and when he left the hour was late. Almost midnight, he saw, peering at his watch in the looming shadow of the Abbey. Looking up, he seemed to see reproach in the carved saintly faces gazing from the west front. Guiltily he realized that for several hours he had not thought about Sir James Delabole in grimacing death, the poison in the head of his cane, the little grave in Calais, the disappearance of Locke – any of it.

And yet he also found that *not* thinking of it had, somehow, cleared his thoughts.

What leaped out at him was this strange business of the man with the hook lingering about Mr Tiverton's house. The man from America, as he surely must be. Fairfax had put this to one side, simply because it didn't seem to fit with anything else. Now he saw that as evasion. If it didn't fit, then he must be looking at it wrongly.

Every other trail, indeed, appeared to lead nowhere. Perhaps this, apparently the most unpromising of all, would be the one that took him to the heart of the mystery.

With that in mind, he turned back and bent his steps to Orchard Street – to Mr Tiverton's house.

A small chance, he thought, but not impossible. Caroline Delabole had seen the strange visitant hanging about the yard at the rear of house around midnight. If a man was going to do something so peculiar once, he thought, then he might well do it again.

The front windows of Mr Tiverton's house were all in darkness. Fairfax waited until a duet of young blades, singing a drunken bawdy song with their arms linked, had staggered on their way; then he slipped into the brick-floored passage that ran along one side of the house.

It was very dark and a little slimy underfoot: he slipped, banging his elbow painfully against the wall in trying to keep his feet. He should have refused Mr Bassett's nightcap, a powerful glass of shrub. With tingling care he went forward. Ahead there was a smear of light in the yard, revealing the shapes of water-butts, a stack of firewood, the haphazard roofs of outhouses, some belonging to this house, some to the adjoining one: here behind the facades you could see the jumble that was the old medieval city of Bath, before the new architects had laid down their smooth lines. The light came from a latticed ground-floor window, projecting out: Mrs Jessop's private room, no doubt. Was she waiting up for the same purpose? It might not be: somehow he couldn't imagine that sturdy tireless woman ever going to sleep at all. Fairfax inched forward until he was just at the mouth of the brick passage. There was a bad smell from a privy here, and his right foot was in a puddle that he hoped was rain not drain. Well, he would wait a little while: probably it was pointless . . .

Then, a footstep behind him – something nudged him in the back – a grunt of surprise. Fairfax wheeled round and looked for a moment into the unmistakable, startled face of the man from America.

But before Fairfax could recover from his surprise, the man was running back down the passage with remarkable swiftness. Fairfax urged his stunned limbs into action. Halfway down the passage his feet slithered in dampness again, and this time there was no stopping his fall. He fell with shattering impact on his behind.

For several moments he could only groan and curse, until

a hand touching his shoulder made him gasp again.

'Mr Fairfax.' A woman's voice, speaking in a tone of mild reproach. 'Really, I had supposed you might be more expert at this kind of thing. Was it him? Well, I dare say he has gone now; and with no moon, and so many courts and alleys hereabouts, and you so unsteady on your feet, there is not much use in trying to pursue him. Here – can you stand?'

Caroline Delabole put a firm hand under his arm, and helped him to his feet.

'Miss Delabole – what are you doing here?'

'Well, as I live here, and you don't, I might with more propriety ask that question of you. But leaving that aside, I imagine we are both on the same errand. I was on the look-out for this nocturnal visitor of ours. If you weren't, and were intending burglary instead, I think I'd rather not know. But come, are you hurt?'

'Shaken,' he said, easing his back, 'but all right, funda-mentally.'

'That's a terrible pun,' she said; but he saw her smile, and he was susceptible enough to be pleased at that. The smile was extremely beautiful. 'I had a better vantage than you,' she went on. 'The old coach-house – just there. The perfect place to see him – and tackle him, if need be. Oh, and please don't tell me I shouldn't have been so brave, or foolish, whichever.'

'Well, I can still think it, though in fact I don't believe that man is a danger. At least . . .'

'You know him?'

'I know of him, slightly. But not his name or where he can be found. If I did—'

'You would seek him out, of course, because like me you think it very odd that he is about, just when my father has been killed. Yes, I can speak of it. Well, at least we know that, like Hamlet's father's ghost, he reappears: but I wish we could have done a Horatio and spoken to him.' She was wearing a shawl, and now she shivered and wound it tighter around her. 'A damp night – and not very sweet here. Come, let's step into the coach-house.'

'Will Mrs Jessop not see?' he said, with a glance at the lighted window.

'Only if we cross the yard. Step round this way – follow me – and do try to stay upright, Mr Fairfax.'

He followed her, carefully, to a low door in a stone wall that he would never have spotted. Inside, there was a musty smell, great hanks of cobwebs, heaps of lumber, and a scuttering sound that was surely rats; but thankfully she had placed a burning candle on a shelf.

'A pity, isn't it? Grandfather did keep a modest carriage once, but he gave it up. He said it was a piece of vain extravagance and affectation.' Her voice was tart but she had turned to inspect the candle-wick and he could not see her face. 'Mrs Jessop, by the by, would not make trouble even if she did see. She is really an excellent creature, though she seems so fearfully severe . . . Who do you think that man is, Mr Fairfax?'

'I can't say.'

'You are being very careful. Quite rightly. But you have your suspicions of him, as I do, else you would not have been *lurking* here. Unless you had some other aim in view?' The look she gave him, turning from the candle, was not quite flirtatious, but almost. 'I also have my suspicions, Mr Fairfax. About everything that is going on around me. Ah, look!'

Amongst the piles of lumber she pointed to a little child's walking-frame of walnut, wheels still intact.

'I learned to walk in that. There is even a rather bad portrait of my infant self tottering about in it – put away somewhere, thank heaven. Not thrown away. Nothing ever is here. See all this rubbish: it is the accumulation of my years. Old toys and spelling-primers and birdcages and frocks . . . You'd think they might be given away, wouldn't you? But Grandfather doesn't do that. We keep the past, here: the past is our household god. And yet the curious thing is we never speak of it at all!'

In the silence and the fitful candlelight the heaps of lumber gave a faintly sinister impression. Fairfax averted his eyes from the mutilated face of a cloth doll and said: 'You spoke of your suspicions, Miss Delabole.'

'I did, and they are unworthy ones, I am afraid. You will not think well of me for them. Now why that should matter I don't know, but it does. I believe people are great hypocrites when they say they don't care what others think of them. Now you, for instance, probably think me rather spoiled. Well, I won't deny it, but I will say I think it's unfair when *spoiled* is used as a reproach. Being spoiled is not something you choose: it's something that's done to you. As well reproach someone for being beaten or bullied.'

'Perhaps so. There is the question of collusion, though.'

'You mean if care and attention is lavished on someone, they should say "No, no, stop indulging me, it's not good for me"? You have an optimistic view of human nature, Mr Fairfax.'

'On the contrary, I have a pessimistic view of human nature.'

She studied him, half-smiling. The sculptural quality of her beauty was emphasized by the candlelight: her neck and throat were soft curving shadows, whilst the clear planes of her brow and cheekbone stood out in glowing relief. 'Because of . . .?'

'Because of – experience.'

'Your experience – or experiences – must have been sad indeed, to give you such a bleak outlook, for you are not very old.' She lifted her arms to rearrange her shawl, and for a moment its winged shape blotted out the light and seemed about to enfold him.

'I would not say bleak. More a matter of always expecting the flaws in human nature to reveal themselves.'

'Original sin?'

'Perhaps. Candidly I have always thought that notion a piece of seminarian's chop-logic. The darkness at the heart of mankind is something altogether more puzzling. It is common to talk of the madness of love: but it often seems to me that self-love is the greatest passion. And just as with the other kind, people will cheat and lie and manipulate and even kill for the sake of it.'

'*All* people?'

'No. But I believe the capacity is always there. Like . . . like the reformed drunkard, who knows that he only has to taste one glass to be lost. So you see: I am not likely to think ill of you, Miss Delabole.'

'Very well. But you are in the business of proof and evidence, Mr Fairfax, and all I have are intuitions. You may well detect the flavour of sour grapes in them, too. But come, you have probably thought this already: that my father's death suits my grandfather and Mr Pinner very well. There! Not so bad, is it?'

'You speak of some – connivance between the two of them?'

'Oh, if I do, I speak only of what has been going on for

years. My grandfather has long approved of Mr Pinner in every way, you know. He treats him like a relative and I think it is the dearest wish of his heart that he should actually *become* one. By marriage at any rate. Oh, that is quite plain. As for Mr Pinner – well, suffice it to say that I think he would do anything for my grandfather. His feeling for me I should not speak of. A woman is supposed to be modestly oblivious of such things.'

'You say it suits them very well that your father—'

'Well, of course it does. Grandfather could certainly never forgive him in any case. And as for my joining him in London, and being taken into society by him, and being set up with an independent fortune – well, Mr Pinner would not like that. He is a sincere man, I suppose, even a thoughtful one. But his mind . . . moves along very narrow paths, let us say.'

Fairfax hesitated. 'These intuitions—'

'Have no grounding in proof. But they make sense, wouldn't you say? As I waited here I was trying to fit them to this strange man with the hook. All I could come up with was: accomplice of some sort. Perhaps he was the one who procured the poison—'

'Perhaps, but there would hardly be any need for such a complication. Why employ a third party, adding to the risk of exposure, just to procure something that is freely available in any medicine-chest or druggist's shop?'

Her smile glinted at him. 'You can see I am new at this. Very well – perhaps he is a party to their secret in some way. And threatens them with it. There must be a reason for his haunting our house like this.'

'Very true . . . But you must be in some difficulty, Miss Delabole – living at home and entertaining such suspicions. How do you—'

'Oh, there is no very agreeable atmosphere between Grandfather and myself just now. And of course, he has his suspicions of me in turn.'

'Of you . . .?'

She was silent and still for a moment: then the smile glinted again. 'Of course. He thinks I pine for my lost prospects. For riches and grandeur, snatched from my grasp.'

'Do you?'

'What an impertinent question. But no, a very pertinent one, of course. What do you suppose, Mr Fairfax? Did I want my father's fortune? Or put it another way – do you think I did *not* want to be made a wealthy and independent woman, able to do everything I wanted, to drink the cup of life to the full? Do you think me a plaster saint – or flesh and blood? Which is this, do you think?' She took his hand, and placed it on the warm skin of her forearm.

'That is – there is no doubt of that,' Fairfax said, removing his hand. 'But there is another question. Would your grandfather really seek to deny you that?'

'That depends on just how much he hated my father. Whether he saw anything that came from Sir James Delabole as – as a poisoned chalice. An unhappy comparison, I know. Oh, but there are others who would wish to deny me the inheritance, of course. His family – that is, the ones who considered themselves his *true* family. And who can blame them? Now, you are thinking me a cold-hearted, fortune-hunting minx, to be talking of the inheritance. But one can hardly *not* talk of it. My father – let us be plain – was about to change his will in my favour. Then he was killed. To me, the connection between those two things is so obvious as to be undeniable. Indeed the only question that remains is whether he had already done so.'

'It would appear not,' Fairfax said gently. 'The only extant will is some years old, when your father's only acknowledged family was Lady Delabole and Selina.'

'That is the only will anybody knows about. But I repeat, there are several people who do not want me to inherit. Would they be above taking away a new will, concealing it, destroying it? I doubt it. You, with your pessimistic view of human nature, Mr Fairfax, can surely not doubt it.'

He hesitated. 'Again it is a question of proof . . .'

'Oh, I know. And that I don't have.' She laughed softly. 'Now I am conscious of appearing a rather hysterical creature. Conspired against!' She rolled her eyes in mock melodrama. 'Like some mawkish Richardson heroine. But I fear it is true that everyone thinks they know what is best for me. And that if I were rich, that would somehow be a great evil. Would it? I don't see why. The money is not particularly tainted or ill-got. Most money surely is as ill-got. It comes from someone's death – or from someone's bitter labour, or self-denial, or hoarding, or from buying cheap and selling dear, or gouging holes in the earth. If it is an evil, then I see no way of making it good.' Her voice, which had taken on a harsh edge, softened as she said, 'Well, Mr Fairfax? Am I mercenary?'

'I suppose that is tangled up with another question,' Fairfax said. 'What did you really think of your father?'

She took a deep breath. 'I hardly knew him.'

'Perhaps. And yet your whole life was shaped by him: what he did, what he didn't do.'

Caroline picked up the candle and stared into the flame: he saw the pupils of her eyes shrink like a cat's.

'I have led a sheltered life,' she said. 'But I have learned enough not to expect perfection in anyone. My father . . . fell short. At the last, it seems, he was trying to make it up to me.

But that – that was not to be. Perhaps it might have been better if he never came back.' The candle guttered, and she blinked. 'This light is nearly spent, Mr Fairfax. I'm going in. You had better go too, unless you want to stay here in the dark.'

He followed her out of the coach-house. Mrs Jessop's window, he saw now, was dark. He had a feeling of terrible furtiveness, as if the single touch on Caroline Delabole's bare arm had been something far more intimate; and from the way she glanced back at him, he felt she knew it. He tried to be brisk.

'A great pity – that stranger giving us the slip,' he said. 'Of course, there's probably an innocent explanation. But if you should see him again, Miss Delabole—'

'I shall let you know, Mr Fairfax, never fear. I am wide awake, in every sense. You have given me the taste for it. And if I do not look out for myself, who will?'

Eleven

Fairfax, when he lay down that night, was afraid that he
would be wide awake too. Instead he slipped almost at once
into a deep though not very refreshing sleep. He dreamed of
Caroline Delabole – perhaps unsurprisingly, as she had
thoroughly disturbed his equilibrium – and also of her dead
twin Maria, buried in that lonely grave in Calais. He found
himself in Edmund Pinner's place, kneeling at the gravestone,
running his fingers along the incised letters; and then a hand
fell on his shoulder, and a voice said that he was under arrest.
Jumping up, he found that the hand was a hook, and the man
from America had hold of him, while Mrs Jessop with tightly
folded arms stood by and watched with seeming satisfaction.

All nonsense, though: he regarded dreams as merely the
mind's idle trifling with the detritus of the day, and they had
never furnished him with any sort of decisive insight. Still, as
he shaved and dressed, he found that the man from America
was at the centre of his thoughts. He was the one person who
had not given an account of himself, and the one person he
could not get hold of. What a cursed blockhead he was,
losing his footing in that passage! The man was still in Bath,
that was certain – but that wasn't much help. Bath wasn't
London, where a man could disappear into its immensity

like a phantom, but neither was it a country village. It was a busy city packed to the rafters with an ever-changing population and the man he sought did not even have a name.

Nor was it true that he was the only missing piece. With a sigh Fairfax looked in again at Locke's rooms. The undisturbed disorder struck him with a chill now. He hoped to God there was an innocent explanation for the vanishing of Francis Locke, but it was growing harder to supply one. When he visited Mr Goode today, he would have to emphasize that this absence had gone beyond the circumstantial. Perhaps there would have to be posters after all. 'Missing' – or 'Wanted'?

Fairfax hurried downstairs. The thought of Locke had, at last, given him one useful notion.

Locke had talked about needing a bone-setter; when he went to buy Macleod's charcoal, Fairfax had come across one – and, coming out of the bone-setter's premises, the man from America. Unpromising, but it was the only link he had.

He found the door above the milliner's in Green Street, with its little faded sign, *Samuel Fry Gentlemen's Tailoring. Bones set here*, without trouble. He had a little more trouble locating Samuel Fry himself. Someone called out 'Yes, sir?' when he went in, but all he could see were endless coats, waistcoats, and breeches, in various states of finish, suspended from the ceiling on hooks and festooned over every surface. When the voice said 'Sir?' again, he followed it, and at last discovered the tailor behind a thicket of broadcloth, bent over his bench in a window-alcove.

'How can I serve, sir?' Samuel Fry was a short fat man in bob-wig and spectacles, with a little squeezed moist voice. Removing some pins from his mouth, he ran a respectful but professional eye over Fairfax's figure.

'You are Mr Fry the bone-setter?'

'I'm blessed with that skill, along of my trade,' Mr Fry said, jumping up and eyeing Fairfax afresh. 'I don't claim to be a medical man, sir: not a bit of it – I'm not a surgeon nor a 'pothecary. But I'm not a mountebank neither. I have a touch, an ability, and I've got testimonials to that effect, should you care to see 'em. Now, sir, where's the trouble, and has it been set afore?'

'I'm sorry, I should explain. I am acting for Mr Goode, the magistrate. Oh, nothing to worry about, I assure you: I am just trying to trace a man we need to speak to, a man who I believe came here two days since.'

'Oh? Well, I've an extensive custom,' the tailor said, scratching under his wig. 'You can see, sir, from their bodies a-hanging up, as you might say.'

'Indeed. You might recall this man, though. A stout man in middle age, with an iron hook in place of his left hand.'

'A hook? Yes, yes, I have him. I asked him about the injury, as it happens. Hand crushed by a cart-axle, he said, some years since. I just wondered, you know, whether it might have been saved, with the right skill. These surgeons are devilish quick to resort to the saw, to my mind. I knew a corn-chandler once, broke his great toe in a rat-hole – they had his leg off below the knee before he knew it. Not that the fellow with the hook had aught to gain, mind, 'twas shutting the stable door after the horse has bolted, but it was my professional curiosity, as you might say.'

'He came to you for tailoring, then?'

'Not that neither,' Mr Fry said, to his disappointment. 'He was looking for someone, and he'd seen my sign, and he wondered if I might know him. I couldn't be a deal of help to him there either, short of pointing him to the churchyard, for the man's been dead ten year, I reckon. Not that I could swear to the date, but it's thereabouts—'

'Who? Who was he looking for?'

'Well, another bone-setter. I was a mite put out when he said so, and referred him to my testimonials – but he said 'twas the man he sought, and not his services. The man was a farrier by trade, he said, as well as a bone-setter, and came from London-ways to set up in Bath, mebbe thirteen or fourteen years since. Didn't know his name, only that he had a wife called Sarah. Well, my memory's a touch rusty, but it moves smooth enough once it's set going, and I brought him to mind sure enough. A holy praying-feast sort of a fellow, but well thought on: I liked him. He used to refer his custom to me, when his strength went and he started to fail, which was good in him. But then he'd never been blessed with children, as he said, so there was no one to carry on the trade. Jessop was his name, Tate Jessop: lived somewhere around Corn Street. But as I say, he's long dead and buried; and I was sorry to be telling this here fellow, if he'd expected otherwise. Though the widow was still about, I reckoned: last I heard, she went into service with an old wine-merchant. Close-fisted old gent, been retired here for years – damn me, I had his name to mind just t'other day, but it's gone again—'

'Gilbert Tiverton.'

'You've got him.' Mr Fry took off his spectacles and polished them: his eyes, no less keen, quizzically on Fairfax. 'And so you've come from the magistrate, sir? Well, well, I don't know what it's about, but I hope I never spoke out of turn to that man. 'Twas only common information he asked about, and quite civil-like. I didn't imagine I was doing aught wrong—'

'No, nothing like that. Was that all he wanted to know, Mr Fry?'

'Well, that was all I could tell him; and he didn't say what he was after particular. I did mention again that if he needed a good tailor or a bone-setter, he knew where to find me; but he only smiled absent-minded like, and went on his way.' Mr Fry replaced his spectacles and began threading a needle. 'I still think it's a pity about that hook. A man with a hook can make shift to do some things, but there's others he can't do at all, not without hurting himself something wicked.'

'He didn't say his name, or where he was to be found?'

'Not likely to, sir, as there was nothing wanted.'

'I see . . .' Damn it, he was no closer. At least, no closer physically to the man from America: though he seemed to have drawn nearer to the heart of the mystery, even moving through a fog as he was. 'Thank you, Mr Fry, you've been very obliging. Stay – there is something else: you have seen nothing of a young officer – tall, fair, regimental dress – name of Locke?'

Mr Fry sucked his teeth. 'No. I'd remember that, I think. Should I know him?'

'Oh . . . he's someone else we're trying to trace. He mentioned once that he was looking for a bone-setter.'

'Another one.' Mr Fry chuckled and bit his thread with little sharp teeth. 'And was *he* looking for me, or for another bone-setter altogether, I wonder?'

Exactly the right question, Fairfax thought, thanking the tailor and making his way out through the forest of garments.

The man from America was looking for a farrier and bone-setter from London: a man, it turned out, named Jessop. Whose widow was Sarah Jessop. And indeed, hadn't Mrs Jessop spoken of her late husband, at Mr Tiverton's dinner, as a farrier – and a man who did a great deal of good for folk besides? It was not uncommon, as Mr Bassett had mentioned last night, for those trades to be combined, horse-doctors seeming to have a way with human aches and pains, more trusted sometimes than the grand prescriptions of physicians. That, then, must be the explanation, or partial explanation, of why the American was seen about Mr Tiverton's house.

And as for Locke . . . he had been looking for a bone-setter in Bath, and yet he seemed fit as a fiddle. Had he been trying to trace this Jessop too, knowing his occupation but not his name? But if so, what was there about this Jessop that made people anxious to trace him? A farrier, a Methodist, a respectable tradesman according to Mr Tiverton – nothing very striking there. Or was it not Jessop, but his widow they were seeking out? Again, there seemed no obvious reason why.

Well, he had a link between Mrs Jessop, the man from America, and Ensign Locke. Very neat, and yet making no sense that he could see.

And yet, Locke had been in the American colonies too. He had fought and been wounded there during the late wars. So that was a link. Fairfax found his mind returning, as the tongue probes at a troublesome tooth, to his notion of the American as a felon returned from transportation. Even as Mrs Jessop's husband, not dead but called so by his shamed wife. Suppose he was trying to trace his wife, having come illegally to these shores. Suppose he was asking around after her, and that had been his purpose at Samuel Fry's . . . Yet if he was none other than Tate Jessop, wouldn't Mr Fry have recognized him? Possibly not – Mr Fry had said he knew *of* him, but it might have been only an acquaintance between fellow-townsmen, and ten years could change a man. But it was tenuous, Fairfax admitted to himself . . . and besides, if a man with a respectable reputation like Tate Jessop had been transported for felony, wouldn't that have been common knowledge, scandal even?

It was tenuous, depressingly so. A voice murmured to Fairfax that this whole notion of transportation might be one of those false assumptions that had led him astray before. Not every American was a transported felon, after all, though it was a common anti-colonial sneer to call them so. And yet he just couldn't let it go, especially now it had occurred to him that Locke had been in America too. Suppose Locke had encountered the man with the hook during his service in America – and then, just lately, had spotted him in Bath? And had been digging around for information about him – perhaps with the idea of betraying him to the authorities? Years ago Jonathan Wild, the king of the criminal underworld, had augmented his income by regularly turning in returned transportees for the reward money . . . And where did that leave Mrs Jessop? If she knew who the man with the hook was, she was certainly keeping quiet about it. Probably it would jeopardize her situation at Mr Tiverton's. But then her feelings at seeing the man again might be mixed: there might still be love.

Or fear. For if the man was a felon, what had been his crime? You could be transported for stealing a yard of lace, of course; but the transport ships carried their share of truly vicious brutes as well. Fairfax tried to recover his impression of the man who had helped him with his trunk, who had nonchalantly stood up to the bullying of Sir James . . . If anything, he had seemed rather likeable. Yet his behaviour around Mr Tiverton's house was undoubtedly furtive. If he *was* a dangerous man, and if Francis Locke did have some connection with him, then Locke's disappearance was looking more sinister all the time.

Perhaps he ought to speak of this to Mr Goode. Another set of posters, maybe. 'Wanted: a man with a hook in place of his left hand, from the American colonies. Suspected of all manner of things.' Oh, yes. That was just the thing to bring him out of his burrow. Fairfax felt depressed. He seemed to be straying further and further from the point – the solution of Sir James's murder. Your mind is very productive, Robert, he chided himself, but every egg it lays is addled.

Coming down the dingy stairway, wrapped in his own gloom, he nearly collided with a small boy in livery coming up. He stepped aside and apologized, then looked again. No child after all: he saw the mournful crab-apple face of Nolan, Sir James's abbreviated manservant.

'My fault, sir. Hardly know what I'm about these days.' Nolan resumed his bow-legged progress up the stairs.

'Stay – Mr Nolan – you're going to Samuel Fry's?'

'So I am, sir; and I hope he's in, only knowing my luck he won't be.'

'Is it a bone-setter you're after?' Fairfax asked him, thinking: another one? Not that any bone-setter could do much with poor Nolan's wizened frame, short of dislocating everything and starting all over again.

'Eh? No, it's a little tailoring job I want, sir. Just for my own self. Mourning-bands for my old master. Only for my own self, like I say, so I'd be obliged if you'd not mention it, sir. Mebbe they'll have the servants properly measured for mourning some time, but there's no sign of it yet – nor of a funeral; so I'll be respectful out of my own pocket for now.'

'The funeral is not settled?'

'No – there's some talk of carrying my poor master back

to his place in Hampshire and laying him to rest there. But it depends if the coroner says yes, or some such. And 'tis only talk: no one's concerned overmuch with it, sir, nor any fitting respectful things, if you ask me. I know I shouldn't say it.'

'You needn't fear that anything you say will be passed on, believe me,' Fairfax said. 'You look fagged. Come, sit down a moment.'

'Well, mebbe I will. I'm not the man I was.' Nolan sat down on the stairs with a sigh. 'There's a lot of things I don't understand, I dare say. But it don't seem right to me. I was a soldier, sir, and soldiers are a rough and ready set, as a rule; dying's part of their trade, as you might say. But they respect it: oh, yes. I've seen the toughest, cursingest corporal kneel down a moment on the battlefield, and say a few words over a dying comrade, though the shot was whistling round his ears. The words weren't the proper ones, mebbe, compared to what a parson would know; and a few minutes later he was cursing and firing away again, no doubt, like any sinner. But there was a duty to be paid, even if 'twas only a silent thought, and every soldier knew that, because it was a man dead and a life gone. And if a parcel of raggle-tag soldiers know it, I don't see why gentlefolks can't.'

'You mean there is no . . . grieving, at your house?'

'Mebbe there is. But what seems to occupy 'em most is calculating, sir, calculating and planning and bickering – like a pack of crows over a poor slaughtered lamb. And that don't seem right.'

'I see,' Fairfax said, trying and failing to accept the image of Sir James Delabole as a lamb. 'When you say bickering – are Lady Delabole and Miss Selina falling out, then? I thought—'

'Oh, not they. They're fond enough. But now there's this

other one. "The new one", I still call her, though of course she was master's first-born; but no call to go putting her oar in the boat, if you ask me.'

'Caroline.'

'Aye, that one. Mind, I've naught against her: master wanted to make up with her, and I know he was mighty pleased with what he found, and if he was happy then that was good enough for me. But she's hoisted her flag this morning, no mistake; and though it's none of my affair, I didn't like the colour of it.'

'You have seen Caroline Delabole this morning?'

'Came calling early. Well, naught wrong in that, of course: a call to pay her respects, as it seemed, for she is family after all, and the mistress received her very kindly on account of it. Then she wants to know about the arrangements – which ain't very forward, as I said – and it turns out it's not just the burying she's talking about. She wants to know what's to do with the master's will. Oh, all very smooth and calm she was: I know because I was, well, I was doing something in the hall, and couldn't help hearing. But cool and plain as you like. She'd been given to understand that Sir James was going to settle his property on her, she says, and if it ain't the case, she wants to know why. Well, mistress can be cool too, and she says she don't know nothing about that. Master made his arrangements years ago, she says, and that's the way it stands. Well! "The new one" – Caroline I mean – says she don't believe that, if you please: says she's afraid there may be something crafty afoot to cut her out of her dues, and if there is, she'll nail it. Her grandfather has a very good lawyer, she says, and they ain't going to let it rest: come what may, she's the master's eldest child, and any amount of people can testify that he meant to do something handsome for her.

Well, I could tell the mistress was struck dumb; but she spoke up at last, *very* high, but a mite shaky too, and said was she being accused of hiding anything, like a will? Caroline says she's not accusing anyone of anything – didn't sound like that to me, mind – but there was something not right. And if it turns out she don't inherit, she says, then it will not be uncontested. Those were her words, sir: cool enough to shave a Jew. And such a young 'un, too! I heard Miss Selina call out: she said something about Caroline being a jealous cat, and dangling after what was rightfully hers, and such – things I regretted, really, from a young lady's lips, and to a sister and all, but then Miss Selina's always been a passionate creetur. It didn't seem to bother "the new one" though: I'll swear she just laughed, and then she took her leave, sweet as if they'd talked of naught but new bonnets.' Nolan put his head in his hands. 'I'm a goose to let it trouble me, no doubt. But it did – thinking of the master laid out upstairs, and downstairs such hard-faced goings on . . .' He looked at Fairfax in puckered appeal. 'A man put out of the world should leave – well, more of a gap behind him, shouldn't he, sir?'

It seemed to Fairfax that Sir James Delabole had left quite a sizeable gap – and one, moreover, that teemed with darkness. But he knew what Nolan meant, and said so.

'Thank ye, sir: I'm glad to have got it off my chest. No, no – I can manage.' Nolan got up, a complex and laborious process. 'I'm spry, thank the Lord . . . Of course, what would settle it for me – make the pack lighter, at any rate – would be if we knew who did it.' His eyebrows wrinkled like a hound's in hope as he looked at Fairfax. 'Is there any hint yet, sir . . .?'

What could he say? He mumbled that enquiries were in

hand, or something of that sort. But it was with a burning consciousness that he did *not* know that Fairfax went out into the street. He had a lot of tantalizing shards and fragments, but they seemed strangely assorted; and for all he knew they might never fit together to make a whole vessel. It had taken that direct question from Nolan to bring home to him just how lost and baffled he was. He felt gloomier than ever. Gloomy enough for his ears to prick up at the clank of tankards from an inn-room across the street. He wrestled the temptation down after a minute, but it was a close fight.

It wasn't just his failure, of course. What he had heard about Caroline's behaviour had affected him. More than it ought, he told himself; but he couldn't help it.

It was because of last night. And that was another absurdity – there was no 'last night', not in any sense that anyone would think important. If that meeting in the old coach-house had made any impression on his heart, then his heart was ridiculously impressionable. Even if he could claim to himself that Caroline had flirted with him, then that meant nothing much – nothing except that she must have done it for a reason. And as he was investigating a murder for which she was one of the suspects, that must be a highly dubious reason. Instead of warming to her, he ought to be on his guard.

Yes: he knew all that. But he had felt something all the same. Perhaps an echo of what he had felt when Locke had made friends with him: a kind of flattered gratification that someone who was young, good-looking, and fully in the *stream* of life as he was not, should nevertheless find something in him that was sympathetic.

He thought about that for a moment, looking at his pale reflection in the milliner's window, sober now rather than gloomy. This self-revelation was not a happy one – but nor was it unfruitful. If he wasn't in the stream of life, wasn't that as much because he had wilfully stepped out of it, as a comment on his prospects? He was healthy, educated, and not wholly without useful reputation: he could always get by. But since the loss of Cordelia, he had seen the world as one great extinguisher of hope, lowering over him. So, churlish and piqued, he had withdrawn from it – taking a bottle with him, of course. It was because he held himself bitterly aloof from human sympathies that he had experienced that extra-ordinary initial reaction to Sir James's murder – a sour questioning of morality, a brutish *Who cares?* And for the same reason, the touch of a hand and the glint of a smile in candlelight had this exaggerated effect on him, throwing him off balance, distorting his precious reason.

I must change, he told himself. It was not a resolution but an acknowledgement.

But, even purged of its adolescent glow, he found his disappointment with Caroline real enough. He didn't like to think of that intelligent and cultivated young woman as a money-grabber after all. But then wasn't that close to sentimentality, like Nolan's maunderings about soldiers on the battlefield? (From what Fairfax had heard, the usual reason for a soldier to kneel by a dead comrade was to rifle his pockets.) She had been apparently offered a fortune, and then seen it snatched away. In highly suspicious circum-stances, indeed. It might well be that Caroline was pursuing some subtle plan of her own to uncover the truth, and that challenging the Delaboles was part of it. Certainly she seemed to have her suspicions about another will. That, alas, was a chimera: he had discovered as much from Pinner yesterday.

And yet . . . The mysterious paper was accounted for now; but that didn't necessarily mean there *wasn't* another will, somewhere. Was Caroline actually on the right track – and even perhaps far ahead of him?

He preferred to think that, even now.

But how was he to catch her up? First, he supposed, he should see Lady Delabole and Selina, and judge for himself how ruffled their feathers were. He would be interested to know, also, whether Lady Delabole had known about Caroline's unfortunate twin, interred in that Calais graveyard. Obviously she had no illusions about Sir James's character; but that pathetic death somehow made the colonel's past history even more unsavoury. He wondered if Lady Delabole had ever feared that her husband would abandon her and Selina, as he had his first wife and their children.

But then, in a way, that *was* what he was doing in cleaving so ardently to Caroline these past weeks. Abandoning them: heartlessly leaving them behind. He hadn't thought of it in those terms before, but now that he did it struck him forcibly. Sir James had destroyed Lydia Tiverton's life that way. If Lady Delabole had decided to stop it happening again, in the surest way possible, then . . . Well, he wouldn't say he couldn't blame her, but he could understand her. If Lydia's ghost were looking on, she would surely understand too.

Lady Delabole . . . His pulse beat faster as he realized that she was perfectly placed to answer that other nagging question: the whereabouts of the paper that Pinner had tried to retrieve. A paper bearing the inscription from the grave of Maria Delabole, Caroline's twin. Suppose Sir James had never told her about that; and suppose, going into his study that morning after he had left, she had found the paper. What would she think? Well, if she knew nothing of the twins, she might well come to the same erroneous conclusion as Pinner had – that Caroline must be an impostor. But if she thought that, then there was no apparent reason for her to murder her husband: the paper would destroy Caroline's claim on him anyway. No good.

Very well, suppose she did know about the twins, and saw that paper. It would not be news to her; but it might be a cold and timely reminder of what her husband had done in the past. The spur that pricked her to action. Of course, in order to have put the poison in his cane, she must have found the paper before he left the house. That was possible, though. Sir James hadn't gone out directly after his interview with Pinner. For one thing, he had come down and discovered Selina in a compromising position with Ensign Locke; after which there had been a row; after which, Fairfax recalled from Nolan's first account, Sir James had gone down to the servants' quarters and given them a roasting about letting Locke into the house. Yes, opportunity then for Lady Delabole to have put in the poison. And as for the paper – well, perhaps she was keeping it to herself, or had burnt it.

All unproven. But it was a relief to hit on something plausible at last, and he set off up Milsom Street with a spring in his step – until a voice called his name.

Dodging horse-puddles, Fairfax made his way over to Mr Goode's carriage, out of which Mr Goode's birdlike head was poking.

'Sir. I called last evening, and received your message,' Fairfax said; but Mr Goode, he found, was not looking at him, though he had definitely called his name. The magistrate was directing an urbane smile over Fairfax's shoulder.

'Lord Tregowan! How do you do, sir! I heard the Abbey bells this morning – that must have been your arrival. Do you find yourself well, sir? And Lady Tregowan? Dear me. Dear me, I did not know. My condolences, sir. Oh – oh, to be the new Lady Tregowan? Oh, my congratulations – I'm honoured, ma'am. Ha ha, yes, as you say, Lord Tregowan, why wait indeed? Yes – I will not detain you – delighted to welcome you to Bath again – I hope to have the honour of seeing you in the Pump Room anon. Good day, good day . . .'

Fairfax waited, impatiently enough, for the magistrate to finish toadying across the street. He took the disappearance of the smile as the signal, and stepped up into the coach.

'My apologies, Mr Fairfax, but Lord Tregowan – influence at the Treasury, among other things. A widower again – confound it, I should have known about that – dear me, he does have exceeding ill luck with wives.'

'A blessed release for them, I would have thought,' said Fairfax, who had only glanced back at Lord Tregowan, but had seen more of the peer's warty nose, mottled teeth, and dewlapped jowls than he wanted to see on an empty stomach.

'Tut tut, how droll, Mr Fairfax, you are quite the flaming republican. Now, my dear sir, my time is short, as I have calls to make, among other things, but I am glad to have caught you. First, have you made any progress with this extraordinary case?'

'I have,' said Fairfax, a little uneasily, 'though nothing concrete that I may present to you as yet—'

'Well, well, press on: it is, I repeat, an extraordinary case, and I have just seen an instance of it, which is the second thing I wanted to say to you. What think you of this young woman – the one Sir James came here to claim – Miss Caroline Delabole?'

Fairfax hesitated. 'Think of her . . .?'

'Her character, among other things. I know more or less

everyone in Bath, of course. But her grandfather has lived rather retired and she has not been seen much socially. I had supposed her brought up somewhat delicately. But I have just seen her in the Pump Room – promenading publicly on the arm of a young man, dressed very well, all smiles. I confess I was much surprised. I know her acquaintance with her father was short, but still I had thought her more affected, and that the decorum of mourning would at least be observed. Instead she strolls about like any young town miss with her beau – and unchaperoned, I might add. They were most confidential with one another. I can assure you there were looks. Bath, you know, is not Covent Garden. We pride ourselves on our propriety.'

'Who was the young man?'

'His name is Pinner, I believe. The young man who came to Sir James's house on that dreadful day of his death.'

'Good God! Are you sure?'

Mr Goode's sharp nose twitched. 'My dear sir. Being neither blind nor idiotic, I can confidently assert that I'm sure.'

'I'm sorry. I'm just – as surprised as you are.'

'Indeed? Well, you know them better than I. Is there some long-standing attachment, engagement even? One did not suppose so. If not, the exhibition is distasteful at best. At worst . . . well, you tell me. Do you suspect some intrigue in that quarter?'

'I did not. I thought Pinner's suit was one of those hopeless and unrequited ones.'

'Hm! It would appear not.'

'Yes . . . No, rather. It's not that I don't believe your account, Mr Goode. What I can't conceive is . . .' Caroline a bare-faced liar and deceiver? Never mind that. 'Well, if the two of them do have something to hide, why are they so flamboyantly not bothering to hide it? It doesn't make sense.'

Mr Goode shrugged. 'Perhaps they feel they are safe.'

Some extra acerbity in his tone made Fairfax look up sharply.

'What do you mean?'

'Sir James has been dead three days now. No one has been accused or arrested. The murderer – whoever he or she may be – may well feel that he has got away with it. There are no signs that the matter is resolved, and—'

'That doesn't mean it won't be,' Fairfax said shortly.

'My dear sir, I mean no reflection on you, not at all. For my part, I am utterly baffled. And it may well be that our chance has passed: vital evidence may have eluded us, and been lost for ever. Surely with each passing hour the possibility recedes. There are limits to human ingenuity—'

'No, there aren't,' Fairfax said, rapping on the carriage roof. 'That is precisely where you're wrong, sir. And with each passing hour, I grow more determined to bring you Sir James's killer. The Pump Room, I believe you said?'

'Yes,' Mr Goode said, looking at Fairfax rather as if he were a peaceable dog that had suddenly showed its teeth. 'Yes, but that was a while ago. They may have gone—'

'I'll find out,' Fairfax said, stepping down from the carriage before it had finished swaying to a halt. 'Good day, sir.'

I'll find out, he thought, heading at a trot for the Pump Room. I'll find out what every one of these damned cagey, slippery-tongued set of people are hiding from me. I'm not blind or idiotic either.

Though it was past noon now, the Pump Room was still crowded. Fairfax threaded his way through, but the stately passing and repassing of the throngs of people made his head spin. Finding himself by an empty bench near the bar, he stood up on it and scanned the sea of powdered, curled and beribboned heads. Faces turned to look at him in surprise – including that of the Master of Ceremonies, whose displeasure at this breach of decorum was plain – but there was no sign of Caroline or Pinner.

He got down and got out. They must have left. Perhaps, like many others, they had gone on to promenade in Harrison's Walk or Spring Gardens or Kingsmead Fields . . . Well, he didn't intend haring about like a lunatic on the chance of finding them. He didn't doubt Mr Goode's account, anyhow, even though the magistrate's insinuations had touched a raw spot. Pinner was in Bath, and Caroline was content to be seen with him in the most compromising way.

And someone was being deceived, that was for sure. The only question was who.

In the meantime, he had a call to make.

He was not the only visitor at the Delabole house. In the drawing-room a well-fed clergyman was just taking his leave of Lady Delabole. Half a muffin remained on a large plate, with an empty wine-glass, by his seat. The clergyman bowed low over Lady Delabole's hand, casting a sidelong glance of regret at the half a muffin. Coming away, he gave Fairfax a look as if he knew him to be a very bad man, but forgave him.

'Lady Delabole. I hope I haven't interrupted.'

'No, sir. I have had a long talk with the reverend gentleman. I have felt the lack of spiritual consolation, keenly. It has refreshed and restored me.'

Fairfax was going to say the parson looked pretty well

refreshed and restored too, but didn't. He saw that being satirical wouldn't do: to his surprise, Lady Delabole was devout.

'You have certainly not lacked visitors, I think.'

'People have continued to be very kind,' Lady Delabole said, extending a boneless arm to pull the bell-cord.

'But not all.'

'Oh. You have heard. I wonder how. From a servant again? You really seem to prefer speaking to them, Mr Fairfax: it's most odd.'

'Servants are people, are they not?' he said, irritated. He made a gesture at the door where the parson had left. 'They have souls, surely, for a start.'

She looked at him frostily. 'We have always treated our servants very well, Mr Fairfax.'

That wasn't his point, but the fact that she missed it revealed a great gulf between them, quite as much as the religion. A footman came in to clear the plate and glass, and Lady Delabole thanked him in a loud voice. It made him jump.

'I heard that Caroline came to see you early this morning,' Fairfax said. 'A bare account. But it seemed not a happy meeting.'

'It was not. Yes, she came, and spoke to us in such a manner as . . . Well. In a way I'm almost relieved. She has revealed herself and we know where we stand. Before, I did feel a certain obligation to the girl.'

'Obligation?'

'As my husband's child, of course. I can hardly say step-daughter, in the unusual circumstances. But yes, an obliga-tion . . . in view of her unhappy history. She had some grounds – some – for feeling that she, or her mother at least, had been ill-used. I couldn't help that, of course; but being married to James, and sharing his life, I could not be indifferent to it.'

He hadn't heard her use her husband's name before. It had an effect of subtly shifting ground.

'When you married him, Lady Delabole, you were aware of this – unhappy history?'

'It was common talk. And common talk, as it usually does, had distorted it.'

'In what way?'

'Come, Mr Fairfax. If my husband was a mere villain without conscience, do you think I would have married him? He was not proud of what had happened with his first marriage. You have heard him yourself trying to brazen it out; but in private, it was a subject he could not speak of without pain and regret.'

'Did he speak of it often?'

'No. Nor did I press him to. But we were never less than utterly confidential together, Mr Fairfax. You look as if you don't believe me.'

'Not at all. But this unhappy history of Caroline's birth – as it happens, I have discovered more about it than I guessed. And I wondered—'

'Yes? Come, out with it. If it is something I know, then no harm done. If it isn't, then I ought to, as his wife. His widow.'

He studied her. 'Caroline was not Lydia's only child.'

'No. Is that it? I can tell you the rest, Mr Fairfax, if you are unsure. Lydia gave birth to twins. One died before she could return to England, and was buried at Calais. James went to see the grave a little while after, and had a headstone raised. Yes, he told me, when we were first married. He wept, as I remember; and we never spoke of it after. Not amongst ourselves, and not to Selina, certainly. It is horribly sad, is it not? But then the whole tale is horribly sad. It made me a little angry also.'

'With your husband?'

'No. He never pretended that his first marriage was anything but a mistake and a – a damned mess, in his words. But I felt a little angry with Lydia's father – Mr Tiverton. He must bear a good deal of the blame, I think, for those tragic mischances. He was so stubborn. He refused to be reconciled with his daughter because she had gone and married James; and he refused her help even after they had separated. That is a proud, malicious sort of stubbornness, I think. Even when she had made her way back to England, with her surviving baby, he would not extend the hand of forgiveness. She lodged in London for some time, in quite severe poverty, before he relented and came to her, and took her home. You are about to say, James did not help either. But he had stayed in France, and did not know the extent of it. He and Lydia had, besides, bitterly quarrelled. And at that time James had no money. Mr Tiverton did. But he was determined to punish. When he did finally take her in, you know, Lydia did not survive above a year. It's my belief that the privations of that time in London broke her health – and Mr Tiverton could have stopped those.'

'I see.' Well, this was Sir James's self-justifying version, no doubt. But what interested him was something behind the words, like a gleam in a dark place. There were many kinds of love; and whatever kind this was, fleeting or lasting, clouded or untroubled, he could not deny its authenticity. Lady Delabole had loved her husband. 'And . . . no one else knew of the twin who died?'

'I think not. Certainly not the servants, Mr Fairfax,' she

said with a wry look, 'so I cannot help but wonder how you came to hear of it.'

He hesitated only a moment: already he had radically revised his thoughts, and a new idea had seized him. 'Mr Pinner,' he said. 'He came upon the grave at Calais. He drew a wrong conclusion about it, as it happens, and supposed that Caroline could not be your husband's daughter; and for reasons of his own tried to challenge him with it. Your husband set him straight.'

'I'm sure he did. So that was the reason for Mr Pinner's call that morning. How very distasteful. Well, I can only ask, Mr Fairfax, that you don't speak of it any more than you need to. I see no need for Selina to know the unhappy tale. She is highly-strung at the best of times.'

'Well, I see no need . . . But you have not been quite frank with me about Selina, Lady Delabole. The row that took place that day was about her, wasn't it?'

'I prefer the word disagreement.'

'You may do, but it was a row nonetheless. Sir James flew into a passion, I gather, excessive even for him. He found Selina and Ensign Locke together. He turned Locke out of the house, forbade him from coming anywhere near it again, and generally made it clear he did not approve of the attachment and never would.' As Lady Delabole did not speak he added, 'You, I think, felt differently.'

'I . . .' She smoothed the dove-grey silk of her gown with long white hands. 'I am very far from approving of rash or headstrong attachments in young people. My watchword would always be caution, prudence. But I have always defended Selina, too: we are close in all things. I was aware of her partiality for Mr Locke. Indeed I knew she was quite in love with him, and it seemed he felt the same: she was certainly happy. Or rather, caught up in that strange, troubled sort of happiness that being in love produces. I winked at their being alone together. Lovers must be at some point. As for my husband . . . he made something of a boon companion of Mr Locke: military men, and all. But yes, it was plain from his reaction that day that he did not approve. Mr Locke has no very great prospects, perhaps, and my husband was a man of great pride in his position. He thought Mr Locke not good enough for her, and said so: I am afraid he called him a fortune-hunter. Well, I supposed Mr Locke quite hardy enough to weather that, but I protested when James spoke cruelly to Selina on the point, and called her a fool and worse. Yes, he was in a passion, as you say, sir, but I would not allow him to be unfair on his daughter. And we had words. A private and domestic matter. You do wrong to make too much of it, Mr Fairfax.'

'You do wrong to treat me like a fool, Lady Delabole. I'm charged with finding your husband's killer; and if you choose to hide things from me, then I can only conclude that you don't want the killer found. Which is odd, at best. There was a violent quarrel over Locke's intimacy with Selina, and a few hours afterwards your husband was dead. Meanwhile Locke has disappeared. And you prate of private and domestic matters! A court of law would tear you apart, ma'am, as well you know.'

At once he was pricked with regret. Not exactly at losing his temper with her – he couldn't help that. But he saw her quail. And he realized that she was a woman used to being browbeaten by a domineering man; and that made him feel bad.

'I – I'm sorry, Mr Fairfax,' she said, in a pitiably shrunken voice, 'I am a very private person. Perhaps it's wrong, I don't know . . . And you must understand we had had disagreements before. I thought this one could be repaired – indeed, I was sure it would be. After Selina had cried a little on my shoulder, I urged her to go up and try to make peace with her father – I thought he had gone back to his study – but he had gone down to the servants to tell them not to let Mr Locke in the house any more, and the next thing I knew he had slammed out of the house and was gone and . . . and that was the last time we saw him alive.' Lady Delabole pressed her hand convulsively to her lips. 'So you see . . . that quarrel could never be made up. But we didn't *know* that then: I had thought we might all be friends again by suppertime . . .'

Fairfax stared. Tears, very Lady-Delabole tears, neat beads of translucence, were falling on her cheeks, and he knew he should be offering a handkerchief. But he was too preoccupied with his sudden discovery. He knew now where the paper had gone.

As if in answer to his thoughts, Selina's breathless voice broke in on them.

'Mama! He's doing it again! He's upsetting you!'

'No, no, my dear,' Lady Delabole said hastily. 'Nothing of the sort. We were only—'

'I know what you were talking about. Locke – I heard his name.' Selina stalked in with a swift rustle and planted herself in front of Fairfax. 'I spoke to you about that in confidence, sir. You are an unfeeling brute to bring it up. And to upset Mama so—'

'Nonsense, my dear, it is no great secret now,' Lady Delabole said dabbing her eyes briskly. 'It's best to have everything open, I'm sure you agree.'

'Oh, I always have – I detest concealment! But—'

'But you concealed something very material from me, and I think from your mother too, Miss Selina,' Fairfax said. 'When you went at your mother's urging to try and make up with your father, the day he was killed, you went into his study, did you not? And you found a paper on his desk. A curious inscription in charcoal-rubbing, commemorating the death of one Maria Delabole in 1744. And you took that paper. Did you think it might be something you might use against your father in some way, for thwarting your romance? Or was it something that seemed to discredit Caroline Delabole? Whatever it was, it was worth getting hold of. Do you still have that paper, Miss Selina?'

For the first time, as she gazed at him, there was no pout of disdain on her lips. They were open in astonishment.

'No,' she breathed. 'Mama—'

'I think you should be truthful, my dear, whatever it is,' Lady Delabole said.

'You don't have the paper, because I surmise you showed it to Locke, and he took it. Isn't that so? I saw you had overshoes on later, and you said you had been for a walk. A walk to meet Locke, somewhere in the town: he made a rendezvous in that note I brought you, yes? You showed him the paper from your father's study. What could it mean? And what did Locke think it meant? Did he come to the same false conclusion as Mr Pinner, who had brought that paper back from France? That Caroline Delabole could not be your father's child?'

'Well – well, yes, that's what I thought it must be. The child had died, it said so, and . . . oh, I don't know: you are trying to trap me!'

'Selina,' Lady Delabole said, 'Papa's first wife had twins. Maria was the one that did not survive infancy. Your papa never spoke of it, because it was an unhappy memory for him and best left in the past. Unfortunately Mr Pinner brought it up, and so . . . Believe me, my dear, it was not a secret: just a memory better left veiled. It could make no difference to us.'

'Oh!' Selina sat down heavily. 'Oh – that poor woman . . . She must have suffered terribly.'

'The sentiment does you credit, Miss Selina,' Fairfax said. 'But tell me, please. Did Locke draw the wrong conclusions also? I think he could not fail to be interested – as you were. Because it seemed a means of severing your father from Caroline – quite rightly, if it were true that she was not his daughter at all. You have made no secret of your dislike for Caroline. As for Locke, he would, of course, be looking out for – your interests.'

'Of course he would – always,' Selina said with a toss of her head. 'And as for that cat – well, it wouldn't have surprised me if she wasn't Papa's true daughter, for she has no more feeling than an iron bedpost. Look at her this morning – coming here so high and mighty and laying down the law—'

'So I understand. But Locke, now – what did he say? Did he propose acting on the evidence of this paper, making it public perhaps – what?'

'No. He said it was all very strange. Important perhaps. And he took the paper away with him. He said I was to trust him and let him take care of it. I did, of course.' Selina produced a glowing defiant storm-tossed look, the kind that had been practised in a mirror. 'I would trust him with anything. I was glad: I didn't care overmuch for the paper or what it meant. Yes, I would be happy to see that cat have her claws thoroughly trimmed: I don't care who knows it. But the thing that mattered to me just then – that mattered in my *heart –*' Selina put her hand emphatically on the place, in case he thought she meant her elbow – 'was Francis. My love for him. It broke me in two to see him turned out of the house. All I cared about was showing him that I would not change. Raging fiery horses would not quell my love for him, let alone this mean prohibition of Papa's.'

Fairfax was distracted for a moment by trying to picture raging fiery horses. 'So . . . so Locke took the paper. What then?'

'Why, then there were – avowals, and embraces, and leave-taking . . . You surely do not need to know about *that*,' Selina said, giving him a look as if he were a lecherous old man.

'I mean, where did he go?'

Selina shrugged. 'He had to go away for a short time. Pressing business elsewhere – I don't know. I didn't care, because I knew the moment would come when I would see him again, and for that the world could go hang. Our mutual flame was unquenchable. We had plighted our troth.'

'Well, you can't argue with troth,' murmured Fairfax, who had never heard a living person say that word before. 'Miss Selina – I don't doubt the sincerity of your feelings. But the fact is, there is still no sign of Locke, and—'

'Ho, what it must be like to know everything!' Selina cried triumphantly. 'Oh, you do divert me, Mr Fairfax. You are so delightfully sure you're right.'

'Mr Locke has been here this forenoon,' Lady Delabole said gently. 'He left us not an hour ago.'

'My God, he's back . . .?' Fairfax put a hand to his head: for a moment he simply felt sapped with relief. It still looked bad for Locke, and he had some hard explaining to do at the very least: but nothing had happened to him, and for that Fairfax was thankful. 'Where the devil has he been?'

'I told you, he had business elsewhere,' Selina said complacently. 'Francis is a man of affairs, you know.'

Fairfax grunted. Ensign Locke was no more a man of affairs than a goldfish in a tub. Unless it was a different kind of affairs . . . but that was a suspicion he would keep to himself.

'So I don't care what you say, Mr Fairfax. It is a terrible thing to say with Papa gone and all, but now that I have seen my Francis's dear face again, I am happy.' Selina certainly looked it. 'Of course, it was a great shock to him, hearing what had happened. He went quite pale.'

'He didn't know of your father's death?'

'Well, of course not: he has been away.'

'Yes . . . But you say he came here – as in, knocked at the door, called openly? Yet he had been strictly forbidden by Sir James to come here again. If he didn't know of your father's passing, how was it that he—'

'Oh, how drearily nit-picking you are! He supposed my father out, perhaps, or perhaps he thought his temper might have cooled by now. *I* don't know. I do know he was prodigiously knocked back by the news. Oh, and most tender and solicitous for our situation, wasn't he, Mama?'

'Mr Locke was very good, certainly.'

'And of course he was more shocked than ever when he heard how that cat was behaving. I do believe, you know, that nothing short of seeing Francis could have lifted my spirits, after what she said this morning.'

'About making a claim for your father's estate?' Fairfax said. 'Tactless, indeed. And yet, Miss Selina, I had not supposed you covetous of worldly things. This is only a matter of money, after all.'

'Oh, I see she has fixed her claws into you, Mr Fairfax.

Have a care, that's all I can say,' Selina said loftily. 'She flings herself at men's heads: that's her way. I taxed her with it this morning. I had seen her, at Mr Tiverton's dinner, trying to snare Francis. Oh, the look she gave me this morning, when I faced her with it! She didn't like being caught out in her little game. But there, I know a heartless self-seeking flirt when I see one. I told Francis. We could only laugh at the poor creature. Mind, he was truly concerned at these envious schemes of hers. He does have our interests at heart, Mr Fairfax, whether you believe it or not. He urged us to be on our guard. Even if Papa's will was quite clear in our favour, he said, there could be legal challenges. Especially if a sharp lawyer was brought in – and no doubt that cat's grandfather could manage that. "Be on our guard", Francis said, and we shall.'

Yes, Fairfax thought, Locke would say that: if he had his sights set on a profitable marriage to Selina, then he would be very concerned. Their loss was his.

Or was he misjudging Locke? If only he could talk to the man, he might find out.

'Well, I hope you let Mr Locke know that he is wanted,' he snapped. 'The fact is, he is under suspicion in the matter of your father's death, and this curious absence of his is one of the things he must account for. The law—'

'Why, Mr Fairfax, I thought you accounted yourself Francis's friend,' Selina said.

Fairfax sighed. 'I do. I suppose I do. But . . . I have a duty.'

'Why?' Selina asked him – with genuine interest, it seemed. 'You aren't a lawyer or a constable. You don't have to do it.'

'Mr Fairfax has a difficult task, my dear, that much is clear,' Lady Delabole put in. 'You make it no easier with these questions.'

'I do it,' Fairfax said, remembering his resolution, 'because I hope someone would do it for me.'

'Oh, well,' Selina went on with a sniff, 'I told Francis you were looking into Papa's death, anyhow. You may as well know that he said "none better for the job, I'm sure". And he said he was sure to run into you, and you could quiz him all you liked. You lodge in the same house, after all.'

'Is that where he said he was going?'

'Well, I assume, at some point. He had more business to see to. But he said he would call here again later.' Suddenly Selina's sulky face broke into a smile so brilliant it unnerved him. 'And of course there is nothing to prevent him now.'

Fairfax got up. 'I'll try and find him. If he should call here, please tell him to present himself to me or to the magistrate.'

A different girl altogether, he thought as he left the house and crossed the Circus. When her father was alive, she scarcely dared to open her mouth. His death had been a liberation for her.

A strong wind was blowing up, and caught in the bowl of the Circus it whipped itself up into sharp little eddies, hurling handfuls of autumn leaves vertically in the air, whisking off the wig of an elderly man and sending it bowling in skittish circles. Fairfax found his thoughts were the same, scattered and rapid, difficult to catch.

Selina liberated. Of course, that didn't mean she had encompassed her father's death. A happy accident: a fortunate tragedy.

Moral dubieties. He had invoked morality as the reason he did this work. But if we were talking in Christian terms, he thought, wasn't it a vice or sin that pushed him on: pride? Couldn't bear not to find the answer: couldn't bear to think of himself being beaten. And somehow he disliked the thought of Francis Locke running rings round him most of all. Locke the young, dashing ladykiller.

And man-killer?

He still couldn't see it. Why kill a man, make yourself scarce for the best part of two days during which you knew you would be under suspicion, then come back and feign astonishment at the man's death? It made no sense. But then nor did much of Locke's behaviour. The fact that he had taken Pinner's paper suggested that he had been up to something: perhaps the same sort of scheming as Pinner himself, and with the same aim of detaching Caroline from Sir James. That in itself suggested he hadn't known about Sir James's death. But why this delay? What was this 'business' he had been about? And then there was the matter of Tate Jessop and the man from America. Fairfax had had a notion of Locke and the American being linked somehow. But the American had definitely been in Bath these past two days – whereas Locke had been 'away'. But where?

The afternoon was getting on, and Fairfax's stomach was growling at its emptiness. He took himself to the White Hart, the coaching inn in Stall Street. A waiter was just laying a cloth for him in a corner booth of the public dining-room when a voice shouted his name.

He didn't recognize the voice as that of Edmund Pinner at first. Indeed he thought he was being accosted by a drunk.

'Here, sir – here – take a seat here, Mr Fairfax, and dine with me. Never mind that cloth, man – the gentleman dines with me.'

He *was* being accosted by a drunk. They talked of a man in liquor as being 'disguised'. Edmund Pinner, a brimming glass of brandy in his hand, his pale eyes glittering, his every gesture terribly expansive, was a different man indeed.

'Mr Pinner. This is – unexpected.'

'Everything is, sir! Life is a – a parade of the unexpected. One thing follows another and each one is something that it shouldn't be by rights. Isn't that so? Don't you find it so? But sit, sit, sir, join me.'

'A moment perhaps.' Fairfax sat, careful not to put his sleeve on the cloth, which was sodden with spilled brandy. 'I only came in for a bite to eat and then—'

'Eat here – eat some of this. Before God, I can't eat it all. Look – here's veal-and-ham pie, here's hog-puddings and cold chine and currant tart . . . Sirrah, another plate, here, if you please! And brandy, sir – you'll have a glass of brandy, of course.'

Pinner slopped brandy into a glass. His neat linen cuffs were stained with it. Fairfax took a slice of the pie – the dishes covering the table had hardly been touched – and tried to find a tactful way of saying it.

'You are – out of your normal habit, I think, Mr Pinner.'

'I am,' agreed Pinner, with a great empty smile. He rubbed his eyes with the heel of his hand. 'But it does a man good, I think, to step out – to break out a little . . . I feel a touch queer,' he added, his hand to his mouth, 'but it will pass, you know.'

'Perhaps if you ate a little,' Fairfax said, not liking Pinner's colour. 'Just a slice of bread to begin with. You are not used to liquor, I think, and—'

'I've only had three glasses. Drank them down one after t'other. That's how it's done, isn't it? It has affected me a little, though, I think. Yes, a little. You're right, of course. I am not accustomed to liquor. That is, drinking it. I ship it and store it and sell it, you know, but usually I never taste it. Does that make me a hypocrite? Sir James said something like

233

that, you know, at that dinner – do you recall? No fool.'
Pinner brought his glass on a roundabout path to his lips.
'No fool, that man. He knew his daughter all right.'

'Caroline.'

Pinner winced at the name, then summoned another
horribly beaming smile. 'Isn't it remarkable how wrong a
man can be? Isn't that the most remarkable thing, sir – truly,
now? Oh, come. You have no doubt what I mean. Long-
headed fellow like you. Why, you saw through me in a
twinkling.'

'I fear I don't understand.'

'Ha! Of course you do. Heredity, Mr Fairfax. Now *I'm* my
father's son. I'm like him – I'm diligent, you know, and
trustworthy I hope, and sincere – always sincere – but that
isn't much, you know, when it comes down to it, is it?'

'I think it is a good deal.'

'You're kind enough to say so. You don't mean it, but
you're kind enough to say so and I thank you, sir, but it don't
alter the case. I'm never going to be the high-flying, knock-
you-dead sort of fellow. I'm nobody's gallant. No, no, don't
say anything. I'm merely being – illustrative. Heredity, you
see. Now this is what I mean when I say how idiotically
wrong I was.' Pinner lowered his head and tapped his nose.
'With that gravestone, and so forth.'

'You mean – in surmising that Caroline was not Sir James's
daughter.'

'Exactly!' cried Pinner, so loudly and with such a flailing
gesture that a man at a nearby table clucked and gave him a
long hard look over his newspaper. 'You have it, yes, that is it
exactly, sir! How absurdly wrong I was to even think that for
a moment! How fantastically wide of the mark! Don't you
think I should be put in the stocks, and pelted with rotten

fruit, and held up for a ninny and an imbecile?'

'Yes,' said the man at the nearby table, audibly.

'It was a hasty conclusion, perhaps,' Fairfax said. 'But in the circumstances—'

'Oh, hang the circumstances. Don't you see what I'm saying, Mr Fairfax? Heredity. Family traits. Is she like her father? Of course she is. Just look for vain, self-seeking, cold-hearted falsity – there's your resemblance.' Pinner set down his glass, folded his hands in his lap as if he were about to pray, and began weeping. In contrast to the tipsy gesturing, it was very quiet and contained: tears seeped from his tightly closed lids and his shoulders trembled very slightly. 'She is false,' he croaked, 'she is false, Mr Fairfax.'

'Mr Pinner . . .' Fairfax waited a moment, swallowing a piece of pie that had suddenly turned to cardboard in his mouth. 'Mr Pinner, tell me. Tell me what has happened, please.'

'Sorry,' Pinner gasped, taking a great shuddering gasp of air like a man surfacing from deep water, 'sorry, gave way, couldn't help it. Gone now. Gone. Like the hiccoughs. Tell you, Mr Fairfax? Not a pretty story. Grubby. Idiotic. All forgot a year hence.' He choked back a sob. 'Sorry.'

'You . . . I did hear that you were with Caroline this morning. In the Pump Room. From what I heard, you were – well, this is surprising, after that.'

'You'd think so, wouldn't you? Ha, but I didn't know. Didn't know she was her father's daughter. Heartless and false. Oh, God, I don't mean that . . . But what am I to think?' Pinner took a convulsive swallow of brandy, coughed. 'I came to Bath this morning to – to see her. I'd hardly slept. Thinking and thinking. After the almighty fool I made of myself – that business with the child's grave – all that – well, it set me to thinking, looking into myself. What did it say about me? I claimed to love her . . . yes, love her. And yet how did I think to win her? With nasty little intrigues behind her back, with trying to *change* things to my advantage . . . What did I fear? Did I fear that she wouldn't have me, as I was, and as she was? I must have done. And so I thought I was beginning at the wrong end. What I should do was simply tell her how I feel. And so I came this morning, and she – she was quite friendly to me, and when I suggested we go a walk together she agreed. Yes, she agreed!' For a moment Pinner's face shone. 'And so it seemed promising. It seemed my instinct was right. We went to the Pump Room. We talked. That is, I talked of my – my great regard for her. And she did not silence me – no, no. She was receptive. When I mentioned my ultimate hopes, she did not put me off, not at all. She said it was something she must give thought to. That is hopeful, surely, Mr Fairfax? There she was on my arm, saying she must give it thought, and suggesting we go on and take a turn in the Walks? Was that not grounds for encouragement?'

'It would seem so,' Fairfax agreed reluctantly, as Pinner seemed to demand an answer.

'Oh, yes. But this, don't forget, this was before I realized she was her father's daughter. Well, we strolled along the Walks, and I could see people looking at us, and my heart felt ready to burst with pride. And she said she had many things to think of just now, and that I must understand that. Of course, of course I did. She had gone through some strange reversals of fortune just lately, she said. She had been led to believe she had prodigious expectations, only to find them vanish. What did I think of that? I said I thought it was a pity, but . . . Well, she wouldn't hear any buts. She said she couldn't be sure who was being truthful with her any more. She feared people weren't being frank with her. And could she trust me to be frank with her? Well, I said yes, of course . . . And then she said she suspected someone was swindling her out of her inheritance from her father – and did I know anything about that? Well, I – I was taken aback. I said to her it wasn't a thing I cared about—'

'That was not quite truthful on your part, Mr Pinner,' Fairfax said gently. 'As you did not want Caroline to have that fortune.'

'Well, but that was *before* – before I'd seen things aright. Well, she gave me a strange look; and she said that if there was a new will, someone must have taken it or hidden it – and did I know anything about that? I couldn't speak . . . but she went on that I needn't be afraid, if I had been urged by someone else, her grandfather perhaps, to act as I did. I said I didn't understand. She said very harshly that I must do: that I had gone to her father's house very quickly, when the news came of his death, and there was this odd story of a document that had gone missing . . .'

'Did you explain about that?'

Pinner shook his head. 'I hardly knew what to say. I was smarting so, thinking she had – had some tenderness for me, when all she wanted was to find out if I knew about her father's will. I was a little angry, I think: I said I knew nothing about any will, and said again that I didn't care. Then she laughed and said she found that hard to believe. She said I was like her grandfather – the two of us never wanted her to be reconciled with her father, that we had our heads together over it all the time. And now that her father was put out of the way, and her prospects robbed of her, did I think I could just step in and claim her hand – and she would agree because there was nothing better on

offer?' Pinner reached for his glass, trembling, and knocked
it over. Brandy spread on the white cloth like a red hand
unfolding. 'It hurt. Perhaps I am a great fool, but it hurt so
very badly . . . I reproached her: she had said she would
give thought to my suit. Yes, she said, and she had: she had
given thought to a lot of things, and they all indicated that
she was being conspired against, cheated of her rights . . .
Can you believe this, Mr Fairfax?'

Thinking of the night in the coach-house, Fairfax found
that he could. It was just as Caroline had said: she was doing
a little investigating on her own account. But her quarry was
her father's money, and her methods not very scrupulous. It
was sad. He felt sorry for Pinner – and yet hadn't the man
seen, long ago, the simple fact that she was not for him?

As if in answer, Pinner said stonily, 'Well, I had heard
enough: I went away from her, there in the Walks, and that
was the end of it. But I did ask her one last question. If not
me, then who? I've said I'm no high-flyer, Mr Fairfax, but
I'm no innocent neither. If a woman won't even consider a
man who's – yes, perfectly eligible, I will say that of myself –
if she can simply dismiss him out of hand, then there must be
another man somewhere. That's my belief. No: I *know* it. So
I said to her.' Pinner wiped his hand across his face. 'She
smiled. Just smiled.'

'This is a hard counsel, I know, Mr Pinner,' Fairfax said.
'But in such a case, when the refusal is so – definite, then
there is truly nothing to do but turn your back and resolve to
forget—'

'Oh, I have.' For a moment Pinner looked almost sly.
'Believe me, I have done that, sir. I just want to know: if not
me, who? That's all.' Abruptly he fumbled for his purse and
scattered coins on the brandy-soaked cloth. 'Could you count

that money, Mr Fairfax, and settle up? I – I think I must find a privy . . .'

When he had lurched away Fairfax paid the bill and gathered up what was left. The coins were unpleasantly sticky in his hand. He went out to the stable block, looking for the privy. He ought to make sure Pinner was all right, as well as returning his money: the man was an emotional ruin. At the slatted door of the privy he waited a minute and then called out 'Mr Pinner?'

'I ain't,' said a man's voice. 'Go away.'

Damn the man, where had he gone? To drown his sorrows elsewhere? Well, in truth Fairfax was relieved. He didn't much want to play nursemaid to a man weeping boozy buckets over a lost love. An uncomfortable reminder of the figure he had been cutting just lately, perhaps.

He gave the remaining coins to a down-at-heel young woman with a baby who was patiently waiting for a carrier's cart, and was about to leave the White Hart when his eye fell on the coach schedules, pasted to the wall within the archway. There was much coaching out of Bath, to various destinations in the West, but above all to London. Tuesdays and Thursdays you could depart early in the morning or at half-past noon, breaking the journey at Newbury . . .

Locke had disappeared about noon on Tuesday. Could it be that this mysterious 'business' had involved a trip to London? He had borrowed money from the painter Macleod: for a coach fare, perhaps?

A possibility. But what was he doing in London? Fairfax did have an idea. Sir James Delabole's lawyer was in London. Locke had a paper which, as he thought, revealed Caroline Delabole to be an impostor. Perhaps he had gone to see this lawyer, presenting his 'evidence' . . . Oh, but a family solicitor was hardly likely to receive this total stranger and talk about a client's confidential business. Locke was clever enough to know that.

But he had another uneasiness about Locke. He didn't share Pinner's egotistical belief that if Caroline wasn't in love with him, then she must be in love with someone else. And yet Selina had been spitting with jealousy too . . . All along he had been tentatively putting the names of Locke and Caroline together: now he tried again, hoping to hear the smooth click of a key turning. But no: nothing.

'Francis Locke,' Fairfax said to himself, 'you must tell me your tale. And who knows, perhaps you will be the one who *doesn't* lie, hide, mislead, and generally hoodwink.'

He hoped so: the hope cheered him. He set out for home. If Locke was back in Bath, he would have to return to his lodgings at some point: even rackety half-pay officers must change their linen occasionally. All Fairfax would have to do, if Locke wasn't at Avon Street now, was sit tight until he came in, and then collar him.

The sky was like murky iron, and in the old streets of the lower town the hanging shop-signs were swinging and groaning in the gusty wind. Here and there panelled interiors were being lit with early candles and tapers, and the glowing glimpses gave Fairfax a mildly wistful feeling. He had thought of going home – but 'home' was a warm plump word for a thin chill reality, he reflected as he came to Avon Street, where his dreary lodgings awaited him. He was glad when David Macleod called to him from his rooms on the ground floor and asked him to step in.

'Well, Fairfax, how goes it? Why, man, ye look fagged.'

'Do I? I suppose I do. Macleod, has Locke been here?'

'He has. And gone again, half an hour since.'

'Damn. Did he say where he'd been, what he'd been doing?'

'Not to me. He just made a smart remark about me not finishing Niobe yet. I've no interest in the whelp's doings. I'd like my money back, mind, but no doubt I'll have to whistle for it.'

'Did he say when he'll be back?'

'Oh, he said he'd see me anon. Ah, *that* is what's needed,' Macleod said, stabbing yellow impasto on Niobe's flowing locks. 'Volume, volume is what's wanted. Ah, yes. Odd how something can be right in front of your eyes, and yet you've looked and looked at it so hard that you don't see it any more – there, an improvement, d'ye think?'

Niobe already seemed to have more hair than even a mythological heroine could reasonably manage, and it seemed to be blown about by at least three cross-winds to boot; but Fairfax agreed that it was an improvement.

'Well, you look as if you could do with reviving, Fairfax. Pull up that chair to the fire, if you will, and you'll see there a kettle of water, a jug of wine, sugar, and nutmeg I think – d'you see nutmeg, sir? – excellent. Then there's the making of a good negus, if you'll be so good as to mix it for us. I fancy there's seed-cake there too, if the turpentine hasn't got into it.'

The warmth of the fire, the negus and seed-cake, and congenial company, were all precisely what Fairfax found he needed to lift his spirits. Stretching out his legs, watching the young painter dart about his great turbulent canvas, he let his mind simply drain like a sink. It was a surprise to recall that life could be like this: no anxious brain-work, no wearying alertness. Life properly lived, he thought, as the negus went spicily down, really was a gift.

And of course he could not quite forget that a man had been robbed of that gift, and the crime was unforgivable, and the criminal was somewhere walking free.

Stretching again, he heard a popping of joints, and thought of Sam Fry the bone setter. And then he realized that something Fry had said was haunting the back of his mind like a half-forgotten tune. Fry had said Tate Jessop had had no children. Yet Mrs Jessop had admitted to having a child many years ago. What did that mean? Could she have had a child out of wedlock? Or had she been married before? He gave a start. That might explain the mysterious American. A first husband transported, a bigamous marriage after . . . And the child? Suppose it had not really died . . .?

'Well, now, if you're sufficiently revived, Fairfax – say if you're not – I'll make so bold as to remind you of a wee suggestion you made. You recollect I love to hear Shakespeare while I work . . .?'

'Of course – I said I'd read to you. No, no, it will be a great pleasure.' Fairfax shook his head, still in thought. 'This volume?'

'Aye, *Macbeth* will suit very well. Dark deeds and terror and pathos. Like Niobe weeping for her murdered babes. 'Tis apt as may be. Lay on, Macduff.'

Keeping an ear cocked for the sound of the front door, Fairfax began to read from *Macbeth* – a little self-consciously at first, his mind still chewing on the matter of Mrs Jessop's past, but with growing relish and abandon. Macleod pitched in with him at favourite passages, fairly bellowing out: ' "How now, you secret, black and midnight hags!" ' and adding in an undertone that that was for the benefit of their landlady, who was entertaining some other matrons to tea. When they came to the appearance of Banquo's ghost, the painter stole about his easel on tiptoe, shuddering: at the grief of Macduff for his murdered family, he stood sombrely back from his painting with knitted brows, nodding to himself.

'Aye – that's the touch. "All my pretty ones?" ' he repeated. ' "Did you say all? O hell-kite! All? What, all my pretty chickens and their dam, At one fell swoop?" That's the pathos, melting but noble, I look for in my Niobe. 'Tis the loss not just of a child, but all her children – that utter loss. Indeed, now that I think of it, I wonder if I have put too much resignation in her grief. There would surely be madness in it.'

'Yes,' Fairfax said, staring into the fire. 'Yes, there would be madness.' A shiver racked him, as if he were starting a fever. But it was not that.

'Are you all right there, Fairfax? You look as if you've seen Banquo's ghost yourself.'

'I . . .' Fairfax shook himself. 'I have just had a thought, and . . .' *All my pretty chickens. That utter loss* . . . He was thinking of Lydia Delabole, abandoned, burying one infant in Calais and bringing the surviving child to London in wretchedness and poverty: Lydia, who had never been the same again and had gone to an early grave. Loss and grief. *My God*, he thought, *I believe she lost them both* . . . He lifted his head sharply. 'Was that the door?'

'Eh? No, I don't fancy so. Our landlady falling off her broomstick, perhaps. You're sure you're quite well, Fairfax? You're feared that Locke won't come back again? Never tell me you lent him money as well. Best resign yourself, if so. "Neither a borrower nor a lender be" – there's the Bard again. Well, Locke's one of nature's borrowers. He even begged a piece of charcoal off me before he took off – luckily you'd fetched me a new supply – God knows what he wanted that for. The man's a gadfly—'

'Charcoal?'

'Aye. Perhaps he fancies going into my line. Fairfax, what the devil is it?'

'Sorry, Macleod – I can't read any more. I've got to – I must find Locke.' He went to London, taking charcoal with him. Why? Surely, like Pinner, to visit a grave . . .

'Whisht, man, he'll be back soon enough. He wouldn't have had yon fellow wait for him if he wasn't coming back.'

'What fellow?'

'I told you, didn't I? Oh, perhaps not. Well, some damn crony of his, I don't know the name and I didn't ask. I'm not Locke's keeper, thank God. He brings this rum devil home and stows him in his rooms and says he'll be back. I don't know—'

'What sort of rum devil?'

'Old fellow, hook in place of a hand – I'd say sailor but he didn't have the tarry look somehow. Fine sketch, if you like the grotesque. The poor wretch is waiting still, no doubt, so you're not the only one, Fairfax – unless he's given up and gone. Maybe Locke owes him money as well . . . Wait – will you not read to the end of *Macbeth*?'

Fairfax sprinted upstairs, flung open Locke's door.

The jumble as before; but a candle was burning on the mantelshelf and he caught a faint odour of old broadcloth and tobacco. No one here, though. Deserted.

He returned downstairs, slowly, stood in irresolute thought in the shadowy hall. Macleod had come out and was asking him what was wrong . . . something like that. His voice faded in Fairfax's ears.

A draught was whipping round his legs. The front door stood a little ajar. Some deeper shadow was visible at the foot of the door: something shiny too, shiny with wetness.

He didn't want to open that door, though he did: he didn't want to see the long splay-legged form there, though he did.

'Oh dear God,' Macleod said over his shoulder. 'Oh sweet Jesus. Who could have done this?'

Below the leaded porch, his head on the threshold, Ensign Francis Locke lay face down in a luminous pond of his blood. The ivory handle of a knife stuck out at an awkward, casual angle from the back of his neck. There was an abrasion on his forehead, with a corresponding dash of blood on the door-panel – God, that had been the noise – where he had gone down, collapsing forward, from the killing blow of his attacker.

Killing: there was no doubt of that, though Macleod, half in tears, kept murmuring about a surgeon. Fairfax, after feeling in vain for a pulse in the throat, brushed the young man's fair hair gently back from his battered forehead. Then, taking a deep breath, he searched in his pockets. A purse with a few coppers, a handkerchief.

No papers: as he thought. But Locke had surely come back from London with some knowledge, and that had sealed his doom.

'Macleod,' he said, hearing his own voice thick and unrecognizable, 'I fear there is nothing to be done. Not here, anyhow. But if you would – go to Mr Goode, the magistrate, at Queen Square. Tell him what's happened, and that I have gone on ahead.'

'Where?'

'Orchard Street. To take a murderer.' Fairfax straightened. 'Who could have done this, you say? Someone driven by the same urge that led her to kill Sir James. Someone trying to protect her child.'

Twelve

It seemed to him that he had never run so fast. Headlong through the dusky streets, Fairfax pushed aside pedestrians and dodged the lacquered poles of sedan-chairs and once nearly went under the wheels of a carriage. Someone speculatively cried 'Stop thief' after him: a dog as vicious as his former landlord's pursued him part of the way barking and snarling. When he got to Orchard Street his lungs felt as if they were bursting with fire. But he had made good time. Ahead of him, he saw the American, disappearing into the brick passage that ran alongside Mr Tiverton's house.

Fairfax followed.

The passage was dark. He reminded himself that it was slippery underfoot, and moved cautiously, his accelerated heartbeat drumming in his ears.

He emerged into the yard. There were no lights at the back of the house, and it took him a moment to make out the burly figure of the American. He had his back to him. He was standing at the window of Mrs Jessop's room, his arms up against the lattice, trying to peer in.

The figure of the woman came with startling swiftness from its hiding-place in the old coach-house and flitted across the yard. Fairfax saw the weapon in her hand, a rusty fire-iron tightly gripped, uplifted, arcing downward as she flew at the American's back.

It seemed to take his last, lung-searing gasp of strength to hurl himself at her, seize her, wrestle her back. She fought him with squirming strength, coming on and on, the fire-iron still clutched in her hand though he squeezed her wrist until he feared a snap of bones, his or hers. It was only when the American wrenched it from her fingers and then with his good hand gave her an open-handed blow across the cheeks that she gave up her struggles, groaning and slumping quite suddenly in Fairfax's arms.

'God forgive me that I should do that, sister,' the American growled. 'But God forgive you too, if He can.'

'Sister?' Fairfax said. 'Then I am in error. I had thought you her first husband, come looking for your child. Then there is more to this than I thought . . . Will you take her other arm, sir? We had better go inside.'

Mrs Jessop, her chestnut hair hanging, a red mark spreading on her cheek, lifted her head, and seemed by some great mustering of will to become the respectable matron again.

'Yes, sir,' she said, 'that would be best. I'm very sorry indeed for the trouble I've caused.'

They went in by the servants' door at the back of the kitchen. Mrs Jessop was all quiet self-command now, telling the maids who gasped and gaped through the steam of the range to hush and attend to their business. But when Caroline came hurrying to the top of the steps leading up from the kitchen, and then stood transfixed at the sight of them, Mrs Jessop's composure gave way. She trembled, and let out a sob.

The American, meanwhile, gazed up at Caroline, and then gave his sister a hard look.

'I want answers, Sarah,' he said. 'I want the truth.'

'Yes, George,' Mrs Jessop said, tremulously. 'Of course. You shall hear. Did you think she might be your daughter? No. There is no one with the right to call her that – except myself.'

Caroline stared at her, frozen.

'I am ready now: I see it has come, and in a way I am glad,' Mrs Jessop said, with a glance at Fairfax. 'I shall cause no more trouble. But let us just sit down together one more time.'

'My name is George Staples,' the man from America said, sitting sturdily upright in one of Mr Tiverton's high-backed chairs, the glass of brandy untouched before him. 'One-and-twenty years ago, I was a weaver in London – in Spitalfields. I had lately married, and we had a little daughter named Lizzie. All should have been well, perhaps, but I was not wise in my choice of a wife, for she was discontented and no manager, and times were hard. I was not wise either in what I did to make things better. I stole from my master – not a bad man, but neglectful – and my theft was discovered. I lay in Newgate, and when they tried me at Old Bailey, I was sentenced to be transported to the American colonies for twenty-one years.' He looked around the assembled company.

'What did you steal?' Fairfax asked him.

'An ell of silk,' Staples said with a faint smile. 'Well, 'twas folly; but I would not have been sorry to leave these shores, but for the fact that I left my little Lizzie, still a babe in arms. My wife was a different matter. As soon as my sentence was known, she put our little girl into the arms of a neighbour, and took herself off. She was handsome and there was a tavern-keeper I knew had his eye on her among others, and no doubt she thought she could do better by herself. It was my great fear that little Lizzie would be handed to the parish before I took ship; but, thank heaven, I had a sister – a good kind creature, who promised to look after the babe. My sister Sarah.'

He looked over at Mrs Jessop, who was sitting with her hands folded in her lap, and who inclined her head very faintly. Candles had been brought, but they seemed to do little to push back the ever-lurking shadows of this creaking panelled parlour, and it seemed to Fairfax that the chief points of illumination in the room were eyes. George Staples's eyes, sober and watchful: Mr Tiverton's, glassy and haunted, and for the first time terribly old: Mrs Jessop's, still bright and birdlike but unreadable: and Caroline's, which seemed to shine with a painful dryness, a denial of tears.

'Sarah Grant her name was then. She was married to a sailor, who was at sea, and she had just given birth to a little child of her own – Amabel. A pretty name, I always thought, sister.'

Mrs Jessop shrugged. 'My husband's fancy. He was full of such notions.'

'Well. My sister took little Lizzie and said she'd raise her with her own. Of course, I was anxious for the expense it would put her to, especially with her man at sea. But Sarah said 'twould be all right enough, for she took in lodgers, and worked as a mantua-maker, on top of what her man would bring her when he was in port, and she would manage pretty well. And so I was thankful, at least, that I didn't leave my little babe a pauper child, when they put me on the ship and transported me to Virginia. I thought she would stand a fair chance, at least.'

'So she would have,' Mrs Jessop said, staring into the fire. 'So she would have, George.'

'Well.' Staples shook his head. 'There was no means of knowing, at first. It takes an age for letters to cross the sea in any case, but neither of us could read or write, not then. It was only in America that I learned my letters at last – for there's precious few in that country, even among the poorer sort, who can't read. Several years had passed by that time, but I tried sending a letter to where Sarah had last been living, in St Giles, just in case it might get to her, and someone might read it to her; but no good. I just had to get on and hope for the best. My life in England began to seem more like one of those dreams that you only half-remember when you stir; but I never forgot that I had a daughter, my little Lizzie, somewhere across the sea. I laboured hard over the years, but I had a fair master in Virginia; and in truth I think I fared better there than ever I could have done in London, where the trade was forever up and down, and naught but struggle from day to day. At last I moved north, to Pennsylvania, and began ploughing and sowing and raising a few pigs on my own account. 'Twas about the time of the French and Indian wars, and there were a lot of troops from England quartered about the country.'

'And that is how you met Francis Locke,' Fairfax said.

Staples nodded. 'I had some work supplying the troops: I had a cart, and I'd go back and forth with provisions, long miles sometimes, so that I'd have to break the journey overnight. Before Fort Duquesne there was a skirmish in the woods north of where I was camped. Come dawn I set out and came across a young soldier who'd got separated from the others. He was lamed, and had taken a blow on his head, and couldn't shift for himself; so I took him up in the cart and carried him to the encampment. He swore that he'd have been a dead man if I hadn't found him – which was mebbe true, mebbe not – and he sought me out after the surgeons had finished with him, and wanted to know what service he could do for me. Well, I didn't want anything particular, as I thought. But as time went by, and the English took Quebec and the French looked to be beat and folk began to talk of the peace being signed, I thought of those troops being sent home again, and how that young soldier would probably be going back to England – where my Lizzie was. And God bless him, he managed to seek me out again, in sixty-three it was, when his regiment had their orders to take ship for England, and said he wanted to thank me once more for saving his life, and was there aught I wanted – something particular sent over from home, mebbe. Well, I didn't want nothing of that sort – but there was something I wanted, very much, as I grew older.'

'You wanted to know about your daughter Lizzie,' Fairfax said, 'and you asked Ensign Locke to try and find her.' He was beginning to see more clearly now, past his own misconceptions. He had thought Staples must be that first husband of Mrs Jessop's, not dead but transported; and that it was their child who had been brought up as Caroline Delabole, Lydia's twins both having perished. Now he saw an even grimmer tale taking shape.

'That was it. I gave him all the information I had, and he gave me his promise he would do it,' Staples said hoarsely, his big shoulders hunched: then he threw a bitter look at Mrs Jessop and cried: 'A good young fellow, Sarah, a rare good one – how could you do it? Have you turned madwoman? What the devil did you fear from him, eh? I just don't understand—'

'What?' Caroline said. 'What is this about Mr Locke?'

'He is dead,' Fairfax said. 'His murder is the sorry end of this tale.' Caroline bit off a cry. 'As for what you feared from him, Mrs Jessop – well, you feared that he would expose the truth, and that truth is what you have tried to protect all along, is it not? Well, I take it Locke was here earlier – Mr Tiverton?'

The old man nodded. 'He was, sir. That poor young fellow.' His voice was papery, empty.

'And brought with him some evidence that he believed you would not wish to be made public. Which you dealt with, Mrs Jessop, by pursuing him and killing him, as you killed Sir James Delabole. A desperate means, the knife, and bloody. At least with the poison you did not have to see the death throes.'

Caroline started up from her seat. 'This is not real – this is some horrible game you are playing – please, tell me what's happening—'

Fairfax put a hand on her arm and eased her back to her chair: he saw Mrs Jessop's downcast eyes lift and they were full of anguish. 'Be calm, Miss Delabole. Be strong: I know you can . . . I think, Mr Tiverton, the story now becomes yours.'

Mr Tiverton stared down at his gnarled hands, shook his head. 'I . . . I can't speak of it, sir.'

'I'm sure you can, Mr Tiverton,' Fairfax said firmly. 'For Caroline's sake.'

The old man cleared his throat, but his voice still seemed to have lost all its power when he spoke. 'You know . . . you know, my dear, that my daughter Lydia ran off with James Delabole, much against my will, and married him. Twenty-one years ago: January of 'forty-four. They went to Paris, where they parted; and where Lydia, alone and deserted, gave birth to – to twin daughters. She named them Maria and Caroline.'

'I had a sister . . .?'

Fairfax pressed Caroline's arm. Mr Tiverton, his eyes averted, went on after a moment: 'Lydia made her way to Calais with her babies, intending to come back to London, where I lived then: intending, no doubt, to – to beg my forgiveness. At Calais, one of her babies sickened and died, and was buried there. She wrote her estranged husband the news, and afterwards he had a headstone raised on the child's grave; and the matter was not spoken of again.'

'It was this grave, Miss Delabole, that Edmund Pinner came across, when he was waiting for the Calais crossing,' Fairfax said. Caroline's eyes were fixed on him now, as if he were a man reaching out for her across an abyss, her one hope. He wished he was. 'Not knowing that Lydia had given birth to twins, he jumped to the conclusion that this was Sir James's only daughter who had died in infancy – and that therefore, in short, you could not be his daughter after all. Misliking Sir James's influence over you, he resolved to use this "evidence", as he saw it. He made a charcoal rubbing of the headstone, unfortunately incurring the suspicion of the French authorities, so that they took him for a spy. But when he returned to England, he wasted no time in taking the paper to Sir James, believing he was making a great revelation. Which he was not, of course. Sir James enlightened him, telling him about the twins, but was very much displeased. The paper bearing the incised words of the gravestone remained in Sir James's possession after he had shown Pinner the door – but not for long. His daughter Selina, coming into the study, took it up. Not knowing about the twins either, her curiosity was similarly aroused. She showed it to her lover – who was none other than Ensign Francis Locke. It was no coincidence that he was in Bath, however. But we will come to that. The crucial thing that happened, twenty-one years ago, happened when Lydia made her way back to London with her surviving child. Mr Tiverton?'

The old man put his hands over his eyes, shaking his head.

'Well,' Fairfax said. 'You must tell me if I'm wrong. But what I think happened is that Lydia lost the other child too. She had come through a most wretched time, deserted by her husband, seeing one of her infants die, arriving at last in London where her vindictive father still refused to take her back. I'm afraid that's so, isn't it, sir? You would not relent; and Lydia and her baby had to take the poorest of lodgings, and survive as best they could. And alas, they couldn't – or at least the baby couldn't. Little Caroline, the surviving twin, died too, in London.'

Still Caroline's eyes were fixed on him, as the abyss yawned deeper.

'It was near Gray's Inn Lane,' Mr Tiverton said abruptly. 'A pestilential courtyard up an alley. That was where I – I went to see her, at last. Yes, I had refused to see her: the pleading letters she sent me at Marybone I had thrown on the fire. I – I was stubborn. She had sowed and she must reap. Then the letters stopped – and my heart misgave me. I took a carriage, and after some searching found out that noisome court where she lodged. It was February of 'forty-five, bitter cold, bleak – cruel weather. Crueller still in such poor places as that. I found Lydia, alone. And I saw, at last, what my stubbornness had done to her. She had buried her babe in the parish churchyard just a few day's past – had stood for the second time, alone, by a tiny grave. She had pawned her wedding ring to bury the child, and she had eaten nothing since. Her thin face was vacant. She wandered in her mind. I feared for her reason.' Mr Tiverton brushed his cheek with his sleeve. 'I had brought no one with me, no servant: I wanted discretion. I consoled her as best I could . . . she seemed hardly to know me. I went out to buy candles, food, brandy, and to see if I could find a doctor nearby. There was none at hand in that dreadful place. So I resolved as I came back that the moment she seemed strong enough, I would put her in a carriage, and take her back home, and – and perhaps we could begin again.

'Well. I went up to her wretched room – and found her much changed. She was cooing and smiling. She had a baby in her arms. I will never forget her face as she looked at me over the little soft crown of its head. "It was a mistake, Papa," she said. "All a mistake. Here's Caroline – see! I still have my pretty babe after all! So everything is all right!" And her eyes were shining in her thin face in the most terrible way . . . Oh, I cursed myself, you may believe. But I cursed James Delabole too, the man who had taken my daughter on the path that led to this. For her mind was all but broken. And now . . . now I had this awful difficulty. For though she would not say so, though in her distracted state I don't think she *believed* so, Lydia had stolen that child.'

'Mrs Jessop,' Fairfax said, 'you told me you had lived in that district. Was that the time?' His pulse quickened. 'Was that how you first came into Mr Tiverton's life?'

'It was,' Mrs Jessop said. 'I lived in that same court. One room, second pair back.'

Staples stirred, frowning. 'Sarah – this is what I can't understand. You were pretty well settled, I thought, when they shipped me out – not rich, but not starving neither.

How came you to be living in such a place . . .?'

'It was my own fault, George,' Mrs Jessop said calmly. 'Oh, there were troubles: my husband didn't come back from the sea, and I didn't know then whether his ship had gone down, or whether he had just skipped off as sailors do. Trade was in a poor way, and I couldn't get much work. But mostly it was my own doing. I took to gin. Yes: I've been a sober woman many years now, and fierce against drink. I have my reasons. I've known what it is to be swallowed up by drink, so that there's nothing left of you but the wanting. This was in the days before the Parliament made that licensing law, and made gin dearer and harder to get. In London in those days every chandler's shop sold gin: you could buy it from a street-barrow. It was everywhere. It was cheap. Twopence bought you forgetfulness. Even as drink goes, it was wicked poisonous stuff – but you didn't care about that, once you had the taste. Because you didn't care about anything, then. It was a shocking time. I've seen good workmen take up gin, and turn idle drunkards so quickly, their families would hardly know them – if they did not take gin themselves. Women, I fear, turned to it as readily as men: they would even quieten their children with it. It made thieves and beggars out of decent folk, and what it did to me was . . . well, call it a typical case, if you like. Mind, I don't excuse myself. I was wrong to fall prey to it. I may say, with perfect truth, that I've never forgiven myself.' Smoothing the neat folds of her gown with her old primness, Mrs Jessop went on: 'When I wanted that drink, I would do anything. Once or twice I went with men . . . not the worst of it. I had the charge of two babies, remember. And no gin-drinker was fit for such a trust. I had already fallen so far as to be living with them in that one mean room in that dingy court; and often I left them alone, crying and dirty. I think I knew it was wrong; but if I could just get another glass, I would be made all right again, and then I would see to them . . . And it was when I was out, that that poor lady – Lydia – must have heard the crying down the passage, and come to my room. And all broken up with grief for her own lost babes as she was, she – she must have taken up that child into her arms, and carried her to her own room; and in her poor crazed way, thought she had her own infant back, and would not be parted from her.'

'That child . . .' said Staples, slowly. 'Sarah. Who was that child?'

'My own,' Mrs Jessop said, locking her fingers tightly together. 'My Amabel, George. There was – there was only she by then. So it is true, George, what I told you when you sought me out here. It is true – your poor Lizzie did die in infancy. You would not quite believe me, I know, and kept coming back to ask me more, but I couldn't tell you the whole truth . . .'

'Tell me now,' Staples said, with a growl in his voice, 'tell me now, Sarah.'

'You found me out, sir,' Mrs Jessop said to Fairfax, 'as a mother – and as a murderess. But this you could not know – that I first took a life many years ago.' She turned to Staples. 'In drink I began to resent your poor Lizzie. She was trouble and required expense that could have gone on gin, and she was not even mine. I fancied she did not like me, and cried and whined at the mere sight of me. You left her supplied with clouts and caps and clothes, George, d'you remember? The last thing you were able to do for her. I thought of the money they would raise, and so one night I smothered Lizzie.' Caroline gave a sickened cry, clamping her hand to her mouth. 'And I put on tears, and told the parish officer she had had fits and died; and in that time and place, where so few children lived beyond their first birthday, he made no remark, and had the parish bury her. And I sold her little clothes, and spent the money on gin, and thought no more about it, as I was then.'

Fairfax, trembling with shock himself, moved to stand between Staples and his sister, but the big man just sat slumped, staring, as if he could not take it in.

'I am sorry, George,' Mrs Jessop said. 'If I could take hold of the person I was then, I would surely kill her. But I am bound for death now, and so there will be justice for you and Lizzie, you see, in the end. And a kind of justice visited me too, back then. Because I am quite sure that my Amabel would not have survived long, as I was. I would have done the same to her, perhaps, or simply let her pine away with neglect, or at best I would have handed her to the parish. Instead, Lydia Delabole came along, and lifted her from the dirty bed where I had left her. And she never gave her up.'

Caroline's eyes – they would not look at Mrs Jessop – sought her grandfather's. 'Then – then you let Mama steal . . .' She could not say *me*: that lay a long hard way ahead, Fairfax thought. 'Steal a baby . . .?'

'It wasn't quite like that,' Mrs Jessop said. 'You must remember, my dear, what I – your mother – was like then.'

'I did not know what to do,' Mr Tiverton said. 'I tried to reason with Lydia – tried to convince her, gently, that the babe was not hers. But she would not hear of it, in her distracted state. And the worst thing was, seeing her embracing that child I saw life in her eyes: a spark, where before there had been only vacancy. It seemed to be the one thing that could keep her from losing her reason altogether

and turning her face to the wall; and yet it did not belong to
her.'

'And then I came back,' Mrs Jessop said. 'Drunk and foul
and quarrelsome. And oh, full of indignation that this woman
should dare to take my baby. The baby that I had left alone,
and that was only a burden to me. Do you see how it was
now, my dear? Mr Tiverton began to explain the circumstances to me – while poor Lydia nursed you and caressed
you, and gave you probably the first feelings of peace and
gentleness you had known. And I looked at Mr Tiverton's
fine clothes, and thought of his purse ... and I was soon
ready to come to an agreement.'

Caroline said, distinctly, but still not looking at Mrs Jessop:
'You sold me.'

'No,' Mrs Jessop said, mildly, 'it was not really like that. I
took money, and Mr Tiverton undertook to give my child a
home, and raise her. It was better than giving you to the
parish, to be farmed out to an ignorant penny-pinching nurse,
and if you survived that to be bound apprentice as soon as
you could work. It seemed a fine idea. I looked forward to
spending the money and to being free. I still do not regret it.
You were not stolen or bought: you were rescued from me.'

'I still had great misgivings, Caroline,' Mr Tiverton said.
'But Lydia's face, when she held you ... It was the only
thing that kept her whole. And yes, I was burdened with
guilt. If I could bring her home with a child in her arms – *her*
child, as she saw it – and cherish the both of them to the end
of my days, then perhaps I could atone for what I had done.
I could not refuse Lydia ... anything. And all she wanted
was you. She called you by the name Caroline; the name of
the child she had buried in London; and so you became. I
took the two of you home to Marybone. It seemed necessary

at first to raise you as Lydia's own true daughter, for the sake of her mind: she grew more lucid during the year she had left before consumption took her, and she remembered Calais, but what had happened in London became a merciful blank to her, I think. And after she had died and I became your sole guardian, I saw no reason to change who you were. For you *were* Lydia's child, as far as she was concerned. And as for James Delabole – your supposed father – well, I preferred that he should think a child still lived from his ill-fated marriage to my Lydia. If he had a conscience, then let it be pricked: he did not deserve the ease of knowing that none of them was left alive to reproach him. He had got away too lightly as it was.'

'Then how do you come to be here?' Caroline said, glancing – just glancing – at her mother. Her voice crackled harshly. 'Why didn't the gin take you to an early grave?'

'I'm sure it would have.' Mrs Jessop was still calm. 'And probably I deserved it. But I stopped the gin, eventually. Not yet: I had the money Mr Tiverton had given me to get through first. But that didn't take too long. Then came news that my husband had died at sea. He left a few effects, and I sold them of course, and drank the proceeds, and was so drunk I fell down a stairway and hurt myself. I was in the work-house infirmary for a time. I didn't intend doing anything except drink when I came out. But an old woman I met in there persuaded me to go to a meeting of Methodists at Clerkenwell. I don't know what made me go. But that was the beginning of my remaking. It was slow at first: my good intentions sometimes fell by the wayside. But at length I left off gin-drinking, and began to take care of myself again, and got steady work. The knowledge of what I had done in the past was always with me, of course; but it came to seem to me quite right that it should be there, like a pain in my soul. That pain was my punishment.

'At one of those meetings I met my second husband. A farrier and bone-setter called Tate Jessop – a good man, older than me, pious and hard-working. I did not expect such a second chance, but he wanted a helpmeet, and so I resolved to be a good one and married him. We were comfortable in a quiet way: we had no children.' Mrs Jessop smoothed her gown again. 'Then he decided to move to Bath, where he thought trade might be better. And here in Bath, I saw a man I recognized – the man who had taken my daughter to raise up: Mr Tiverton.'

'I had been retired here some years,' Mr Tiverton said. 'I preferred to be away from London, and to concentrate on – on Caroline. For of course, I had grown to love her as my own granddaughter.'

'And when you saw me, and recognized me, sir, I think there was perhaps a little alarm, was there not?' Mrs Jessop said with a faint smile. 'A little concern that I might – well, make trouble. But you very soon saw that I was not as I was. I felt I had caused enough trouble in the world for ten sinners: I had only remorse. And yes – curiosity. Of course. To see how my child had turned out.' Mrs Jessop tried in vain to catch Caroline's eye. 'And when Mr·Jessop died a year or so after, worn out from good labour, and going to his deserved rest, I very quietly approached Mr Tiverton, and asked if I might just see her, no more. He saw, I believe, that I was wholly to be trusted: I believe he felt a certain pity. And as he felt the need of a womanly presence in the house as the little girl grew, we came to an arrangement. It was strictly on the grounds that I did not reveal the past – but that, indeed, was the only grounds I wanted. So I became companion-housekeeper here, and –' for the first time, her voice faltered a little – 'and through Mr Tiverton's goodness, I was able to watch my girl grow in to a beautiful woman.'

Fairfax rose to trim a smoking candle. 'You have filled in the gaps, Mrs Jessop, in a way I could not have guessed at. But from here, I think, I can see my way. Here you were, happy with Caroline, your past life buried – or far away in America. And then two events took place that altered this comfortable state of affairs. Ensign Locke returned to England and, true to his word, began to look for Mr Staples's daughter. Not an easy task. He knew only that the child had been left with one Sarah Grant, mantua-maker of St Giles, London. But he made enquiries; and though Sarah Grant was long gone, he must have found someone who remembered her – who remembered, certainly, that she had married a man who did bone-setting, and moved away to Bath. Well, it was a trail of sorts. And as Locke was a young half-pay officer without prospects, Bath was as good a place as any for him to come to. He would ask around for bone-setters here, and perhaps be in luck. In the meantime, though, he had had a fateful meeting with Colonel Sir James Delabole, and began a romance with his daughter Selina.

'Sir James Delabole. That was the other event. The long-delayed return of the prodigal father, in poor health, contemptuous of his second family and full of sentimental longing to be reconciled with that long-lost daughter whom he had never seen: whom he knew only to have been gathered to her grandfather's bosom after her mother's death, and raised by him in retirement. And who turned out to be beautiful, gracious, talented – the daughter of his dreams. And surely a worthy heiress for the fortune he had garnered over the years.

'But a lot of people did not take kindly to this notion. Mr Tiverton could never forgive the man. Edmund Pinner, her childhood friend and would-be sweetheart, saw Sir James's grand promises as a threat. Sir James's wife and daughter saw themselves neglected in favour of a stranger, and even their future comfort in jeopardy, as he spoke of settling the bulk of his property on Caroline. And Locke did not like that idea either. He hoped to marry Selina, and he preferred to marry a rich Selina. Human, I suppose.

'Oh, and there was a third event, unknown to all. This year, Mr Staples, your twenty-one year sentence of transportation was up, was it not, and you were free to return to England if you so desired? I kept thinking you perhaps someone who had returned illegally – my apologies. I gather you *did* so desire: and having heard nothing from Locke about his search for your daughter, elected to come to England, and conduct a search yourself.'

'Aye,' Staples murmured, 'once I had it in my mind, I couldn't rest, couldn't wait . . . so I took ship.'

'And you found, I should think, the same scanty clues in London as Locke had – your sister had married a bone-setter and moved to Bath. So you came here. You made enquiries of Samuel Fry, who told you about Tate Jessop, and more importantly his widow, who was housekeeper at Mr Tiverton's. At last, you had traced your sister.

'And Locke too, I surmise, had traced her, by a different route. At the dinner here a few evenings since, Mrs Jessop, you spoke of your late husband as a farrier, and someone who did a great deal of good for people. Farrier *and* bone-setter is a frequent combination. So Locke must have thought that evening, and realized you might be the woman he had been looking for. After the dinner he returned here, supposedly to retrieve a glove. I suspected him – I'm sorry – of intriguing with you, Caroline. But I think he came to see you, Mrs Jessop.'

'He did. We spoke in my private room. I was – much surprised, and flustered, when he said what his errand was, and that my brother in America wanted news of his daughter. I suppose I had come to think of George, across that great ocean, as – not dead, but dead to his old life. I never expected to hear from him again. And of course I – I could not say what had really happened to Lizzie. What I had done to her. And so, in some confusion, I just told the young man that Lizzie had died as an infant. Colic, I think I said. He was very – alert. Looked as if he did not wholly believe me. And he wanted to know all the details, so that he could let his friend in America know, he wanted to know when she had died and where she was buried . . . I said St George the Martyr, near Gray's Inn Lane. It was all I could think to say. That was where they buried Lizzie, after I – after I killed her. In a parish plot. But it was also – it was also where Lydia laid her poor Caroline, that terrible winter.' She raised her eyes to Fairfax. 'And that, I fear, the young man went on to find out.'

'I see,' Fairfax said, in sombre thought. 'And so you directed him to the very place . . . In the meantime, there was a growing storm around Sir James Delabole. The morning after the dinner, Mr Pinner took his supposed evidence to Sir James, which made him angry. Sir James caught Locke and Selina together, which made him angrier still. Having turned Locke out of the house, he ordered a servant to send for a lawyer: it looked as if he was making his decision to change his will in favour of Caroline. And indeed he set out for this house, to see her, the apple of his eye, the one thing that would gladden his heart on this infuriating day.

'But all was not well here, I think, Mr Tiverton. You had forced yourself to have Sir James to dinner – but he was every bit as hateful as you remembered him. Worse, Caroline behaved warmly to him, and showed every sign of wanting him to be her father – even perhaps going away with him to London. You pressed the claims of Mr Pinner, whom you had always favoured as a husband for Caroline, but she was dismissive. It was a horrible prospect. Sir James looked set to take away all you loved, and destroy all you had hoped for. And yet this was all based upon a lie! Caroline was not his daughter at all! Sir James's real daughter Caroline, like her twin, was long dead, and lay in an obscure grave in a London cemetery. And so there was a very simple way out. It meant revealing a secret you had guarded all these years: it meant, perhaps, hurting Caroline herself; but it would solve the problem. Just tell him. Tell Sir James the truth, and he would be out of your lives for ever.

'And so you did. You took him into your private office, where he began by being as obnoxious as ever, telling you of Mr Pinner's failed little plot, and speaking no doubt very contemptuously of your favourite. But you had something that must have silenced even him, for a moment. You told him the truth about Caroline's birth, did you not?'

'I did, and it was – God help me, it was a satisfaction to me,' Mr Tiverton said. 'Just to see his face . . . I told him that his daughter had died in London, and that I had brought up Mrs Jessop's child in her place. You should be aware,' he added harshly, 'that such was all I knew. I did not know that the woman had smothered her own brother's child in drink. I thank God, indeed, that Lydia did take her child from her: but I would never have allowed her in this house had I known the whole.'

'Well. The truth as it stood was certainly enough to – ignite Sir James, should I say? He was furious, I should think?'

'He raged, and swore, in his usual way,' Mr Tiverton said scowling. 'Accused me of imposture, whatnot. I didn't care. I had done with him, at last, for ever. Even when he ranted that he would advertize the truth – that he would let the whole world know who Caroline really was – I didn't care.'

'No,' Fairfax said. 'You didn't. But someone else did – someone who was listening in growing alarm. Mrs Jessop. You are greatly proud of your daughter, aren't you, ma'am? Proud and protective – perhaps even more so, because your care has had to be kept under a veil of disguise. You have watched her grow, as you said, to a lovely young woman; and a young woman, moreover, who now had great prospects – fortune, society, eminence. And she wanted them very much: that was plain. Never mind the rights or wrongs of that: who are we to say we wouldn't be dazzled too, in Caroline's place? And yet now – now Mr Tiverton had let out the secret and destroyed it all. Worst of all, Sir James was ranting about telling the truth to the world. Your beloved daughter's life was about to be shattered.'

'Yes,' Mrs Jessop said decidedly, 'and I knew Sir James would do it, too – every malicious thing in his power. And so I would stop him. It might be that she would still get her fortune: he had spoken so much of it that I thought he might already have made the arrangements. But even if not, the main thing was to stop him spreading the truth. If he died now, the world would still know her as his daughter, Caroline Delabole: she would surely have some claim, and she would keep that sense of herself . . . I wished Mr Tiverton had not let it out, but I understood: he was much provoked – and I believed I could talk him round afterwards, and make him see it was so much the best thing for Caroline not to know, and keep it secret once more. All that was needed was to kill Sir James. And so I took some arsenic from the drug-chest in the store-room and put it in the little flask in his cane, where it stood in the hall. And that was that.'

'And you did talk Mr Tiverton round afterwards, did you not? You have grown close over the years, I think, and have come to rely on one another; and I'm sure you spoke very sensibly. But as for you, Mr Tiverton – when the news of Sir James's death came, did you not suspect . . .? Even in your innermost heart?'

Mr Tiverton covered his face with trembling hands. 'I can't say any more,' he muttered.

'Well, you acted coolly, Mrs Jessop, and averted the crisis you feared,' Fairfax said. 'But then you must still have been in a highly anxious state all the same. Locke coming and questioning you about George's poor Lizzie must have unnerved you. Here was the past nosing up, breaking the surface . . . And to confirm that, George himself appeared. He had tracked you down. He came discreetly to you, by the yard at the back, not wanting to cause trouble, no doubt – though Caroline did glimpse him, and begin to wonder. It must have been a great shock to you to see George in the flesh, even though Locke had in a way prepared you for it. You told him the same tale, I suppose – that Lizzie had died of natural causes . . .'

'And I didn't quite credit it then,' Staples said. 'You were a pretty good liar, Sarah, but not a perfect one. I knew something was up. That's why I kept coming back: there was something you weren't telling me . . .' His voice rose to a roar. 'God curse you, Sarah!'

'Yes: He will,' Mrs Jessop said, quite casually.

'Though you could not yet know it, Mrs Jessop, a danger remained,' Fairfax went on. 'Selina, remember, had passed on Mr Pinner's paper to Locke. It appeared to show that Sir James's daughter had died in France as a baby. And Locke did not know, mind, that there had been twins. So who was Caroline really? The poor fellow is dead, and cannot tell his own tale, but I think this is what went through his mind. He thought Caroline must be an impostor – and very much hoped so, as that would benefit Selina. He knew that Mrs Jessop had had the charge of her brother's child Lizzie years ago; and though Mrs Jessop said Lizzie had died, there was something uneasy about the way she said it that raised his suspicions. I think he came to the conclusion that George's Lizzie had *not* died: that she was alive – and that she was none other than Caroline. But how to check this? Well, I think I see it now. Mrs Jessop, you told him where Lizzie was buried, is that not so: the parish churchyard of St George the Martyr by Gray's Inn Lane in London? And so he took a coach to London to find out. And he took with him a piece of charcoal – an idea suggested by the ingenious Mr Pinner's paper – I think in case he should find Lizzie's grave after all. A rubbing of the headstone would be something to send to you in America, Mr Staples – a sad proof, but it would show he had kept his word, and you would at least be free of uncertainty. He didn't consider, I think, that such a poor grave as Lizzie's might not have a proper headstone.

'And in London, I think, he did find Lizzie Staples's grave. So much for his grand idea! But no. You said, Mrs Jessop, that Lydia's daughter was buried in that same churchyard. Here there was something else, something more revealing. I believe Locke found that other grave: a grave which must have borne the words "Caroline Delabole", and the date of

February 1745. Did he work out now that there had been twins, both dead? Perhaps. The main thing was, the living Caroline was *definitely* not who she was claimed to be, as he had suspected all along. Lydia pawned her wedding ring to bury her child, so I am sure there was a headstone, and that Locke took a rubbing from it.'

'Aye – I have it,' Staples said, and drew from his pocket two crumpled pieces of paper.

'Here it is,' Fairfax said, 'together with Mr Pinner's. Sad remnants of two short lives, that should never have caused so much trouble . . . Well, when Locke came back to Bath today, he cannot have been aware that Sir James was dead. It must have been a shock to him. And also, it must have seemed at first that his odd quest had been pointless. He had set out to discredit Caroline as Sir James's heiress, and that was why he dared to come back to the Delabole house today – because he had evidence to show Sir James and knock him back. But now Sir James was dead and his will was apparently unchanged . . . Except that you, Caroline, had been to the Delabole house this morning, and talked of claims and lawyers, and made it clear that you meant to put up a fight for Sir James's estate. I think you may have genuinely believed that there was a new will that had been taken or suppressed, perhaps by Pinner, and you had turned detective yourself in search of it: wasn't that what was behind your rather cruel behaviour to Pinner today? Well, no matter: the fact was, there still seemed to be a threat to Selina's inheritance. And that, Locke could deal with very easily, he thought.

'I believe he stowed the papers away safely at his lodgings – and at this point, I think, he must finally have met up with you, Mr Staples.'

'That's so. I had been here to see Sarah again – I still

couldn't let the matter of Lizzie rest. Plainly she wanted to get rid of me. We had talked of the young soldier who had come asking about Lizzie as well – my young soldier, I knew. I was pleased and touched that he had kept his word and tried to find her. Well, Sarah said, she had told him exactly the same, and I was welcome to go and ask him myself. I was glad of the opportunity to see Locke again, and so I went to his lodging, and met him there.'

'He had told me where he lived,' Mrs Jessop murmured, 'when he first questioned me. Said I could come there if I had – anything else to tell him.'

'He showed me that rubbing – Lizzie's grave,' Staples went on. 'I suppose I had to believe it then . . . But then he asked me more about Sarah. He must have worked out, as you say, sir, that this young woman couldn't be who she was claimed; and he must have been casting about to think just who she was. Not my Lizzie: but hadn't I said my sister had a child of her own? Aye, said I: and then he fell to thinking. He had to go out, he said, but he pressed me to stay in his rooms, and asked me to take care of those papers, and make myself easy until he came back.'

'And so Locke came here to sound you out, Mr Tiverton – thinking that you were behind the plan to contest the will. I doubt that he was threatening or even unpleasant: he was a clever character. I imagine he spoke of Sir James's death, and the inheritance, and how he hoped for his future wife's sake there would be no difficulties made over it.'

'Yes,' Caroline said. There were tear stains on her cheeks, but she had done her weeping silently, and she kept her voice firm. 'He was – he was not unpleasant. But insinuating . . . I'm afraid it was me who spoke up: I said that I most certainly would make a claim on my father's estate, and nothing would stop me. And he said that was a pity, as he could lay his hands on certain evidence from London that would prevent me in law from any such claim. I thought it was bravado – I said, "Very well, then," and challenged him to produce this evidence. And he – he just smiled in a curious way and said he would. Then he left.'

'To return to his lodgings, and fetch the papers,' Fairfax said. 'And you, Mrs Jessop, must have guessed by now just what that evidence was: it was even you who, unwittingly, had pointed him to that churchyard in London where he found Caroline Delabole's grave. And so, it was Sir James all over again: a man leaving the house, threatening to bring your daughter's great palace of dreams crashing down. But this time there was no opportunity for poison. Instead, you followed him, and on the threshold of his home you stabbed him. But the papers had been entrusted to Mr Staples, who was still waiting inside for Locke's return – while I, God help me, was spouting Shakespeare . . . You heard the noise at the front door, Mr Staples?'

'Aye. I went down to see what was up – found poor Locke lying there. Terrible . . . And now I bethought me how Locke had asked about Sarah having a child of her own, and a horrible suspicion settled on me, and I lit out for this place to find her . . . And I did,' he said, shaking his head at Mrs Jessop with a grimace of loathing, 'and she damn near killed me too. You realized I'd smoked you, did you, Sarah?'

'Locke meant, certainly, to reveal Caroline's own true identity to her,' Fairfax said. 'But only to safeguard Selina's inheritance, I believe. I don't think he intended to shout it abroad, as Sir James did. But I suppose you had no time for such niceties, Mrs Jessop: all you thought was to protect your child.'

'All I thought was to protect my child,' Mrs Jessop said, her hands still mechanically smoothing. 'It sounds strange, perhaps. But I wanted nothing for myself: since my reform, I never have. Only for you, my dear.' Her eyes begged Caroline to look at her. 'Everything for you – the best! I hoped I might hear of you – not see you, of course – taking the arm of a duke, as you opened the dancing at some great ball at St James or Ranelagh or some such place. Miss Caroline Delabole, the belle of the season! And I'd know in my heart that that was my Amabel, and that after all, I'd done right by her.' A strange look came over her eyes, as if they were covered with something hard and translucent like watch-glass: after a moment Fairfax realized they were tears that did not fall.

Caroline turned full away from her mother. She looked with a sort of desperation at her grandfather, and then at the grim face of George Staples, and at last at Fairfax; and for want of anyone better, she cried at him: 'But what about me? Who am I? I have nothing to do with Sir James – nothing truly to do with – with my grandfather. Nothing! I have nobody, nobody in the world. Only a mother who is – is—'

'A shame that will soon be gone,' Mrs Jessop said, as a knocking sounded at the house-door. 'I know what must happen to me: I am quite ready. It's only what should have happened to me twenty-one years since, George, for what I did to your Lizzie. It's caught up, that's all. But listen to me, Caroline, one last time: you always did when you thought I was just Mrs Jessop your starchy old companion, so pretend I still am for a moment. You say you have nobody: it is not true. You have yourself. You are clever and beautiful, accomplished, determined: you have wit and fire. Many women would wish for as much. And that is who you are, whatever your name: that can't be taken away.'

A servant came and whispered that there was a constable outside sent by Mr Goode. Fairfax nodded, thinking how tired he was, thinking how odd it was that Mrs Jessop, though a murderess, was also a very sensible woman.

Thirteen

'It is astonishing, is it not, Mr Fairfax,' Mr Goode said, pulling on his lilac gloves in the hall of his house in Queen Square, 'how ill-regulated people's private lives can be.'

'A never-failing source of astonishment, sir.'

'And such highly respectable people too! Even the woman herself. Not of genteel origin by any means – but still, the widow of a decent tradesman; and in the household of Mr Gilbert Tiverton too – an establishment always seen as impeccably, sedately respectable, even for Bath. Well, well. She comports herself admirably, they say, at the gaol. Her case will be quite a scandal at the next sessions – but it will, I hope, have lost some of its novelty by then, and will not reflect on Bath too badly. We cannot be too careful of our reputation.'

'The verdict, I suppose, cannot be in doubt. Nor the sentence.'

'Oh, assuredly,' Mr Goode said, pausing before a gilt mirror and settling his gold-laced hat on top of his frizzed wig. 'There can be nothing but the ultimate penalty. But there, apparently she is resigned, and does not fear it. Well, my dear sir. All is settled, most satisfactorily. And you, I am sure, will be glad to return to your pupils, and more peaceable

employment – carrying, of course, my profoundest gratitude
for all your help. Come, let me give you a ride thither: my, er,
the Bassetts will have missed you.'

'Satisfactorily . . .' Fairfax repeated with a sigh as they went
out to Mr Goode's waiting carriage. 'I wish it were so.'

'But it is, my dear sir – you have solved the most puzzling
and, I must say, thoroughly ghastly case I have ever
encountered.'

'Without saving Locke.' That still pained him. Locke had
wanted to marry a *rich* Selina, but still Fairfax believed he
had loved the girl truly: all his intrigues had been to that end.
Even that apparent flirtation with Caroline must have been
designed to divert Sir James's suspicions. No, Locke had
deserved better.

'I don't see how you could have saved him, Mr Fairfax. I
don't say that lightly. It is one thing to seek justice: quite
another to stand on perennial guard between evil and
innocence. It would be a fine thing if one could, but we are
only human.' Mr Goode settled himself in the carriage seat
and pulled from his pocket a silver flask. 'This is not my habit
by any means, sir,' he said, taking a conservative sip. 'But I
am accompanying Lord Marham on a visit to the hospital –
subscription concert on its behalf tonight – Lord Marham is,
among other things, a generous friend to charitable causes –
and I am told brandy is a good defence against infection. Will
you take a nip, sir?'

'Thank you, no.' Fairfax had not had a drink in the past
three days, and found he did not really want one. If ever he
was tempted to self-indulgence again, he thought, he need
only remind himself of these past few days: of Mrs Jessop
selling baby-clothes for gin.

'A pity Lady Delabole and her daughter left Bath so

precipitately. I would have wished to say my goodbyes – but there, I don't suppose they cared to linger. I have hopes they will come back in the spring season, however. Miss Selina, with such a fortune, will be quite a catch; once she has got over the loss of her poor young beau, of course. One cannot say the same of Mr Tiverton's, ahem, adoptive granddaughter, alas, now that her history is known. But then she will have his portion when he dies, and she has other attractions: she may be happy yet.'

'I hope so.'

The carriage pulled up in South Parade, near – but not in front of – the Bassett house.

'I won't step down, my dear sir, if you don't mind,' Mr Goode said, glancing quickly out of the carriage window, then sitting back. 'Much to do, you know, and can't loiter. Present my compliments to the Bassetts, of course – oh, and you may remark, on your next banker's draft, an increase in your remuneration. Quite deserved, I feel. And so I'll bid good day to you, Mr Fairfax, and—'

The carriage door opened. Mr Bassett, Mrs Bassett, and the Misses Euphemia, Felicia and Aspasia stood there, all beaming.

'Well, now, cousin!' Mr Bassett cried heartily. 'We were wondering when you'd come to call on us. We've been a walk, and I saw the carriage, and I said damn me if that ain't cousin Goode, didn't I, Hetty? Come in, come in, and have a dish of tea! You shall see how well the girls are doing under Mr Fairfax here – Spash shall talk French to you, shan't you, my dear? Oh! her ankle's much better now, by the by, Mr Fairfax: we went to see a rum old man called Sam Fry – none of your bobwigged physickers, but a clever devil, and he gave it a squeeze and a turn, and bound it special tight, and she's even fit for dancing, ain't you, Spash? So we shall go to the Assembly Rooms at last – we'll see you there, cousin Goode, no doubt! But come in, come in—'

'No, no,' Fairfax said, suppressing his laughter, and stepping out of the carriage, 'Mr Goode has a most urgent engagement. And *I* have an engagement with you young ladies, and a French grammar-book, that must be kept.'

He heard a sigh from Mr Goode, and then the carriage rattled away at speed.

'Well, that was hello and goodbye, to be sure,' said Mr Bassett.

'Or *au revoir*,' Fairfax said, rolling the Rs in his most extravagantly French fashion at the Bassett girls; and with them shrieking, fizzing, blushing, and slapping each other, and their elders chuckling benignly behind, he went on into the house.

The Devil's Highway

Hannah March

It's 1761. Travelling up to the country home of his new employer, Robert Fairfax is aware that this lonely stretch of road has lately been the haunt of a notorious highwayman. But nothing can prepare him for the shocking discovery of the Stamford to London stagecoach, tipped into a ditch. The driver has been shot through the head and the two passengers inside are dead.

Investigating at the behest of his employer, the local JP, Fairfax soon suspects that this is more than simple highway robbery. One of the two corpses is apparently a wealthy banker, Nicholas Twelvetree. But Nicholas Twelvetree is in the neighbouring town, alive and well – and paralysed with fear. The other corpse appears to be that of a harmless lunatic escaped from a local asylum – a revelation made by a Methodist preacher who is universally disliked. But the coach records state that there were three passengers on board that day. So where is the third – a missing woman whose anxious husband still awaits her return? Fairfax must piece together his most baffling puzzle – knowing that a ruthless killer will stop at nothing to prevent him . . .

'Written well with a great deal of self-assurance' Deryn Lake, *Shots*

'A clever and accomplished first novel . . . for fans of period dramas such as Moll Flanders and Tom Jones, this will slip down like a cup of sherbet' *Scotland on Sunday*

0 7472 6013 3

headline

Death Be My Theme

Hannah March

Recuperating from illness in Chelsea – in 1764, a rural spot outside the jostling city – Robert Fairfax expects to be bored. But a chance meeting with his old flame Cordelia leads to his involvement with a very unusual family: the Mozarts of Salzburg, whose young son is the musical prodigy creating a stir throughout their tour of Europe.

The boy is as inquisitive as any child, and it is this which makes him an uncomprehending but vital witness to the bizarre events surrounding the death of Mr Gabriel Chilcott, an elderly, wealthy and ill-tempered music-lover. His pretty young wife seems to have secrets she does not care to divulge, and the mystery deepens with the horrific discovery by the river of a local maid's murdered body.

Fairfax's investigation of these strange events leads him to a puzzle that seems too great for his powers to solve – unless he can garner a crucial clue from the remarkable little boy whom the world will know as Wolfgang Amadeus Mozart . . .

'Exuberant' *The Times*

'Clever and accomplished . . . for fans of period dramas such as Moll Flanders and Tom Jones, this will slip down like a cup of sherbet' *Scotland on Sunday*

0 7472 6627 1

headline

Now you can buy any of these other bestselling
Headline books from your bookshop or
direct from the publisher.

FREE P&P AND UK DELIVERY
(Overseas and Ireland £3.50 per book)

The Anubis Slayings	Paul Doherty	£5.99
The Field of Blood	Paul Doherty	£5.99
Chronicles of Crime	Ed. Maxim Jakubowski	£5.99
The Traitor of St Giles	Michael Jecks	£5.99
Death Be My Theme	Hannah March	£5.99
The Amorous Nightingale	Edward Marston	£5.99
Half Moon Street	Anne Perry	£6.99
The Whitechapel Conspiracy	Anne Perry	£5.99
A Rare Benedictine	Ellis Peters	£6.99
A Pattern of Blood	Rosemary Rowe	£5.99
Our Lady of Darkness	Peter Tremayne	£5.99

TO ORDER SIMPLY CALL THIS NUMBER

01235 400 414

or e-mail <u>orders@bookpoint.co.uk</u>

Prices and availability subject to change without notice.